POWER

Solar Storms

Mean Spirit

The Book of Medicines

Dwellings: A Spiritual History of the Living World

Seeing Through the Sun

Savings

Red Clay

Eclipse

The Stories We Hold Secret

POWER

LINDA HOGAN

W. W. NORTON & COMPANY

NEW YORK   LONDON

For information about permission to reproduce selections from this book, write to
Permissions, W. W. Norton & Company, Inc., 500 Fifth Avenue, New York, NY
10110.

The text of this book is composed in Waldbaum with the display set in Typeface 7.
Desktop composition by JoAnn Schambier
Manufacturing by The Haddon Craftsmen, Inc.
Book design by Chris Welch

Library of Congress Cataloging-in-Publication Data
Hogan, Linda.
    Power / Linda Hogan.
        p.   cm.
    ISBN 0-393-04636-2
    1. Indians of North America—Florida—Fiction. 2. Indian women—
Florida—Fiction. 3. Florida panther—Fiction. I. Title.
PS3558.034726P6 1998
813'.54—dc21   97-42997
                                                                         CIP

W. W. Norton & Company, Inc., 500 Fifth Avenue, New York, NY 10110
http://www.wwnorton.com

W. W. Norton & Company Ltd., 10 Coptic Street, London WC1A 1PU

2 3 4 5 6 7 8 9 0

ACKNOWLEDGMENTS

My first thanks goes to my daughter, Tanya Park, who did extra work that enabled me to write. I have special gratitude for Brenda Peterson for reading and discussing the manuscript. Patrick Hogan, as always, was one of the best readers. I am grateful to biologist Deb Jansen for offering me a place to stay in the territory of the panther, and to Gary Holthaus and Charles Wilkinson, who brought me into the Endangered Species Working Group. I wish to acknowledge the University of Colorado for the IMPART travel grant for research on this novel, and the Lannan Foundation for their support. I thank Jean Fortier for passing on her knowledge of the depths, and Connie Studer for our many wonderful hours of conversation. Marilyn Auer's friendship has sustained me over the years. I have a special debt to Beth Vesel for her caretaking of my work, and my editor, Jill Bialosky, for helping in the creation and flowering of this book, and Eve Grubin for her patience. I would also like to acknowledge Randolph Stowe for the work that serves as inspiration. And, finally, I am thankful for the support of Dharmaja Raviendran, who has kept me alive in all ways.

FOR THE FLORIDA PANTHER.

MAY THEIR KIND SURVIVE.

POWER

Mystery is a form of power.

1
OMISHTO

This is the place where clouds are born and I am floating. Last night, before I fell asleep in my boat, the earth was bleeding. The red light that began at the edge of earth moved upward until all the sky was red. Mama calls it stormlight, and this morning as I sit back in the boat, it looks like she is right; a storm is coming in. I watch the clouds form. They are high above me, heavy and dark, and they are fast, traveling across the sky.

You'd think the clouds would make a sound moving that quick and full, but it is quiet this morning and the sky is no longer red; it is nearly green now with the first hint of a coming storm. The land, too, is musty and sea-green. An egret stands on one thin leg at the edge of water, and even the water, with seeds floating across it in search of other worlds, is green. Insects walk on it. Spiders drift above it on threads of silk. It's as if I am curled inside an opening leaf in this boat covered with algae, as if I am just beginning to live. But behind all this, a distance away, the trees are dark, almost black in the shadows thrown down by clouds.

It is beautiful here, this place I call mine, where clouds are born from water. Most days the clouds disappear in the morning. They go back to the gulf or they wander in toward land, but today they keep arriving with restless weight, and I watch as they add to themselves, taking in the rich waters of this place. Even this boat is like a cloud moving across water.

I sit back in the boat and run my fingers through the warmth of shallow water. A water snake, a moccasin, curls through the water, and comes toward the boat, trying to climb in. It's too alive and quick for me, this thin life, and I'm afraid of snakes. I push it away with my pole. It turns and slides back into the water and I can't see it, only that the water is darkening the way it does before a storm when it seems to have no reflection, only depth.

I pole the boat to land.

But then, as I near water's edge, a cold chill passes over my back. I feel watched. It's not the snake watching, I can tell. I feel it in my body, something not right, eyes watching from the trees, something stirring about. I feel it in my stomach, an animal feeling, something—or someone—dangerous. I glance into the trees. I know some of the things that live in there. I've seen their eyes shining through the dark nights. But there are other things in shadows I don't know, things that might leap at me or reach out and take hold of me. I don't want to look, but I'm half-minded about this because I don't want to turn my back on it, either. I think something strange and out of keeping, that the trees never turn color here like in other places and that their leaves only fall with storms, but even so they seem almost naked this morning, stripped of protection even though something is hidden in there. As I draw the boat in and bring it aground, I hear my own movements in water. I keep myself from looking toward what is watching me. Aunt Ama says what you look at is what you become, so I don't look into the trees. I don't want to become like the shadows hiding the eyes of animals, harboring insects and lizards or runaways. Shadows do not seem honest to me. But I sense it and stay alert, listening, watching out of the corner of my eye.

A wave of memories washes toward me as I drag the boat up to land. How old man Tate disappeared, and some say he is still out here, wild and hidden in trees and mulch. I remember, too, that a bear bigger than any I've ever seen still lives in the swamps and feeds on horses and cattle, drags them away from ranches and into thick trees.

And the cat. Ama says this is its place, its territory. She always watches for it. She has seen it and she believes in it. In the old way, she says, the cat is her relative. My relative, too, since we in the same clan. She knows it is there. Sometimes at night she looks out into the darkness and they see into each other's eyes.

I've never seen a cat before, except that one time recently when some schoolboys, three of them, had one treed and Ama took away their rifle to keep them from killing it. Or worse yet, from wounding it and leaving it to die. After that last one was hit by a car, Mama said they are all gone from here and the ones left are all sick, but I know one finds its way through now and then. You can feel it more than see it, feel it more than smell it. It feels like space has eyes and ears, and it watches with all its might, listens with ears that can pick up the slightest hint of sound, and it moves slowly, silently. Even when people are around they say it doesn't hurry. It makes the hair on your back and neck rise to think there's something like that out in the dark, something that can sneak up on you but you can never see it. I feel it sometimes, though. I've heard that they follow people sometimes, creeping behind us, trying to figure out what we are. We must mystify them. As animals, I mean.

I try not to think of it because they say that to speak an animal's name is to call out to the powers inside it and because everything, our words, our intentions, travels by air.

Even if I can't see what's in the shadows this time, I know what I feel and there are things I know and feel and see that other people don't. My older sister said she heard that when I was only four days old and my mother was gutting a chicken she pointed at me with the knife and said, "This girl's going to give us trouble. Look at her eyes." She put down the chicken and was quiet a long time, watching me. "They're barely open, she's only a baby and she's watching everything." And then Mama turned her back to me so I wouldn't witness her work, so I wouldn't see her cut the chicken apart. That's why my father named me Omishto. It means the One Who Watches, but nowadays most everyone just calls me Sis or girl. But it's true, I watch everything and see deep into what's around me. I have a strong wind inside me, is what Grandma said. A wind with eyes. They used to call it the spirit, the breath, and the name we have for it is Oni. I feel lives and spirits in the woods, and I see the growing things. But I can't see what is watching me from the trees. Still, I am careful in the way I move, not to be caught unawares, not to turn my back on it.

2
STORMLIGHT

It's a year to the day since Abraham Swallow died. Old man Swallow died either by magic or by fear. People still argue about it, and right now I can't say which one I believe, although most of the time I don't think there's such a thing as magic.

He died in the trees not far from the borrow pit, at the place where land was taken out of the swamp to build a road. Stolen more than borrowed. Now it's also the place, the canal, where sometimes I catch bass or crappie, though you can't eat them. This morning as I walk to Ama Eaton's, I think of Abraham Swallow and I see him in my mind, a bent man, not a kind bone in his body. It was a year ago and it was near this place, I remember, because there's a spring close by and the Spanish once believed it was a fountain of youth. Of course, that's a joke now because everyone around here seems to be pretty old. But we call the spring Immortality anyway. And that's another joke because now it's polluted like all this land and you can't even drink a cupful of that thin trickle of bad water.

But it's a testament to how things used to be. So is this road, the white road I'm walking. Fossil Road is what we call it, although some people call it State Road 59. This road, this whole layer of earth, used to be under a sea, and one ancient day it broke free of the earth and rose up here like all things rise, the clouds that drink our water, the white birds, and even, as Mama claims, the souls of people. Sometimes in my mind's eye I see the way land floated up away from the sea bottom as if it knew the secret of how to fall the wrong direction away from gravity.

But beneath all this, down below us, live the bones and teeth of sabertooths and mastodons, from before there was swamp. Like us, they're down at the bottom of God's sky, only we're still surviving what history has laid down on us and not yet covered up. Just barely, though, we just barely survived the tide of history, and even at that, sometimes I look at myself or the other Taiga people and I think maybe the only things that remain of us, just like with the mastodons and sabertooth cats, are bones and teeth. We barely have a thing, a bit of land, a few stories, and the old people that live up above Kili Swamp.

From the fossil road, near Ama's house, I can just see the tree everyone calls Methuselah. They call it that because it's been there so long with its tangled dark roots hanging on five hundred years or so. They say it's a tree the Spanish brought with them here and planted. It's not from this conti-nent. That's why there's only one. And no one can figure how it took hold in the shallow soil of this place.

Back in from Methuselah is the house of Ama Eaton. It sits on the very edge of our Taiga land, lines drawn by the govern-ment. Today it is partly shadowed by the clouds. Her house looks raw and abandoned, but it isn't; Ama lives in the rickety thing. The place sits on cinder blocks in case of flooding. It's a square, simple house, gray-looking, with a porch that wraps around one side. She uses palmetto fronds on the roof to keep the place cool, so it looks something like a hut sitting in the shadows of a jungle, even though it's close to civilization. It even seems to lean against the plants and trees. I've asked her if she worries about fire with those fronds up there on the roof, but she laughs and says she could build herself up another place that would be better than this one if she had to, and truth be known, it wouldn't take much to build a better place.

Ama's house used to be blue as seawater. You wouldn't know it now except for the fact that there's just enough blue paint left on it to look like clouds scattered across the dirty walls of evening sky. Now the wood itself is so rough that moss tries to grow on it and the blue flowers and vines of morning glories climb up it, hanging on for dear life with their little grasping tendrils. I can't help thinking that yesterday my older sister bought a dress that very shade of blue. She asked me did I want to try it on and I said I didn't. It might have hurt her feelings, but I didn't want to look pretty for one minute then take it off and go to school looking plain and skinny like I always do. I'm my sister's project. She's always trying to fix me up, but I don't want to look pretty in the house with my mother and stepfather looking at me, his eyes always looking too much in places they don't belong, and my mom jealous like she is being replaced by me and it's all my fault, my design. She's half mad at me about it. Mostly, I just stay away from there and no one seems to notice. My mom says it's not good to sleep in my boat and I shouldn't camp out like that, but it's the safest place there is, surrounded all around by water. It's like I am a continent, a whole continent.

As I cut off the road and through the damp tall grasses, the birds fly up from the ground and away from me. Insects jump away from my feet. I look up at the dark clouds that pass over Ama's house this early morning and I watch the shadows of them move across land and trees and water, now dark, now light, as the clouds move. There are always clouds here, snake-like some days, full on others. This, the place where they are born, is Ama's love, this cloudy place with its thick trees and swamps, oak islands, mosquitoes, snakes, and waters. It's my love, too, this place of million-year-old rivers and sloughs and jagged limestone, and I'm just barely getting to know it, learning the land from Ama, and how the underground rivers run.

A frail kerosene light shines out from Ama's windows in the green morning. It's the kind of light that makes you think that Ama, like the rivers, dropped out of time and that the houses of towns and suburbs have not crept forward, draining the swamps ahead of them, filling them in with soil, trying to make our world run even farther away from them until it's gone altogether.

But we, us Taiga people, haven't run. Instead, silent and nearly invisible, most of us have been pushed up against the wild places, backed against them. And some of them are still there, like a dark corner in the minds of the intruders.

I walk as silent as possible toward Ama's.

"Come in," Ama says, and I hear her low, soft voice from inside, and wonder how she knows I'm here this early on a Saturday morning, at daybreak. She always knows, even when I cut through the trees, silent as air. I guess she hears me the way she hears every animal that comes around. You can't sneak up on her. Usually I try to sneak up on the house. Just once I'd like to surprise her. It's become a game for me. But she's never surprised to see me.

The bottom step is made of cinder blocks on which the others rest, the ground washed out from under them in a flood. I go up the two hollow-sounding steps and knock lightly before I open the door. I don't really have to knock because Ama says this house is going to be mine someday, that it already is, and I can come and go as I please, but I like to be polite.

Ama stands at the cupboard, putting away the dishes, most all of them chipped. Her hair is still down. There is warm light. She moves slowly and she looks larger than she is in the low-ceilinged kitchen. We smile at each other, but I don't speak yet because silence is sometimes one of the rules of this house, especially in the mornings. Then I get a cup of black coffee, the kind of good, strong coffee my mama doesn't let me drink at home, and I go out and sit by myself on the front stoop and look at the world.

Pretty soon, Ama comes out and sits beside me, her legs apart, her elbows on her knees, and we both look at the clouds moving across trees. Ama is a wide-boned woman with big, dark-shining eyes, and the gap between her front teeth makes her sound girlish at times. She has long arms, but small hands and small feet. She never seems quite at home in anything, not shoes or clothing, not houses, not even her own muscles, just in the wild swamps and grasses and trees. She wears the kind of dress my sister and I call "state" dresses from the time Mama was in the hospital, the time her husband—not my pa—put her there so he could get her out of his way while he ran around with another woman and never even tried to hide the fact. When I visited I barely recognized my own messy-haired mama from the pills they gave her that made her face swell up. That's how Ama looks today, like she's been crying in somebody else's old cast-off dress, and I think how my mama once called her a human ruin, but it's just that she doesn't fit Mama's idea of what a woman should be. For me, out of those two choices, I prefer the ruin.

I want to ask Ama what's wrong, but she's not the kind of person you can ask things directly. Just like you don't ask questions of the old Taiga people. It's different manners here. She talks, though. She'll chat while I help her chop the deep grasses with a scythe. Or we tear out the kudzu vines while she talks about the dog she used to have that got eaten by a gator or about a book she once read. Mostly she likes history. She used to go to the library in Consodine every so often, but now she mostly reads the land and sky. Sometimes when we visit I don't listen to what she says. I'll listen to the throbbing sound of frogs behind her voice and think they're part of her story, and they are, nature is part of her story, although it seems to me that when she talks it's so soft and calm the frogs and insects would all be as quiet as I am. That's the kind of voice she has. But even so, she always says what's on her mind.

Through Ama's dress, I can see her backbone as she sits there on the wooden steps. She looks large, but I see that it is mostly bone.

Her hairbrush is in her lap. "You want me to brush your hair?" A damp wind is starting up as if it originates right here at Ama's house.

I stand up behind her before she even has a chance to answer, take the brush, and run long strokes through her dark hair the way my sister and I do with each other's hair, the way I used to do with my grandma who'd never once had her hair cut. It's the way of girls and women.

Ama's dark hair is clean and straight and warm, longer than mine, and I see that it's beginning to gray.

Today, as the sky darkens in patches nearly black, as I sweep the brush through her hair, she asks me, because she must be thinking of him, "Do you think they killed Abraham Swallow by using magic?"

It catches me off guard. "I don't know what you mean," I say, but I do, because I saw that man, Abraham, running away from death. My face turns hot as Ama glances at me. With guilt. With fear.

The truth is, my sister and I were close by that day, even though we never told a soul what we saw. We were cutting school. We'd come out to look at a killed gator, the largest one ever found. Donna, my sister, said they might blame us for his death or think we were involved. Or that we should have called the police sooner than we did. We both wonder that—I know we do—but we don't ever say it out loud, not even to ourselves.

That day, a year ago, we heard the sound of Abraham Swallow's breathing coming down the white road not too far from where Ama's house perches. Unlike today, with weather coming in, there was full sun, and it looked too bright in the sky, and then a single dark cloud raced across it. Like an eclipse. I remember how it looked, because Donna said, "Doesn't it look strange out today?" and I took a full measure of it. There was a chill cast over the hot sun. I felt my hands grow cold even before I saw Abraham Swallow. It's the chill I remember most, because it was unusual in all that heat. Then I heard Abraham come running toward us, and when I spotted him I saw his gray hair in a mess and the black birds flying up all around him, startled and making a commotion of sound. I heard him breathing hard, and as he ran closer, I jumped off the road and watched to see who was coming after him, but there was nothing, no one else, just a whirlwind of dust following behind him like it was chasing him. A handful of black-tail boat grackles flew with it. We all know everyone here, so my sister called out and asked did he want a ride somewhere. It was a strange question considering the look on his face, pale in spite of the heat. He looked like he'd just seen the worst thing in the world. It was just after noon.

He looked at us like we were two spirits walking through his world, like we shouldn't have been there. I thought he was afraid of us. "No. No," he said. "They killed me." And he went on past us. Abe Swallow crossed over the fossil road and took off through the water of the borrow pit. He crossed right through it, not even thinking that a gator might be in there, and he looked like he had seen a ghost, he was flying so fast.

Donna and I just looked at each other and then back to where he ran into the trees. Donna said, "I just offered a dead man a ride."

He stumbled as he disappeared into the brambles, his eyes too bright, his shirt and pants too large for him, the whirlwind behind him—I felt it go past—like it was chasing him, his strong brown feet bare and dusty.

Then it seemed the world went still and after a while I wanted to follow him a ways in to see where he was going. He'd turned off toward the small trickle of fenced-off water of Immortality, that spring of eternal youth. Birds were startled out of their nests in the branches of trees, and the monkey that hates humans, the monkey somebody got rid of by putting it out of their car, was jumping from tree to tree down in the swamp, chattering.

I said to Donna, "Let's get out of here," but now she was the one who wanted to follow him into the trees to see what he was doing. He must have known her intentions because he yelled back over his shoulder to us, "Stay back. They killed me. Stay back," and then he went into the trees.

"Let's go," I said, every cell in my body anxious to leave.

"We ought to see if we can help," Donna said. "At least we ought to do that."

But I refused to go with her and she wouldn't go by herself, so she went to the edge of the trees and looked in while I stayed on the road and she said she thought he must be sick because he'd fallen over.

"We better call an ambulance," I said. "Come on. Let's go."

We were going to the store, but we got in the car and Donna started up the engine and when we got to the gas station, we just sat there like we couldn't get out of the car even if we wanted to. It was the worst feeling, like we didn't have any control over it. I kept saying, "We've got to call," but we just sat there like we couldn't move a muscle, and neither one of us could explain it, why we couldn't move.

After a while, we both went inside the store and I stood next to her while Donna called. She disguised her voice so no one would know who called, as if we'd get in trouble. She gave directions on how to find the old man, then we left and we went back to school, trying to pretend we'd been there all day and seen nothing. We pretended we'd never played hooky and never watched Abraham Swallow, the dead man, run away from the wind.

I l o o k a long time at Ama before I answer her question about Abraham, and wonder why in the world she is asking me. Even though I saw the pure fear on his face that day, she knows I don't believe in magic. I don't believe because at school I learn there is a reason for everything. This is what separates me from Aunt Ama, that as smart as she is she never went to high school, that even though she reads, she still swears by old-time beliefs, and she believes in all the Taiga stories, that they are true, that they are real.

The truth is, I am thinking of the way Swallow died and the look on his face, and the whirlwind that followed him, and it gives me chills, but I say, "No, Ama. I don't think magic killed Mr. Swallow. I think he just drank too much." That's all I say, and then we are done with it, done talking about it even though she looks at me sideways to see if I'm lying and it makes me feel like I am, but I'm not a person who believes the way she does, because it's a different world what with the houses and highways.

But even with the storm my mother predicted blowing toward us, I'm quiet. I am still thinking about old man Swallow and how, not long afterwards, his body was taken away from the oaks near the spring by Mr. Willard's place not far from here, Willard's brown trailer with his old white horse standing outside it.

Even though old Abe's body was found without a sign of damage, his wife insisted on an investigation. His wife, who loved him in spite of his attacks on her, said she knew for a fact that the old Taiga people up above Kili Swamp had called him there and killed him by their wills alone and that if the damage wasn't in his body when the coroner saw it then it was some other part of him that they attacked. His soul, she meant, and she wanted the old people arrested. The coroner said old man Swallow's heart just stopped in mid-beat, that he was a worn-out man, and just about everyone around here agreed with that because only a worn-out man would beat his wife. And anyway, how could they cut open a soul, dissect and examine it? But his wife insisted that the old people cursed him or planted fear in him and that's what stopped his heart and wouldn't they be held responsible just the same as if they'd shot him with a gun? She said they had songs that could kill a man, she knew they did. But even though I've heard this before, who could believe there was such a thing as a song with the power to kill or hurt a person? Or even, like some maintain, a song that would keep the world alive.

Still, just to quiet Mrs. Swallow, the police took an interpreter and went out to the woods by Kili Swamp and talked to the close-mouthed old Taiga people. The police did it just to pacify her, and they felt mighty silly about it. They even laughed at it over coffee. I heard them myself in the doughnut shop where the cops hang out. "Someone ought to tell her this is the twentieth century," said one of them. And some of the younger Taiga people, my own cousins, laughed at Abraham's widow and said it was superstition and that she must have drunk too much herself with old Abraham, but after that you could see them thinking it over, whether it was possible to kill a man that way, and Ama says there are unseen forces all around us and we can't know them and that anything could happen in this world, anything at all. And after that, a few young men went to live with those people up at Kili, to help them with chores and to learn Taiga ways from them.

Later I heard from Mama how it was true that Abraham, a man who kept goats, beat his second wife one day, and it was true that the old people, on hearing that he'd beat his wife and his children in the past, and killed does out of season, held a tribal court at the place of old law, at Kili, and pronounced a death sentence on him. She said some people did believe he died by the songs and thoughts of the old people. But I think it was more likely that his fear was as big and tall as the old tree, Methuselah, and that was what doomed and killed him. He died by fear. That's what I tell myself.

A m a i s s i m p l e, not like my mama, who is so complex. My grandmother used to call it grace. Not simple in her mind, but in her ways, and she tells stories. I like the way she tells things, and I am her friend, her sole audience. Once she told me how she saw an alligator chase a butterfly and eat it and then smack its big, toothed mouth. The way she told it made me laugh.

Or she'll say, "Before the making, the great storm. Before the human people entered this world, there was the great cat, Sisa."

Sisa is our name for the cat, the Florida panther. The Taiga name.

"Sisa was the first person to enter this world. It came here long before us."

And I'll see the lithe, tawny brown body of the panther, Sisa, in my mind, the way I never see it in the woods, but only in pictures. Panther is our elder, and this is why we respect it so, even though no one hardly ever sees it, even the old people of the Panther Clan. Even when they were plentiful, you'd hardly ever see one.

I heard one of those gold-colored panthers once. Its cry was so loud I thought it could bring down the world. But now the world's come down without a cry. The panther's world, too, if you could call it different than ours.

Ama loves the panther. It grieves her that it's endangered and sick because she worships the cats. She said one was born alongside of her, to give her strength. That's what the old people used to say, that an animal was born when we were born, that it is our one ally in this life. It lent us its power when we needed it. I often wonder what animal it might have been that would have walked with me, in my footsteps, me in its paw prints, and slept beside my skin if I'd been born in the older days. Ama says it's still this way, things haven't changed as much as they seem, but if it's true I don't believe any animal has done too well by me. It hasn't shown itself or protected me, either one.

But Ama always watches for the panther. She believes it is there. Sometimes at night she looks out in the darkness and I believe it's true as she says; they exchange glances, see into each other's eyes.

Ama Eaton isn't really my aunt. I call her that because it's what my mother called her the first time I came here with my uncles. Ama's about the same age as my mother, and they are cousins in a roundabout way, second cousins I think, but Mama calls her that out of respect for what she knows and who she is. Mama respects her and is jealous. Mama's made her choices and they are different. Still, she'd like it both ways. I can see that now and then. She'd like to learn from the old people, live the way we used to, but she wants it modern, too. Ama says it's not about choices but about heart and heart is what Mama's low on. Because of how Ama lives, she's a woman both admired and ridiculed, sometimes by the same people and in the same moment of time. You could say she's traditional even though she has no healing herbs or roots or songs. Not that I know of. What she's got is herself, and that's all she has. She doesn't even have a stick to shake, my mom says. It's true, she has no lights or television or washing machine, but sometimes, even so, I think she's got more than the rest of us because she believes in herself, in what she does. She lives in a natural way at the outside edges of our lives, and she "keeps up relations," as she says, with nature and the spirit world. I see this firsthand. It's the way she lives in the place where Cuban lizards climb trees and plants look enough like gold in the deep shade and slant of afternoon sun that the Spanish believed there were riches here, in this place that is now darkening with storm and smelling of rain.

Since the first time I was here, I've kept coming back, but I come alone now. The first time I came was when my uncles sent me to ask her if they could cut some trees nearby. I stood in front of her, a small girl, but not as afraid of her as my uncles were. Her eyes were the color of river mud after the wash of a storm, her chest nearly flat beneath her dress, her neck too bony, her collarbone protruding. I thought she was ugly, but I stood here with something like courage, on this very porch, and asked her about the trees.

She looked me over like she was thinking all the same things about me, then asked, "Which trees?"

I could smell fish frying behind her, in her house, the house that was blue then.

I pointed behind me and to the west. "Those ones that are dying out there. We'll bring you back some of the wood," I said. "Uncle Sonny says you could use some."

"All right. Go ahead." And that was all we said. She turned and went back to the fish dinner cooking on the stove. She had a screen door then. I had seen her through the screen. And I saw her older and darker than she is. But when I went back to help take the wood to her, she invited me in and gave me a glass of sweet tea to drink. I sat down with her at the table and we talked while I waited for my uncles to stack the wood, and she looked nice then, her hair shiny and clean around her shoulders, her eyes soft.

"You know my mother," I said, taking in her hair, her hands that looked small and old from hard work. "She's your cousin."

And she said, "Yes, I do, and you're nothing like her at all."
That was what won me over to Ama.

After that, they told me not to be going out to her place. But I come here anyway and I help her out and no one says much to me about it. I bring her ice sometimes, or sugar for her tea, or other small things I pilfer from my mother's place, a can opener or strainer, perhaps.

My mama knows I come and help her out even though she pretends she doesn't, but we don't say a thing about it to Herm, my mama's husband, because he's funny about these things; he's suspicious of just about everyone.

I should be mad at my mama for staying with Herm, but mostly I feel sorry for her. But Herm is one part of why I stay with Ama so much. Him, and the way his cold eyes follow me, the way he looks me down and then up, hungry, and it takes only two seconds but I can read what it means that fast. But that's only part of it. The other part is that Ama is a kind, good woman. I haven't told her a thing about Herm, but she sees it in him anyway, and has told me, in so many words, to stay out of his way. She says he's an attack waiting to happen. And I always wonder why it's me he's after when Donna, my sister, is so pretty.

Ama likes having me here. It's better than being at home. It's like being part of the world. Some days we go out and fish. Or she'll teach me to track the black fox that lives out a few miles past the bend in the road, out in the lightning-struck oak grove. The thing I like about tracking the animals is that it teaches me how to move. I move lean and strong in the shade of trees. And although you can't eat the fish because now the water's poison with the runoff of the farmers and cane growers, fishing has its lessons, too. It teaches me to be still. And holding still is not something that comes easy to me.

I'm learning from Ama how to survive and be friends with this land, and this is a place where a girl can get lost and the swamps and trees would eat her alive. It's a dangerous place with dark corners. On the days when Ama is silent, I learn from her stillness. It's not that she's moody. It's not an empty quiet, either, the way it would be with some people. It's a full silence and I like sitting with it and it's a relief from the chattiness of my sister and mom. I can't say what I learn from it; there's no words for it. Words are such noisy things and silence is something you have to listen to and when you do, it takes you by the hand, it catches hold of you. It tells you how to know things, like how sounds travel, where a certain bird is calling from.

But my feelings about Ama are mixed, I admit. Sometimes I love her, and in those moments I think the gap between her teeth is beautiful. But there are times I don't even like her, and on those days I think she's ugly. I can't account for these feelings, but I think it has to do with how the world catches me up. It's when I've come from school I'm most likely to find her homely and strange. I see her through the eyes of other people and what they'd think of her. Through their eyes she looks wild and crazy. My mama said Aunt Ama was married once and the man left because she wasn't tame enough to be a wife. Still, I always want to stay with her. Maybe it's because I am afraid of everything and she's afraid of nothing and I want to learn this from her. Foolish, my mama calls her fearlessness, and she says foolish people don't last too long around here. But I think it's courage more than foolishness that Ama has, and besides, sometimes I long for, I feel a longing for the old ways she lives by. And that's why I come here. I feel called.

Today is a day Ama is beautiful, but a person has to look for it. If she was a flower, she'd be one of those hard-living ones that hang on to the earth for dear life and have tiny blooms a person can barely see, but they are there.

I sip my coffee and the clouds are darkening. I watch the white goat and kid. They are unnaturally white in the strange stormlight. The kid butts against his mama's head. She ignores it and keeps eating away at the brush. The goat was one of Abraham Swallow's goats. It came here on its own accord and no one could keep it at home, so now it seems to be Ama's. His wife says Ama stole it and she's going to have the law after her. The truth is, Ama and I have both tried to take the nanny goat back to Mrs. Swallow's and it returns on its own. It doesn't like the woman. It likes Ama. It's simple as that. And now I think again how Donna and I were the last ones to ever see Abraham Swallow alive and I don't know why but Donna made me swear to silence so no one would question us. Like we'd done something wrong. Someone's always swearing me to silence, even Mama's husband, Herm, who says she'd be brokenhearted if I ever told her how he keeps after me. And he's right, I'm sworn to silence and betray myself, and if I talk, I betray Mama.

Then I look at Ama and I realize for the first time that Ama isn't as old as I think. It's just that I think she is old because I am so young. I am sixteen. I am young and smart, not pretty, but smart. I am a thin girl whose mother has said not to spend too much time with Ama out in the woods because Ama doesn't ever put her foot down inside a church and she's bound for hell. My mother is of a split mind, too, and she thinks Ama Eaton believes like an old woman, in old things, and it's probably a sin, what she believes. But I think my mother, who tries to pass for white, is really afraid I will love Ama more than I love her. For Mama, love is something we have in small measures and there's never enough of it to go around. She sees everything as a threat that will subtract love from her world. My mama is parched for love. Still, she knows I come here and help Ama out and she keeps quiet about it, as if some part of her agrees with what I do, as if she likes the ways Ama is simple or the ways she's also strong and tough-minded as a mule. Mama says she isn't going to turn to dust when she dies, she's going to turn to grit.

I look at Ama as she stares out into the swamp trees. I wonder why I've thought of her as old when she isn't. I'm right, though, when I think of her as wild. She's wild as the land. Grandpa was the one who said that. He watched her grow up so he knew it firsthand. He said you could see it in her right at the start. How she would go into the swamps and big trees, how she didn't talk much with people or laugh and she always acted like she thought she was royalty when she wasn't even pretty. "Posture," Mama calls it. But Grandpa said it like he respected her and how she held herself up tall and straight, even loved her for it, even with him so much older than she was. I think he meant that everyone who sees her knows she is strong and she feels their knowing this and it keeps her distant and makes her tall.

Ama looks at me quietly. She has honest eyes. "Did you dream?" she says.

I shake my head no. I hardly ever remember dreaming. I used to, though, before Mama married Herm. I used to dream each and every night.

"I did," she says, and I know she's going to tell me about it, but first she gets up and goes inside. In just the few minutes she is gone, the sky gets darker. Birds sound like they are singing from something hollow. A cloud, heavy and thick, is laying itself down on us, muting the sounds of the land.

Long before I knew Ama, I'd heard stories about her. She was a weak and sickly girl until she disappeared from Walker Town when she was only twelve. This is a place where a person can be lost two feet from a road and never be seen or heard from again, but she showed up, weeks later, standing in the tall grasses near a stand of bamboo someone had planted. She was different when she came back. She had a still gaze, unwavering and strong. It was the rainy season and everyone wondered why her clothes weren't soaked clear through and wet on her skin. She'd found shelter of some kind. They were afraid, at first, she'd been stolen by Tate, the hermit that lived south of Kili Swamp. Some of the superstitious ones believed she'd been taken by the little people to learn the medicine ways. That is what the old people say happens in the woods at times, the little people take a person away and teach them things, and when that person returns they know medicine. But this is just another old belief and I don't give superstition even an ounce of weight.

Other people were afraid Ama'd been killed by that horse-stealing, cow-dragging bear that was around even back then and that what returned was not really Ama but only looked like her, like a spirit that had changed bodies the way they used to do when people could turn into animals and animals could transform themselves into a human shape. And some people said she'd done that, she'd met and married a panther, and now she was an animal come back to observe us to see if our manner of worldly conduct toward them was right and kind, and because of this, those people—some of them had been cruel to animals—changed their ways when she was near them because her presence was that strong when she came back, and they were afraid of her strength. But whatever it was that happened to her, no one was ever comfortable with Ama Eaton again. Except me and a few of the older people like Janie Soto, the head of our clan, and Annie Hide, who has healing hands. If I had to believe any one of these superstitious stories, it would be this last one, but only because it's the most interesting. But I suppose what really happened when Ama left was that she went up to the place above Kili Swamp and stayed with the old people. Because I know she's said that Janie Soto, who helped raise her, had wanted her to live up there, but Ama said the old ways are not enough to get us through this time and she was called to something else. To living halfway between the modern world and the ancient one.

My mother was a girl when Ama stepped back into the civilized world. She said she never saw one who looked that calm and what could she possibly have eaten in all that time except wild things and she thought for sure that no one remembered what wild things were good to eat anymore now that everyone shopped in the store for their food, and the swamps were so full of poisons.

Grandma said it was like Ama was from another time when she came back and that she's been out of place in this world ever since, and just about everyone can vouch for that.

All I know, all I figure, is this: she was changed by the wild, by whatever she met or that happened to her out there in those bogs and trees and low-lying clouds.

In truth, I know little about Ama even though I've heard all the stories. I can't say I know or understand her even though I visit her and go about with her, fishing in the boat, listening for snakes in the grass. And while I'm afraid of snakes, she says they must be important creatures to have so many natural, god-given weapons and people ought to leave them alone. Old Janie Soto, the oldest person in our tribe and head of the Panther Clan, the old woman who never speaks a word of English and who always wears strands of red beads around her neck, like fire or the first red of dawn, used to visit Ama and me and sit outside in front of Ama's splintering house on the chair and they'd smile, the two of them, and sing old songs, the kinds that have echoes in them, and I always figured Ama was going to grow old like that, like a true Taiga Indian who didn't mingle with the white world, who knew the songs and dances of the past. She was going to be proud of what she is in a way the rest of us are not, in a way my mother has never been.

———

Ama comes back out with a plate of biscuits. She's

already buttered them. It's hot this morning, even with a storm moving in, and the biscuits are good and sweet. As I eat one and taste the salt of butter, I watch more storm clouds form. There's distant thunder.

Ama tells me, "I dreamed a golden panther. It came to me in a dream. It stood on two feet and said follow me. It stood up like a person and I could see its belly and eyes and it gestured at me, that crooked-tail creature. But it looked so skinny and sick it broke my heart to pieces." It's not the first time she dreamed of a panther, either, but it's the first time one talked with her. Even the elders never see one anymore, Ama says.

For only a moment, as I listen to her dream, a patch of sharp sunlight cuts through the clouds and lays itself down on the road and the plants all around us start rattling in the light, strange-smelling wind that begins to blow in as if the world is also listening to Ama's words.

"You should have seen it. It stood there looking at me. It was so close I could smell it. And when I woke up it was peculiar but that smell was there, inside the room. Like the panther'd been here right beside me."

I'm sitting beside Aunt Ama, listening. Listening, too, to a thousand songs of locusts all around us, and that's when I see the four women from another tribe come down along the road slow as a breeze, shaking their rattles, singing together beneath the heavy clouds that are coming in with them, from the same direction, as if they are forming up near the Kili Swamp. They must be the four women Ama told me about once before, only I didn't believe her then and now I see them for myself, and hear them singing, their voices higher than the locusts, and I stand up and watch them. They are walking slightly above the ground as if they are gliding and have no feet.

I can barely breathe as I see them. The women are straight-backed and move like all four of them are just one person. This early in the day there are already heat waves on the road, so it looks like water is on the ground in places. It is a mirage, a pooling of water that isn't really there. Eyes are like that, I tell myself, always seeing what's not there as real as if it was, but it all looks true to me, the women singing slow and then fast, faster, so fast it is powerful and mighty enough to sing the dead straight up from the ground, even Abraham Swallow, and there is the sound of turtle-shell rattles, and I can feel the song in my stomach as they float above the road and seem to have no feet and come toward us.

The bony cattle in the distance disappear for a moment behind the heat waves, and an old Oldsmobile comes along the road and passes the women like a blur on the straight fossil road. The women in their long dresses vanish a moment behind the car, for only a moment.

"See them walking," she says. She's sitting there and she doesn't even look up and she says, "Look at them." She doesn't turn her eyes toward them. It's like the seeing is inside her.

The women in their dresses are coming in from the highway out of the heat. Dancing almost, in ancient dresses no one wears anymore, drifting and singing toward us. They remind me of ghosts. I think they aren't there, they can't be there, but I ask, "What do you think they want?"

Ama's voice is strange and beautiful. She says, "There must be good news today. The messengers are coming." Says it like she knows them.

I nod as if I know what she means. Then I see the birds flying in and they are noisy and agitated about the coming storm and the sky is growing darker and I can feel the temperature drop. When I look again the women are gone. I want to know where they've gone as much as I want to know where they came from and as I look it is as if I see the space between things like there's a place in between every solid thing where creation takes place. Maybe all life comes from there and then, quick as water, is taken back again.

"Who are they?" I ask again about the women.

She doesn't answer. She closes her eyes and there's a look on her face I can't name, like she has seen something terrible and beautiful at one and the same time.

Later, as we sit at the table with the new, strong-smelling oilcloth on it, she tells me again about the panther she dreamed. She thinks it was guiding her toward something. I half listen, and as I do, I look around her house. Aunt Ama's house is a worn place. My mother says it's time for the house to die. She says houses are alive things and we should respect their wishes and Ama's house wants to die and Ama should let it. Ama's house has termites and a path worn into the floor from the stove to the window where she looks out. The path goes out the door to the porch and down the two wide steps. A stranger could read her life from this floor. They'd find fish scales in the boards if they looked close enough, and road dust and pieces of leaves and stems.

Through the window I see the rain clouds still growing and building and moving toward us from behind the big trees. The temperature has dropped to the point where there's a chill in the air. The clouds will meet the way they do in this place. It's the rain coming. The clouds will join with one another, force themselves together like two fighting-mad people and lend each other the strength to hurl a storm at us.

We go stand at the window in the cool wind to watch the storm come in. The wind is blowing the curtains I made for her out of my mother's old blue cotton flour sacks. Ama holds one curtain still. The others dance with the sweep of wind.

As we watch more birds come in, from the west, there's a noisy excitement in the air.

"How many do you suppose there is?" She asks this as if she can't count. Not that numbers mean anything to her anyway.

They are dark-colored birds.

"There must be at least a hundred or so," I tell her. They light down like ashes, unsettled, some of them shifting to make way for each other.

And then the wind starts knocking at the door like it has knuckles and fists. And soon it begins to rain, a soft rain at first, even carried by the wind. We stand and watch another cloud of rain come toward us. It approaches the way the old women did, with that same above-ground kind of movement and even though I know it's a storm coming in, my skin loves the wet air. There's an overwhelming smell of freshness. It feels good. I smile even though I'm as afraid of storms as I am of snakes, and I close my eyes and breathe. In the distance the soft outlines of the land are breathing in the water, the land not yet brimming with it, the deep green and black of trees taking it in as if they are swallowing. The land and the trees have needed rain. It has been a drought. This is the year of wildfire in places that were swamp, the year Lake Okeechobee was opened and the water level down here rose so much it drowned all the fawns. The wardens had to kill all the starving deer that were standing up to their necks in water, and it broke my heart to see the little deer with their white undersides lying along the high roads in a line, counted out and numbered as if they were nothing more than rocks or coins. It seemed cruel to me, even though they said it was the only thing to do and they tagged them so they could examine their hungry insides later. I told my mom I was mad about it because it was the building and farming and sugarcane that were killing the deer, and she said, "Why do you always have to fuss so much about everything?" She thinks it's the small price you pay for progress. I think it's the way to kill a world. That's how different we are from each other.

Soon I hear the storm strengthen, the rain beginning to bil-
low down, and when I look again, in just that small moment
since I closed my eyes, the ground has grown dirty white with
the rush of the heavy rain, the sky shaking with the sound of
thunder, the sudden lightning breaking open all around us. It
arrives that quickly and I see how it forces Ama's morning glories off the vine. They are on the ground like blue wings of
butterflies, tattered and dying. The water rushes down all
around them and then they are gone, carried away, and the
strong wind fills the rain-smelling room. The curtains are
blowing in and out from the window and they are flapping
there. It's as if everything breathes, hard and desperate, the
land, the house, the water.

The wind is a living force. We Taiga call the wind Oni. It
enters us all at birth and stays with us all through life. It
connects us to every other creature. Standing here at the
window, I think this word, Oni, and I try to close the windows but they are swollen. As hard as I push, two of them
won't go down at all.

More noisy birds fly in. They are just as spooked by the curtains that are blowing in and out of the open windows as they
are by the storm. We can just make them out in the darkening
air. They stand huddled together, stirring and rising and set-
tling beneath the trees like they are trying to tell us something, pushing against each other, displacing one another,
seeking safety that isn't there.

"How many do you think are there now?" she says again.

I look at the birds and in my mind I estimate. By now there
are several hundred, maybe a thousand. They could kill us, I
think, this many birds, they could destroy us, and I wonder
why it is the animals and birds show us any mercy at all, why I
have ever felt safe from them. I wonder, too, why they stay near
or help us, like the time the red wolf showed my mama how to
get home, that time when her husband, Herm, drove her to the

woods near State Line and threw her out of the car in a storm and told her not to come home. The red wolf came to her, she said, and I knew it was true because she's a Christian and wouldn't say anything that isn't the truth. She doesn't believe in animals or any of the stories old people tell about them. She doesn't believe they have souls or power, but she said the red wolf came and took her home that day. She saw it plain as day, and she trusted it because she remembered Janie Soto and one of the other old Taiga women, Annie Hide, telling about how sometimes the animals used to help the humans, how they would teach them the plants that were healing, sing songs for them to learn, how they would show the people the way to renew the broken world.

Ama's dying house sounds like a seashell with ocean wind blowing through it or maybe it's more like wind in a bottle. Outside, the wind and rain are forcing the grasses down flat. It's more than just an electrical storm, I'm sure, because through the heavy clouds and lashing rain, I see the old dog with her puppies and long teats; she sets to howling and looking for a safe place. And it scares me and the birds are flying in now from the east like they are coming out of the shadow of something mighty into a place they believe will hide them. The hair on the back of my neck rises, and a cold chill climbs up my back. I stand up. It's more than just a storm. "It's a hurricane," I say to Ama. I'm sure of it. Suddenly everything feels unsettled and tense. The sky is dark. The house creaks. "It's looking bad. We better close things up," I say. "We ought to go get that dog and her puppies."

But before I say this, Ama has already jumped into motion to tie down the house, and I can't even hear her feet on the floorboards as she moves to close up the shutters, to get the wood to hammer over the windows. "Hurry!" she yells at me over the wind, and I feel my heart in a panic, the wind and rain entering the room, the tablecloth edges lifting, the floor is wet and slick. The old dog scares me, too, running off that way with her puppies, and I don't know if they are safe. I yell, "The dog, Ama, get the dogs." But she can't hear me.

The light outside is so strange, even though there's a patch of sun on the roots of the old foreign tree called Methuselah. In that one patch of moving light that comes down from behind the clouds, that little runaway piece of sun, I see the roots of Methuselah, gnarled like hands grasping mightily at something, like old, old hands, hanging on to the earth.

Ama is headed out to the shed. I follow her, my heart racing. As I run out to the shed to get the hammer and nails, my shadow is long, running over the wet grass. I'm surprised to see that I have one at all and it's such a funny thing to notice, it seems ironic what with the rain and darkness, but that little patch of sunlight is still working its way through the black clouds like someone shining a flashlight through the middle of the night, and I don't know how, but it's fallen across the shaded land as if light travels in a straight line. And then, just as suddenly as I noticed it, it disappears, the shadow, the sun, all of it, and what remains is darkness, the sky is gray lead with low, bruised clouds.

From outdoors, when I look back, the curtains I made for Ama's windows out of my mother's old flour sacks are blowing out of the two stubborn, open windows like sails on a ship. Like we are going to be blown east and away, and I can see the house carried off by the wind, its curtain sails filled with wind, gliding across the land like the women did, easy, barely touching earth.

And then we can just hear that a siren sounds, a fire truck moving up the darkened road to let us know the storm is coming, and we should go to safety, a man's voice through a loudspeaker.

I run back up the steps with the hammer and help Ama nail the shutters. Ama is good with tools. She can drive a nail with only one tap of the hammer so I just hold the shutters closed, wood against wood, with the wind whipping my hair. Fear is ice-cold in me. All I do is hold the shutters and hand her the nails, but even at that it's aching hard work in the wind and harder still to breathe, as if the air has disappeared under the force of wind. In the distance, I hear the sound of sky and trees and water, all roaring, all cracking open and moving toward us, and another strange thing I notice is how even though the skirt of Ama's dress is heavy with wetness, the wind blows it and I see her legs and they remind me of a young girl's legs and she seems vulnerable to me, more than I'd ever have thought, as she nails shut the eyes of the house.

Rain falls harder now, at a slant. I'm wet and chilled. Earth turns into water, the smell rich with loam, and water becomes mud. Everything is wet, soaked, this world turning into another one, as if it is only sand turning over in an hourglass, as if someone just now set it on end and it's starting to fall once again. This is what I think, surprised to be so calm in my mind, standing and holding a shutter closed tight in the driving wind, the rain hitting against me while Ama tries to hit the nail, for the first time missing. And while I hold this shutter is when I look down at the ground and see the rattlesnakes, and my heart moves over in my chest. Rattlesnakes, and they are winding toward us, moving faster than I knew they could move.

"Ama, look!" I say, letting go of the shutter, letting it fall.

The snakes know what is coming. They are afraid of drowning and they are climbing up into the trees. Some are climbing the steps toward the door of Ama's house, looking at us with their unseeing eyes as they move toward safety, the narrow muscle of snakes, their backs wet from the rain and shining, looking toward us as if we are two of the four unreal women floating above the ground, not quite real to them.

Ama doesn't see them.

"The snakes," I say to her again, pointing.

And then she sees them, too. Now some are looping themselves in the trees outside, shining and silver, entwined in the branches, tongues darting out, cold-eyed, but others try to enter her house. She yells over the wind and sound of rain and I think she says that they need shelter, too, don't pay them any mind, but when she nails that last shutter, we go inside and she shuts the door against them, closes us in with the darkness, and even in the noise of the storm I can hear them thump against the walls. The snakes want in. We lock ourselves against the storm as much as we can. Ama closes, and even bolts, the door, but inside the wind and rain and darkness it feels like the house with its bug-eaten floorboards is starting to move, and the storm is getting louder so it's not worth trying to talk and the house groans and creaks. Ama relights the lantern and sets it on the table next to a jar of white flowers. Our shadows fall across the walls. The noise of the storm outside is a roaring sound. It's close at hand beside us and I'm thinking if it's a hurricane we should leave because this little house is going to fall around us. Then Ama gets up and goes back to the door and opens it to look at the sky. From behind her, from where I sit and watch, I see her stand framed in the door, the wind blowing her long hair, her wet old dress. The sky is deep blue to the south, almost black, as if there's smoke.

"Don't let any snakes in," I say.

Ama shuts the door tight, but then she turns to me. "Did you tie down the boat?" Her voice merges with the drum of rain. She's right. I've forgotten all about the boat. I need the boat. It's my life. And it's my real father's boat, it's what I have left of him.

"Oh, no!" I jump up, desperate to reach my little boat before the worst of the storm arrives.

"Maybe you better leave it," she says, before she looks at my face and sees that I could never do that. "Okay, I'll come help you," she says, pulling on a sweater, preparing to go with me. As if a sweater could shield her.

"No. Don't come," I say. "I can get it faster." I don't think she should leave the house. Besides, I'm known for my running. But I'm nervous and I wonder, too, if it wouldn't be best to let the boat go, to do as she says and let the storm have it.

"Then hurry!" she says. She is disturbed at my leaving. She worries about my safety. It's on her face.

And I run out the door, past the snakes, and away toward the water of lakes and glades and rivers. This time the snakes and I don't fear each other. Each of us has a bigger enemy in the storm. As I run into the deepening color of storm, I don't recognize this place, this land that is screaming and drowning and I know this is just the beginning; the full force of the storm has not yet reached us. Only once do I stop. For half a second, I think of turning back, and even that half second costs me in time.

In the rushing water, my hair is glued to my neck and back, my clothes wet and heavy, so much water on my face I can barely see, but wet and breathless, I manage to get down to the boat in the slippery mud of the bank and I'm sliding and nearly blinded and hoping I am not a blood sacrifice to this clay. Soaked to the bone, when I reach the brown water, it is churning and the level is high. Slipping in the mud, pulling my hair out of my eyes, my back strained, my arms aching, I drag the boat up from the water as far as I can, with all my strength, breathing hard and crying, and I drag and push it up to the big tree for all I'm worth, my feet going out from under me, the wind hitting me, and I am crying, my heart pounding like a frightened mouse I once held in my hand, sorry it feared me so. But the storm, this storm, has no apology. It doesn't care if I'm small and frightened.

I tie the boat to the large tree and place rocks inside it so it won't get blown about although it might get drowned, and then, exhausted, I take off running, back toward Ama's, hoping the tree will hold. Then, just then, there is that worst sign in a storm. It is suddenly still, the deadness, I think, just before the worst of it hits. That heavy moment of silence dark gray with weight. It is dead still as if I am in a clear eye of destruction, a calm heart dressed in a skin of fury, but it's not even the eye of the storm, it's the silence before it hits, the time it takes to inhale, to gather itself. I have time, I hope, in this clear space, to make it back to Ama, as if she holds safety in her skin, as if the house will hold me safe even though it's dying and rotting away. Then I wonder again if maybe we should leave that rough old house altogether. But where would we go? One place is no safer than another in these storms that are temperamental enough to make claims on anyone's property, just or not. I take off in a dead run, and then the wind strikes.

The wind has pushing hands, it has a body. It screams like a train coming through. It hits so quickly it stops me in my running and throws me to the ground. It forces the air out of my lungs and I see the dead and drowning insects being blown right off the earth in front of my face. There isn't time to seek shelter in the dark light and slashing rain of the storm. It's roaring and screaming at me. Somewhere there is what sounds like the clatter of chains hitting against each other, and the report of guns. I try to get up and run and it throws me to the ground again. All around me the trees bend, the dark leaves are thrown off. I fall and try to inch my way closer to Ama's and I think I'll be safe if only I can get back to the roots of Methuselah, who has lived through all these centuries of storm. "Please," I say to something, as if I believe in God and am wanting his help. "Please." Maybe I say this to the wind, the wind that is our life, that could be our death. But the wind doesn't listen. It claps against me with the brute force of nature. I want to stand and run, but there is no running from such a storm. I crawl back a little, like I am inching my way to a birth through air, laboring, moving toward Ama, who is in the dark house with the flickering light of the lantern. I try to find the tree that's held its ground through more storms than anyone alive can count. I try to keep my eyes open but the rain and blowing sand cuts at them and I can't see and my ears ache from the wind. My nails claw at the ground, holding to the thin near-roots of grasses, but it feels like I could be blown away from earth just like the ants and beetles. Even flat on my stomach on the ground I could be blown off earth clear up to the black holes and burning stars in the sky.

The trees I can see are nothing more than sticks being shaken. A chair comes flying from out of the storm, strange and not in keeping with this place. Limbs break and fall at the feet of the storm but I can't hear them, only the howling and roaring of the storm that is alive, that has taken all the air from me into it, and my breath makes it stronger and me weaker. But even without air there is a smell, a fish smell from the water that's being taken up, a smell of decay, mingled with the scent of rain and sodden earth.

I try to work my way back to Methuselah, moving against the weight of wind. I grab hold of another tree, feel the wind's body against me, hitting me as I pray at the bottom of the tree that it won't blow down. I grab at the tree roots and it is dark and I ache from trying to hold on.

Just another minute, I tell myself, trying to be calm. Just one more. This is how I survive in my life. By time. Always. Moment by moment. I try to remember that there's a center to every storm, an eye of stillness. It calms me now to remember this, as if I can find that place or it will find me. What else can I do when I'm so small and what's bigger than me now—and everything is—has water running everywhere like something is being born, and so many things are flying past me, pieces of wood, howling things, a bird with its large gray broken wing bent at a strange angle and I know the bird screams in the dark of storm, but I can't hear it. But more than minutes pass. It seems like hours but time has no meaning. Everything is stronger and louder than me now and it feels like it's all against me, everything is blowing in, clothes and paper, fence posts from where they were holding cattle. Nests fly away from trees. Trees break, bend, and fly away from earth. My arms shake. I hold tight to the bottom of the tree. I pray the tree holds. Water slashes like a knife. I ache from the effort of staying on earth.

And then for a moment, a still moment, it all stops and it is eerie and dark as night and it is quiet. I look up and see a circle of dark clouds roiling, tumbling, and in between them I see a clear sky and stars. It is twilight and the stars are shining with peace. And I stand up. I don't know how long I stand looking at this eye, so amazed at the pure sky, before I realize it is my chance to run, and I do, as the eye of this storm passes over, I run back toward the house, and as I do, somewhere along the way it starts up again. I scream and I see that the sky is bruised and unnatural, and the wind is so strong the deer are flying, looks of terror on their faces. The deer are flying in the storm. The hungry deer they have been shooting. They are lifted up by the wind and everything is again dark and wounded and two large trees turn over and fall, black-trunked and shaken out by the hands of something bigger. Fifty-foot trees, they must be, their dark roots in air. I think I hear them crash down but I don't, it's all drowned out by the sound of the storm. I can't even hear the slashing rain or the terrified screams of owls I know are there. The deer are flying and I hear only a loud roar. The deer look so strange and surprised up in the air, legs flailing at nothing but the body of wind. Then there are tree limbs and parts of houses, a piece of the patched tin roof of Ama's chicken coop. I want to cover my head as it all flies by, but I fall to the ground and hold to another tree. There is a pause now and then like the great animal of wind is taking a breath back inside it. In these pauses, or maybe they are more like gusting waves, I try to move forward, try to reach the big tree, Methuselah, my ears aching from the cruel pressure of air.

In one pause I come up behind the house against the wind. Then, afraid of the clearing I'd have to cross, I slowly work my way around from tree to tree, and when I do, I see, can barely make out Ama.

She is standing upright, pinned against the side of her little house by the wind. She was coming to help me or maybe to nail up that last useless shutter and the wind threw her back, changed its direction, forced itself against her. She is straight and looks tall, the hammer still in her hand as if she believes it anchors her. Her eyes are closed and her dark hair is thrown straight back, plastered against the wood as if it is painted there. Her clothes are blown hard against her body. She doesn't look real. Her hair looks like it is part of the dying house, a black vine creeping along the wall, and she is only carved wood. I think I can see her rib cage through the cloth, her belly and breasts. She is against the house like she is nailed there, crucified, and she can't move, she is that held by the power of the storm, and the door is torn off its hinges and open. Several dead birds are also thrown against the house. One of the snakes is cast from the tree against Ama. The wind has pinned her and things are flying against her. It's as if we are in a sea with weeds and debris flung by mighty currents. Ama is being covered by blown-in vines and wet, dark leaves, as if the world is trying to bury her, and her eyes are closed. I see her mouth moving, but all I hear is the scream of the storm.

The moment of my seeing once again passes. I scream out to Ama and do not even hear my own voice, and then I can't see her anymore through the torrents of rain. I see only what flies past, I feel only a branch that hits me. I hear only the roaring voice of the storm. All nature is against us. It falls down on us. It throws itself at us. And then I say, "God!" calling out to what has never heard me before, because through the dark air of storm, Methuselah falls and I hear nothing but only see that what has lasted this long is being taken down now as if it were nothing, as if it had never been anything that counted. This tree planted by the Spanish, conceived on another continent. I think this must be a dream and I'll wake up clammy and flushed, my hair tangled across my face, but however I try to convince myself I'm dreaming, I know old Methuselah lays there black and uprooted from the hole in the ground where it once was held. And then, after what seems like days, after the muddy, racing water, after the roaring voice of the storm has spoken, passed judgment, it turns and runs away, the wind lets up and the ground breathes a sigh of relief that the storm is ending and sooner than most, and I wonder if I should feel lucky.

After the storm, it is strangely quiet. It seems like everything is on the ground. I look around me, examining the damage. The ground is littered and strewn and wet. I am crying. I'm turned around and I don't recognize the place. Then, to the left, I see Ama's house that I had come so close to and realize I was blown sideways, away from it, and never even knew it.

I see a woman hanging in one of the trees that somehow still stands, and I can't even scream when I see her. Then I see it's only a dress in the tree, no body inside it, and I breathe again. Like the ground and the trees, I am relieved.

I don't know how Ama's house withstood the pounding wind and tree limbs because the house was not that strong to start. The fronds from the roof are gone. The shed is splintered. The door is blown off its hinges. One shutter is ripped off, the window broken. But the house still stands.

Stunned animals walk about, unafraid of us. Two herons, unable to fly, walk slowly. We are usually only something visited in their dreams and they must believe this silence is not the waking world, the wakened time, as they look at us without seeing. Ama's goats walk by, no longer white, their fur matted and wet, like sleepwalkers among the torn trees and ragged mosses and debris. It is a quirk of fate, of wind, that they survived, that any of us did, for that matter. There is a chicken, still alive, standing, with blood coming from its beak. A dead horse lies on the ground and it's covered with mud so that I can't tell what color it is. The closest horses, the Spanish horses at the Sanchez ranch, are several miles away, and it must have come from there, but I can't think of how it got here. Perhaps the wind blew it the way it blew the deer, but it's too heavy for that. More likely it ran off in fear and was struck down by a tree and died here. Now the horse sits on the ground, its legs pulled together under it, sitting poised this way, but its head is on the ground, its neck stretched out and bent forward gently. I can see the sloping lines of its body, angles of its hipbones. It is covered with mud and dark leaf, trees uprooted around it and pieces of collapsed houses that have blown in, scattered here and there, in this vine-twisted place.

Then I look down and see myself and I am naked.

Ama is standing at the top of the steps. She looks as stunned as the animals, and I go up to her and say, "That's my dress in the tree. The wind blew my clothes off me. It's *my* dress in the tree." No one could be as surprised as I am. But in the wake of the storm, it doesn't matter that I am naked. Not to either of us. She hears my words but not their meaning and she doesn't yet see that I am naked. Her face is bloodless and white.

I see how the snakes were flung against her house by the rough, angry hands of wind. There are three, one still alive, a brown piece of slow-moving flesh. It, too, is covered with mud. It moves as if just returned to life, delivered out of death. Ama has a bruise forming on her arm where she was hit, perhaps by the snake. The preacher would say this is a bad sign, snakes at a woman's feet, but Ama doesn't believe in the preacher. She believes old Janie Soto and Annie Hide and the old women would say the snakes are a sign of God, they always were, it was always this way and it still is. They *are* God, Janie Soto contends. And Janie ought to know because she's been face to face with this other God all her life. For whatever reason I start to think of this old woman, I wonder how the old people who live in their little settlement at Kili Swamp have weathered this storm. And my mother, I wonder if her house has survived it, if she is okay or worrying about me, or if her faith relieves her of even these concerns.

An osprey, a survivor, flies over. In its claws it carries a fish that has been thrown from water to ground by the storm. This is how God receives us, I think, pulled out of our element, held tight and helpless. He eats us, my mother's God. The preacher thinks different from the Taiga way of thinking. He thinks a snake is the devil. The old ones think it is a god. He believes in angels, children with wings in the sky, but he doesn't believe in what's on earth or birds; he says it's all an illusion, this life on earth, a dream, a miserable place we will one day escape into the golden streets of heaven. I would like to think this way. Then I could believe this storm, as I suppose, as I wish, was not real. The black clouds, the broken trees. I am in the world, the preacher says, but not of it. I used to believe in that preacher, but when it comes to this kind of thing I can't say what I believe anymore. I can't say even what I think or know. Believing and knowing are two lands distant from each other.

The door has been blown off its hinge, but for the most part, Ama's house with its rickety smallness and decay seems to be standing almost unharmed except for the broken window and the door I step through, cautious that it might fall. Inside, from the shutter that has come unnailed, the curtains of that window are tattered threads and heavy and wet with mud. There are mosses and leaves and shards of glass on the floor and the windowsill and all I can think to do, naked as I am, is to take up the broom and try to sweep away the things that blew in.

The floor is wet and a dead chicken lies just inside the window, glistening with its wet, red feathers and a yellow open eye. I'm too stunned to cry or do anything but say, "I should go bury this," as if there is only the dead bird, as if there is no dead horse outside looking like it is asleep, covered with mud. But I can hardly hear my own voice, my ears injured by the storm.

Then I look down at myself and say again, "Ama, the wind has blown my clothes away." I don't try to cover my body. I'm too much in shock to be embarrassed at my thin little body so vulnerable-looking and young and bare. Still naked, I head back outside to find the shovel beneath the debris and mud.

"Wait," she says, sounding far away.

I don't wait. I go outside. I'm skinny and small, digging through the rubble of the shed, the branches and leaves and sticks of the world, and I think how the shed has been destroyed although the curing barn stands, the foolish barn built by some squatters who believed they could clear the trees and grow tobacco in this wet place. But even thinking this, all I really want to do is to dig holes for the dead animals. It's the only thing I want, to hide the dead.

I find the shovel by its handle sticking out of a mound of rubble and mud, but Ama comes to me and takes the shovel from my hands, gently.

"Come with me," she says, and she sounds calm, and leads me from the ruins of the shed.

Naked as the day I entered this world and breathed my first breath, I do as she says. I am breathing hard with exhaustion and I follow her to the house. Like I thought of God and tobacco, I think again of breath, and how we Taiga people have that word—Oni—for breath and air and wind. It is a force. Oni is like God, it is everywhere, unseen. I think I heard this word spoken in the rush of weather. I'm sure of it. The wind said its own name, "Oni." But I don't tell Ama that; she'd think I'm crazy. I just follow her to the house, quietly, peacefully past the yellow-eyed goats who are now sitting wet and flat against the ground and watching me, looking at the first human nakedness they have ever seen.

Ama goes inside and gets me a dress. "Here, put this on." She puts the dress in my hands.

I read her lips more than hear her. I am stupid standing here before her. The dress is pale green with buttons. It's so clean and innocent-looking and out of keeping with the storm and all that's just happened that I have to laugh even though I sound shrill, even to myself. "You want me to wear this?" There's a dead horse out there and the world is ruined and she wants me to wear this nice-looking, clean dress.

Ama smiles, too. Maybe we are happy to have survived.

I step into it and pull it up. "It's too big," I say, no longer laughing, but I wear it anyway. It seems to be getting dark, so I think it is evening. I button the dress. It's fresh-pressed. And while I smooth the skirt, I feel how the air is heavy about me. I feel its breath and heaviness against me, even inside my chest, like it's clamped down on me, and I think it's talking to me, still breathing out the power of the wind, and when I look up I see that the sun is in the wrong side of the sky as if a day snuck past the storm. Ama sits me down in a chair and wraps a blanket around me. Then she stands at the unhinged door and looks at the ruined land where nothing moves and all is rubble. It looks like everything is dead, the ground, the trees, all of it. She stands there, quiet, looking out. And I look at her and think to myself, yes, she is Taiga, my thoughts coming back from the storm, and it's just like she came from some of those people, the Calusas, I think they were, ancient people who made mounds out of oyster shells and killed Ponce de Leon with a plant, and now we are cying, both of us.

This was how the world was created, Ama told me once, out of wind and lashing rain. "We were blown together by a storm in the first place." It was all created out of storms. The mud was blown in with the trees and the seeds of growing things already planted in it. She said, too, that the white egrets were carried here from Africa in the eye of a storm that bellowed in from across the ocean in 1927. There were no white egrets here before that time. They were carried in the eye of that storm. I look about me and wonder if it was a storm that carried us Taigas here, lifted us up into its all-seeing, calm eye, and dropped us down in this godforsaken place. Mama used to say I looked like something the wind blew in.

Ama looks into the distance a ways. It's as if she looks for something, something out past the downed old tree. And then she points. Her hair is still wet and matted from the storm. She looks out over the land and she sees a deer. She says, "See that deer over there with the broken leg?"

I look to see where she is pointing. The deer limps and moves with pain. It breaks my heart just to see it.

"That's the one we're going to follow," she says. "It's the one."

I think she means to hunt that skinny, starving deer. It seems right, all hungry and injured that way. It only seems right to kill it, to put it out of its misery, to eat it. But she must be tired, I think. Where could she get the strength to go after it or kill it or dress it out, even a small deer like that one, when the wind has just about blown the life right out of us?

On three legs, the deer moves into the remaining trees and vanishes.

My own legs are heavy. I sit down, shaking, holding the blanket tight around me. And I remember now that I did dream, after all. I can see a piece of that dream, and something in my chest moves. I dreamed this storm with the flying deer. That's how it feels, like I've seen this before. I remember it, and the downy fine hair on my back moves with a chill. And I remember that Ama already said, as if years ago, in another time, when she saw the deer with the broken leg, "That's the one." As if all this has happened before and could happen again.

Then I get up and go stand next to her and pull the blanket tight as I can and watch the place where the deer has vanished. I say to her as I did in the dream or in another time—and I don't know why I say it. It's as if something speaks through me—I say, and don't even know what it means, "I know what will happen," as she moves the door, struggles with it, pulls it over the doorway and tries to close us in. She looks at me with no falseness anywhere on her face, and she says, "So do I."

3
TAKE

Some days the clouds rise up from water like breath or ghosts, and from the trees you can hear the bird that talks like an old woman. Other days the clouds look like a river flowing from a valley of sky. But today, after the storm, the clouds are low on water and land. They are ashamed of what sky has done and they try to hide the storm's damage from our eyes.

After the storm, even the sky lies exhausted. It seems dark in the afterlight of the storm, and Ama once again has lighted the lantern. The blue oilcloth is neat on the table, yet it seems we are not in a house at all. The storm has blown twigs and leaves through the open window, plastered them on walls and the muddy floor. It's as if we are in a forest. The door has fallen open. And yet the house feels strangely untouched, safe in a way I can't say. Maybe it's in the way a Hills Brothers coffee can full of bacon lard sits beside the sink and how the dishes are so neatly put away, and how I wash my hands and dry them on my skirt like on any other day.

Attracted by the dim lantern, June bugs and millers arrive at the unshuttered window and fly into the house around us.

They want to become light. They come through the window the same way the storm entered, and through the door blown off its hinges. How easy it is now to enter this house my mama says is dying.

I look out through the broken window and watch the clouds begin to lift. The strong winds have blown water all across the land. There are no edges, no borders between the elements because everything is water, silver and glassy. The whole ground moves and shimmers as if it is alive. The roads are nothing more than reflected sky. Fish, thrown out of water, have been able to swim out over land and there is an occasional, desperate flash of a white belly. Heaven has fallen.

In the distance are cloud-dark swamps. A heron cries like a lost soul and usually they are silent birds. I can just barely hear it; the screaming wind of the storm is still inside my ears.

I want to know how my mama and sister made it through the storm. It gives me a pang of guilt that I am not with them. There's no way to reach them for now. From Ama's I could walk down the road a half mile or so to the gas station, but I can see from here that the roads are closed, covered with fallen trees and other debris, and that the phone lines, too, must be out. My eyes scan the stormfields. There are new streams and bodies of water from the storm, and I worry about the wounded deer and all the other animals and creatures that have no shelter.

Soon a storm tide begins to come in and the water begins to rise. We are inland some distance from our dangerous neighbor, the gulf, but that's how strong a storm it was; water comes from far away in a wave, and from lakes above us, too. Slow and wide, it brushes across land, rising. Water is natural here. This land wants to be beneath it again, as it used to be not so many years before our time.

When the storm tide reaches Ama's dark, rickety house, I say, "It's rising." I look at her, but she doesn't move, not even to come watch the approach of water. She has given in to nature, or to something inside herself. She's unwilling to fend it off. But then, it has always been Ama's skill to live with the world and not against it. Still, she looks mournful.

The rising water and foam cover the palmetto fronds that blew off Ama's roof, and then the water climbs up, brown water up the cinder blocks the house rests on, and comes up the two steps like someone coming to visit, calm as you can think. It moves across the porch, laying itself down, brown and murky.

I look over at Ama. She's quiet, as if she's preparing herself for something, calling her soul to her as sure as if she's saying out loud, "Will all the parts of Ama Eaton come here, come home." The kettle heating on the stove is boiling, steaming up the window above the sink and she doesn't notice this any more than she notices the intruding water along the floor.

So I go over and turn off the stove, pick up the boots and put them on the table, then I pull the heavy, broken door as closed-tight as I can. By myself I take towels and an old blanket and put them at the bottom of the door against the floor, but the brown water still comes in the house along the sides of walls and there is nothing to do but watch it and lift my feet off the ground, sitting in the chair as it creeps toward me, gray and muddy. We are still in shock and we do not behave as normal. But I think of the snakes, one more time having to find shelter in trees, and this time I feel sorry for them. One day someone will find this world, our world, our time, our pieces, beneath a layer of limestone or silt. They'll find snake bones with their hundred ribs. They will be fossils in lime the way the old bones of mastodons are still beneath this land. At least that's what they say now. They'll find us like the treasure hunters who were searching for pieces of a wrecked Spanish galleon off the Keys found the sabertooths and mastodons. They broke through a layer of limestone and found a tusk from something large that had lived and walked before we were here, creatures whose remains dwell beneath the warm, clear waters, the newer mangroves, and the heat of sun. There are layers to the world. And with time, the world changes, a new layer forms, an old one falls or drifts. This much is always certain.

"Why are you so quiet?" I say to Ama, regretting the words as soon as they're spoken. I don't want to invade her thoughts. But I'm nervous about her plan to follow the deer and how she just sits there unaware of the water covering her feet. I study her face. It's as if she is preparing herself for something, as if she's left her body, entered some other place. Even though the storm is gone and the trees are becoming visible, I feel danger outside where everything is out of its place and water has come to fill it.

She says nothing, but her mind is busy. I look out on the world turned-over-on-end. Everything smells wet, of wood, of clay.

After a while, as the water seeps back away, Ama gets up and begins to sweep the floor as if mud and water can be brushed away, easy as dust. I am overwhelmed with the sadness of so much destruction, but more than that, I am exhausted. Without wanting to, without willing it or even thinking it, I go lie down on the bed and before I know it I dream of the flying bodies of deer and dogs. I dream my sister in her new blue dress being tumbled by the storm like she's no more than a weed. I dream tree roots growing upward, toward the sky in an upside down world, and they take root in air and bloom with their deep-scented flowers beneath them in the ground. And I see white snails under the layer of sleep, moving slowly over leaves like stars in a dark sky.

When Ama wakes me, I can't tell if it's morning or evening or how long I've been sleeping. A darkness hangs over us, the room full with moist air and the smell of mildew. I'm cold.

"It's time," she says, as if I've rested long enough. My first thought is of Methuselah, gone after all these years, the tree we expected to be there always.

I have the pillow in my arms, sheets around me, and I think I've only dreamed this whole story, the storm with the flying deer and Ama saying, when she saw the deer with the broken leg, "This is it, this is the one we'll follow."

The dress I am wearing feels damp. I get up and look outside. I'm open and soft the way early-morning people are, before they put up their walls for the day, and I look out into the gray light, half expecting to see Methuselah rooted back in the ground, but nothing is there except devastation and over-turned trees, although some of the younger ones have survived. It seems there is light in between the young trees. A chair with broken arms sits upright near the fallen Methuselah as if someone had been sitting there, and I think I hear from some-where inside myself a sucking sound of roots tugged out of earth by invisible hands.

Behind me, in the near dark, Ama prepares herself. She says, "Old Grandmother, I am coming." And she packs some of her clothing inside a red cloth and ties the bundle with twine.

I turn and look at her, but I can't see what she means by her words, and I can't see why she is packing her clothing, her comb, into the square of red cotton, as if she is planning to go away for a time.

"Where are you going?" I ask.

The house smells of wet wood. It isn't warm enough. I shiver.

"Here, put this on." Ama hands me a sweater that's been washed too often. Her eyes shine in the light of the lantern. Our shadows are moving along the wall like unformed twins of ourselves and it makes me think there are four of us, like the four women who came down the road a day or so ago.

"Where are you going?" I ask her again. I am still sleepy, my hair uncombed.

"We," she says, to correct me. "We are going." She sets down a cup of coffee on the blue tablecloth. She doesn't answer my question. She takes the knife from the drawer and puts it on the table beside the cup, then wraps it in a buckskin cloth.

"What do you need the knife for?"

In the gray light, without answering, she goes down the steps outside, splashing through the water and mud. Without knowing why, I follow behind her to the curing barn—it's still standing—and when she goes inside, a big white barn owl flies out so silent I can't hear it even though it brushes past me close enough that I can feel the air that moves away from its flight.

I wait outside and after a moment, she comes out carrying rope and a burlap bag. The insects in the remaining trees start to sing as if she woke them.

"What are we doing? What do you need the rope for?"

I suppose it's to hang and bleed the deer, but she doesn't answer.

I follow her back to the house and along the way I feel pity for the landlocked fish because the water is already receding. I pick some of them up and put them in the wettest places I can find, then I go up the two steps behind Ama, wondering if the fish think it was the hand of God that saved them, and the insects by now are so loud it almost scares me. Maybe they're calling out for loved ones, displaced by the storm.

Ama takes a last sip of her coffee and rinses the cup in the sink. She picks up the rifle my grandfather gave her. She moves quickly, as if we are running out of time, and maybe she's nervous. She has the rifle and knife in hand. She places the knife and rope inside the burlap bag. And still, she doesn't tell me what she's doing.

Because I'm still cold, she hands me another jacket, worn-out, blue. "Put this on. Then get us some fresh water."

I do what she says. I obey and go to the sink and push the pump handle and fill two plastic bottles with water.

"Here. Put on my boots. You should wear them," she says, moving quickly, setting the boots on the table closer to me. Then she takes out a blanket from the top of her closet and puts it in the bag.

I pull on her boots and watch her every move.

She ties a small length of rope around the bottles and puts it over the back of my neck, under the collar of the jacket, so I can carry the bottles and still keep my hands free. "Let's go," she says, and that is when she goes down the steps and begins to walk away, her rifle in hand, carrying the bag with the blanket and knife.

And though I don't want to go, don't know where she's going, I follow her. "What if we don't have enough bullets?" I ask, behind her now. I ask this because I saw my father shoot a deer once and it didn't die and he'd run out of bullets and it haunted me after that, how long it took the deer to die. He could have cut its neck and let it go faster, easier, but he didn't. I always wondered why, but the only thing I could think was that he didn't have the courage to do that deed by hand, up close.

Again Ama doesn't answer. And then we just head out, me behind her. She is already following the wounded deer as if, even after the rise of water, she can see its tracks.

The ground looks at first to be evened by the storm, but it isn't. In places there are deep pools of water. In other places it's nearly dry already, as the water seeps into the ground. That's how the soil is here; it's limestone, humus, clay, each with its own thirst and need for water. Limestone swallows it quickly. Water falls through it like through bone hands that have nothing to hold it with.

Some of the trees must have been cleared while I slept, because on the road now, a car passes by us, leaves and branches on its top. The headlights are on, and in the gray cast of strange light that could be morning or could be night, they remind me of the eyes of a wild animal. The driver honks at us but we don't even wave and I follow Ama as she heads out to hunt the skinny, lame deer, and I think it's a shame to hunt such a pitiful thing, that maybe it could live on three legs the way our old dog, Pup, did.

All around us as we walk, everything is in ruins and broken. In front of me Ama is almost graceful even though it's difficult to walk over the downed trees and through mud. I see a dead deer beneath a fallen tree, and I ache, not just in my body, but my heart is aching, too, as I look around at the wreckage, the buried trees, the fences blown in as if they were nothing more than little sticks, rather than the keepers of order they were designed to be. The oil rig equipment in the distance is tossed down, too, and all the tallest, oldest trees are downed by water and wind. Methuselah, gone after these five centuries. It is the young trees that have survived. It is the young that continue and I worry again now about my family, my sister and mother and how they fared with the storm, and everything smells of drowned earth.

Ama is muddy. She looks at me. She has the rifle in hand. "Do you hear that?" she asks, like someone is calling out. "Do you hear something?" But I hear nothing and her question scares me. Clay and twigs stick to her old shoes. She looks like some kind of creature. She looks not human. I call to her now and then. I say, "Ama," and wait for her to slow. Or in a small voice I ask her what she's going to do. But she doesn't answer. She doesn't even look back at me. It's as if I'm not here. The only voice I hear is a bird crying out from the direction of the oyster shell mounds from another tribe, of long ago, and I follow Ama, follow her like I can't leave, like I'm her shadow rooted tighter than Methuselah was to earth even though I know it would take more than wind to whip me free of following Ama, to uproot me, because I feel compelled, held by something, like the day Donna and I couldn't for the life of us get out of the car to call for help for Abraham Swallow.

From time to time I recognize where we are. We pass by Willard's brown trailer which is across from the spring near where Abraham Swallow died. A side of Willard's trailer has fallen off and I can see the kitchen counter and sink and stove exposed to air like it was always meant to be out in the open that way, like I could walk right up and take a glass out of the cupboard and get a drink of water and it would be the most natural thing in the world. Willard's skinny white horse stands outside, wet and tense, spooked by what he's never seen before.

The grasses are laid down flat by the storm. They are moist and dank-smelling. A tree branch falls right in front of us. I hear it fall, but realize it is louder than I hear. The loud storm has damaged my ears. More than hearing it, I see it, but I don't even jump back and away from it. In this disturbed world, it is as if I'm in a trance and I feel no danger. Soon, in no time, my walking becomes automatic and I don't stop. By a canal of water, bird tracks are delicate in the mud, beautiful as stars. And behind the canal there's another sea of bent grass. From somewhere there's a sound like oil pumps in the distance, the pulse of machinery that can't possibly be this close to us as we step through a wilderness. The sound seems to come from the ground itself.

Ama keeps an eye on the tracks of the deer. I can't see them, but she can; even though they have been washed by the storm tide, she can see and smell them as if by magic. She knows where an animal has walked. I used to call her Bloodhound, to tease her, but it is her gift and try as I do to learn it, I never see anything but fresh-made tracks or newly broken twigs. She has a sense I lack. Now she seems to catch the scent of the deer; she picks it out from the smell of fish that were thrown out of water by the hurricane, the wet smell of the storm on the ground.

I don't know how long we move or how much time has passed when Ama stands still and senses the land, feeling her way into the brush or saw grass around her, into the oak hammock. I stop now and then to drink water but Ama never does. She walks as if pulled by something, drawn, as if she has no choice, the way we are drawn and held by gravity.

Sitting on a reed is a blackbird. It flies up as we pass.

I think it is the past we travel, even though there are Spanish horses and skinny brown dogs that once were wolves, dogs that now stand back from us as we pass. They growl, unowned and hungry. I keep my eye on them. I, too, am unowned, untrusting.

We pass a fallen citrus grove where the trees were planted in measured feet from each other, and the green oranges are on the ground, the broken branches and limbs a jumble of sticks, mocking such things as feet and inches and yards.

I look back at the tracks we've left in the wet ground, as if we've grown from them, as if they created us and we grew upward, rose up as if from the footprints of our ancestors, to become the flesh of a woman and a girl. Ama walks as if it's easy, and her steps are nearly silent. Behind her I keep an eye on her back. It is straight.

Then, soon, I recognize that we are in the place where the stones look like backbone. Some people say this is God's back but we call it the Taiga Birthplace. In this place, the place of second creation, you'd think all this is true and that we walk toward the feet of that spirit, toward what meets firm and solid with the ground. It could be another world, another time, except that in the distance I hear a radio, and it sounds so strange to me. Stranger still, there must be a house behind all the trees that remain standing here, and a house is out of place here because it seems like we are walking in a time before houses and wires. I have already forgotten such things as music exist. Ama doesn't hear it, though, she only hears the deer walk. "Listen to its hooves," she says, and I wonder how, always, she puts this world away as if it never happened and how she hears the little feet of the deer.

It's this my mother fears most about Ama, that she lives as if nothing's ever come to pass, no America, no schools or churches. But it's this I like about her, that even though there are only twenty years between us, we live in different worlds. We do not even hear the same sounds. I try but can't hear the sounds of animals walking and she doesn't hear a radio. Still, I saw the four women and I heard them, too. That must mean something. Perhaps it means that in at least one way I am as connected to the past as Ama is. Ama once said that space is full and time is empty; I think now I understand this. We are surrounded by matter, but time disappears from us. Or maybe, as Ama says, there are other worlds beside us all the time and every now and then we cross over and enter one, and every so often, too, one passes over and enters ours.

Looking up, there is a hole in the sky, the way the old stories say about the hole pecked by a bird, a hole through which our older sister, the panther, Sisa is what we call her in our Taiga language, entered this world. And the anhinga birds with wings draping down have just come down through that hole; I see several of them as they sit in the trees and sun themselves. They don't move when we pass beneath the angle of their wings. We are that determined; we are that in nature. They can read us. Through that hole there is also an unbroken ray of sun, but even as it shines, the rain begins to fall again, lightly, on the already glutted, sodden land. A person would think that with all this water, there would be no thought or hope of solid earth, but the land absorbs it. Except for swamps and bogs, the land takes in all the water. It is thirsty land. It is also honest land. It doesn't lie or hide anything. Neither does Ama. Everything she is, everything she is about to do, is clear in her face and in her movement and in her words. The way everything is open to view when sunlight comes down through the hole where all life entered this world.

Smaller birds are noisy on the overhanging trees that seem

to lean down toward us like everything, all of nature, knows what we are doing; we are hunting, we are old.

Then the rain leaves and the hole in the sky widens. I see the cloud of rain move away from us and it begins to rain to the south, where I think it must be my mama's house, the wall of water falling from sky, moving away from us. And now the opened world is hot sun. It feels good on my back and skin because I ache all over from the damp and from holding to trees during the storm. My skin is chafed and tender from wet clothing. But soon it is stifling and hot, without even a breeze, and in one place I hear the rattles, a slow shaking of a snake in the brush. I never see it, but it, too, is being warmed back to life.

I don't know when it became evening or how long we have been here, but the sun seems to lower itself in the sky. We move from place to place slowly; it's hard going with some of the old trees upended and twigs and bushes all moved to where they hadn't been before. I am sweating, following Ama as she picks her way around water. I scrape my legs on broken branches. I cannot tell time or how it passes, but the sun is in pieces on the ground, broken by what must be evening shadows and yellow light.

And then there's a sound in front of us. The damp grasses part. Something is ahead of us and I hear it, see its traces. I hope it's the deer so we can be done with this. It is the only sign of anything moving, and then there is a crying sound behind me and maybe it's the deer but the grass makes a sound behind my back. I turn. It is following me, something in the grass. I am breathing loud and heavy. I am afraid and tired and my arms and legs are bruised and scratched. "Ama," I say, and she has already turned, and she, too, watches what is following me. She walks a ways toward it.

Then beside me, there is a crashing of brush. The deer starts. I see its dark eyes, so soft and alive.

But Ama ignores the deer, looking instead at the ground. "Look," she says. One of Ama's hands is on my arm, the other one pointing. In the fading sunlight I see it, the paw print. The prints have materialized as if from thin air. And it is now that I realize for the first time that we are not hunting the deer, that we are hunting, she is hunting, the cat, that the deer is only the bait, that the big tawny cat will follow such easy prey as a broken-legged deer. I am surprised I didn't think of it before, when I said, "I know what will happen," that I didn't see that we have been inside the cat's territory all along. Ama has talked so long about the panther that I don't remember back to when the talk first started, but now, suddenly, all her words come forward, her dream of one calling her toward it. It has been in her face all along, what will happen, but I have only now seen it clearly.

She. She has always watched for it. She has always believed it is there. Sometimes at night she has looked out into the darkness and seen its eyes. They have exchanged glances.

Ama tries to place her foot inside the track of the cat. It has large paws, it is a large cat, but Ama's foot is larger; it is too large, and I think how delicate, how small is the footprint of the fearsome cat, the hated creature now being covered by, overshadowed by, the human.

I've never seen a cat before except that one treed last month by those white boys from my high school. I saw its eyes shining like stars behind the tangles of leaves. No expression in them except one that told us, Go away, but it wasn't afraid of any of us. I believe they would have killed it, too, those boys, except that Ama sent them away, took that one boy's rifle and sent them away.

The boys were noisy, like they were drunk. And they didn't see me standing behind Ama in the brush, even though when Ama started toward them, I said, "Don't." Because I know young men can be so dangerous. I guess they got a glint of her rifle in the dark, because they grew silent, gave her their rifle, and left like they were spooked. They hightailed it out of there, too. Like she'd just grown out of the darkness, a ghost or an apparition, that's how they must've seen her.

My mother and most other people say the cats are all gone, but one finds its way through now and then. That's just what people like to think. It makes them feel the world is safe and tame. The cats can hide themselves, but you can feel them there. It's as if space has eyes and ears. It watches with all its might. It listens with ears that can pick up the slightest hint of sound. Something like that out in the dark, it makes the hair on your back and neck rise. Like what I felt the day of the storm, leaving my boat, something watching from the trees. There are nights, too, I have felt it watch me, even through the windows of a house. The first time I heard one holler I couldn't tell where it came from and it sent that same cold chill up my spine.

I don't know why I think these words, that this is the end or the beginning of something. I don't know why, but inside myself I say it. What will happen has been in the air all along, and in Ama's face, and now it's in my mind. And still I follow Ama. She hears something speaking to her, calling, and I hear nothing, but I go with her as if I have no choice. Or maybe it's just that the scent is strong and that's what she follows. Whatever it is, I look at her and she is all drawn into herself, concentrated, her skin, back, hands, all pulled in and small, and she is drawn into the movement of the cat as it follows the pitiful, broken-legged deer; she is connected that close, knowing the way, and I know what she will do and I don't want any part of it, but I follow her. I want to split in two, so part of me can turn back, can go home to where there are radios and schoolbooks full of knowledge that will begin my life, but there is no turning back. And then I tell myself that she is not hunting the cat, she couldn't be; there are so few of them, as few as there are of us. Thirty of them left, maybe less, no one knows for sure, but they're endangered and I don't want anything to do with taking one out of the world.

We come to a hole where they've taken the rock out of the ground to make a highway and then we cross over the highway. There are car lights in the distance, far from us. I want to laugh, that we are in wild nature this way, that we are caught up in something that is driving and pushing at us like invisible hands at our backs, and we are passing over a highway, following a wild cat and a deer that have also crossed this highway made of tar.

Then we walk along the canal beside the road for a ways. Something splashes into the water, and it sets my heart to beating. I am sure it's an alligator. I watch for it. They're fast but they don't look it. I know how quickly it could run toward me on its muscled legs, could open its wide jaws and take me apart.

I hear a dog barking. Again, as before the storm, I feel watched. By nature, I think now. It's what I felt watching me, all along. It knows us. It watches us. The animals have eyes that see us. The birds, the trees, everything knows what we do.

Ama cuts through the brush. I hear her moving and I want to turn back, go home, but I follow the sound. She knows the cat is there. She isn't afraid of it. She talks softly to it all the while she walks. She tells it she is coming. Its paws are large for a cat even though they are smaller than Ama's feet and I am more afraid now of what we're doing than I am afraid of the panther.

I can still see the eyes of that one bayed up in a tree by the boys. It was a cat Ama said she knew. She'd been keeping an eye on it for years. They'd been watching each other, she said.

The next night I was at Ama's when they came back. The boys stood outside and yelled at her to give them back the gun. I was afraid, then I recognized them from school and I stepped out the door and stood on the porch and told them Ama Eaton wasn't there. "What are you doing there?" one asked me. "Taking care of her animals," is what I told him. They looked at the chickens, me, and the goats and then they turned around and left. Afterwards, Ama said that was a crazy reckless thing for me to do. But I am more afraid of this thing I follow, although my fear is mixed, in the strangest way, with excitement.

It is just now becoming night and we are surrounded by darkness as we walk, nearly soundless, on the white road, the road that looks as if it's been painted with whitewash but it is really made of limestone and old fossil animals, fish, and seashells.

In the moonlight I see the eyes of the black fox. It has lived for years at this bend. It gives me a sense of where we are. We have walked a good, long distance into the trees with moss hanging down from their branches as if left there, untouched by the storm. Maybe even the wind doesn't want to go there.

All around us the darkness is full of strange white things. There are birds; ibis, the white egret, a stork, all white at night and roosting in a dark world of trees and at the edges of black water. I catch glimpses of the white piles of gravel left from the road-builders. Earth's bones turned inside out. Every so often there is a rumble of heat lightning that reveals the pale undersides of clouds above the darkness of earth. In the pale, quick lightning in the black sky, my eyes mistake the rocks and broken trees sticking up from the ground for animals. It startles me at first, the stone that is a bear, the tree that is a deer with branching antlers, the owl standing on the ground. My eyes play tricks on me and it scares me and I am starting to cry. I see them and I feel like weeping, at least a part of me does; the other part feels more awake and alert to the world than I have ever felt.

Ama turns and looks at me. "We'll rest soon," she says, dry-voiced, more to comfort me than really meaning it.

Then I see that she is also crying. The tears don't want to stop. Her face is wet even though she knows what she is doing and she knows why. Everything about her says she doesn't want to do this thing, but that there is no choice, as if it's destiny, as if it's fate, as if all the stories are true.

I look at her and even though it's dark, I can see her. She looks far away but she is present and awake. She is transfixed like they sometimes say about people at Mama's church. I see her in the moonlight, and not once does she stumble or lose her hold or her bearings. Not once, even crying the way she is. She walks like a strong woman chasing her God and I'm surprised how fast she moves. My feelings about her change. One moment I think she is a stranger and she is insane. I don't know her anymore. She is a stranger to her own self, too. The next moment I am surprised and proud, wishing I could believe like she does, follow the blood, the tracks, wishing I had such a calling. Then I try to keep up with her, surprised and proud at her strength, and that her uncovered arms are not cold, that she still carries the rifle, the blanket, and bag, all heavy by now, with no signs of weakening while I walk behind, exhausted and wanting to go home, stumbling from sheer exhaustion.

I stop for a moment and stay behind to take a drink of the last of our water and listen to the low, loud drumming sound of frogs. Then we are again in the thick trees, in deep, ragged cover, fireflies clustered in the brush and the blackness. Their lights are beautiful and summoning, calling us forward into near silence, into what looks like a starred universe in movement that is not orderly. Ahead of us, as we walk, frogs leap into the water, and sometimes as a cloud passes away from the moon's face, it brightens and I see the water ripple, and as we move, tears run down Ama's face even though she doesn't look like she is crying when you look at her. It is just wetness falling down her skin. I think I must be wrong about her crying and that it is raining so light I don't notice. It must be rain on her face. But I look up at the sky and no rain is falling.

She knows the cat is ahead of us. She talks to it all the while we travel. And then she turns for the first time and really looks at me, and talks to me as if she knows how much I want to turn back, how much I don't want to witness what she is going to do. She says, "We have to. Letting it die the way it is dying is worse." By hunger, she means, and illness. I follow her voice, glad she is speaking to me at last, and quicken my pace to move closer to her. "This way is God," she says, and I wonder if she means the way we travel or the kind of murder she is about to commit.

Once I said to Mama that God was what we call what we don't know. Mama said not to think about such things when I am so young, but I think Ama Eaton is following this kind of unknown thing, moving toward it. I try to understand her. By what she says, by her words, I think she doesn't want the outsiders to kill this cat. She doesn't want it to die by poison or be hit by a car like the others. In this, maybe she is right. But she is also wrong. I look around me at this world. Even in moonlight, even changed by the storm, this country doesn't lie. There's no one to steal here in this honest, decent land but us, and I am already sick by this act Ama has entered into, this act I don't yet comprehend except that it is both grace and doom, right and wrong. But whatever it is, it is killing and I think, can't a human decide what to do and what not to do? Can't Ama turn back now and can't I turn around and go home to my mother and sister who might even at this moment be homeless from the storm? I can't and I don't. And neither can Ama and I know this. We are carried in something larger.

Ama knows we are close. She isn't afraid. She isn't even short of breath. I can't hear her breathe. I can't hear her steps on the ground. I hear only myself breathing, walking. She is more careful now. I slow my pace behind her, walk softly and quietly. We cut through near saw grass and thickets and again I am scratched, and I think some hungry thing could smell this blood I am bleeding, anything could follow me. Out there is something, we are following something that moves without noise and is drawn by blood. Again, as before, I feel watched and I look back over my shoulder, then turn and hold still a moment, listening, remembering how Ama said that in the earlier times, in ceremonies and to cure disease, they used a panther claw to scratch the skin of the Taiga people.

We are in the deep cover of trees with black Spanish moss hanging down from their branches when I see the cat. It is standing, bending to drink water. I see it now, clear as the moon that shines out between clouds. It is vulnerable and beautiful and bare. I hold still and watch it with fascination. It is an easy shot, but Ama, too, only watches. She could shoot it but she doesn't take it now when she can, when it's so easy. And I am relieved. I think she is not going to kill it, after all, and I breathe and stand and watch it. So beautiful, as it raises its head and seems to look right at me, its eyes turning to light, round and glinting, its body all animal and lean muscle, its face so thin.

The tawny cat bends once more to drink from the water as if it has not seen us. Ama moves closer. She walks so quietly, even a snake makes more noise in the ground. I don't hear a thing when she moves, not the sound of her feet, not a brush of cloth against bush, nothing. I only see her in the shadows moonlight throws down, bending to a crouch.

The cat knows she is there and I see it draw her forward, looking back once before it turns and plunges into the water, silent as it moves across to the other side. Ama follows a distance behind it, stepping like the cat into water. In front of me Ama dips and submerges her whole body like she's being baptized, holding the rifle out of water, so for a moment the rifle's all I see. When she rises up and walks out from the skin of water, her hair is wet and long down her back and the moon is reflected on her wet outline and I notice for the first time how womanly she is, that she has a strong and curved body.

And then I follow and the water is lukewarm, strange, like the temperature of skin, so it feels like I am not in anything at all but my dress is wet and the scratches on my skin sting. I look around me at the surface of water, afraid. I listen for the sound of alligators, the large breath and splash that will tell me I am the prey.

Then it is quiet. The cat looks back at us. It doesn't run. In the darkness its eyes shine and that is what I see. Eyes. It seems to look right through us. It sees through us. Then, at ease, as if certain we will follow, it moves slowly away. It is calling us forward. I can see this in the way it looks back at us from time to time, and in the fact that it is calm. It does not hide itself the way it could. It does not run or take to the brush. It is sure of us, and that we will follow.

At times it disappears from view and I don't know how Ama traces it. Everything she does is all under the surface and secret, I think, unlike the land which yields itself and is open in the bright moonlight, unlike the cat that could conceal itself but doesn't. Instead, it appears every so often to lead us forward, as if it knows what it is doing. It could vanish at any time, and every now and again, its eyes give off a light. That light is its only outcry. That eyeshine is its testimony, its voice, its words.

And I think Ama is deadly more than I could know, stalking, crouching, slipping, dangerous and hungry under the brush and limbs. The hunted knows this about her and looks again toward us and reveals itself in the little bit of moonlight there is.

"These cats are like ghosts," Ama says, and her words cut through the night.

We are at the place of false channels and several inlets from the south. We move alongside the water for a while. Then, at the place where a river enters, we head west, following, and I no longer know where we are. There are pug marks in the sand and mud. A cloud of rain passes over briefly and I am thirsty so

I turn my face to the sky and try to drink the rain as it falls. The rain cloud continues on its way and the moon is once again above us.

And then there is a deer. It bursts out from under a tree and Ama says, "There." And she stops walking and waits awhile and we no longer see the deer but after a while as I try to breathe without sound, I hear a cry in the darkness and I know it is the deer. Then I hear the singing. I hear it come out of the grove and I'd be lying if I said I am not afraid. Because it isn't her voice. It isn't her singing it. The sound is like old women, a song I feel I remember, but cannot place. I stand straight up then and I see her and she is standing like royalty, like Grandpa said. She stands still and she quits looking for the tracks or smelling the deer or even the cat and now she closes her eyes like she feels something strong, like her skin is feeling it or her hands or her heart. She doesn't have to look with her eyes. She doesn't even know I am here with her now. Watching her.

Before long, it is silent, and Ama sees the cat, once again, in the shadows. At the edge of trees. I see it, too. It has taken shelter in the tangle of trees. It is still, its eyes partly closed, breathing, but it looks toward us with that light. It is guarding the dead deer, half on it, claiming it. The pale underside of the deer shows in the night and I smell the meat and fur. Ama stays back and lets it eat. I stand still in the shadows of a tree, a little away from her. We say nothing. We are still, perfectly still. Ama watches, listens, and waits. And then Ama says, "Omishto, come stand beside me," and I do. The cat looks up and she shows me to the cat, and what she does is, she introduces me to it, it to me. She says my name as she looks at me, as if I am both an offering and a friend.

Then, when Ama fires the gun, I jump back and cover my mouth with my hand and the world breaks apart in the terrified screams of small animals. Birds wake in trees and call out. But after the noise, everything goes quiet. A great silence spreads over the place. It is bleeding silence. Like everything in this place, the trees, the birds, the ground, they all know a death has been opened here. The frogs are silent. Then Ama is on her knees in the mud, crawling toward the golden panther in the trees. She stays a moment looking to see if it is hit.

I am afraid to breathe. So is the rest of the world. Now even the insects are quiet. There is no sound, but Ama lowers her head and her hair falls forward. She listens as if there's something to hear. It's so still that even the nearby water has hardly a ripple. Everything is that smooth. I don't feel right in the midst of this stillness and death, and Ama knows it and says, "You don't have to look," so I look at the sky and I am sorry to be a human and I hope we are forgiven.

Ama breaks the silence again by speaking to the cat but I don't know what she says. And then lightning comes and when it comes it looks clear as daylight for a moment, only a moment, with a clear blue sky, and you'd forget it is night. It reminds me of looking up into the clear eye of the hurricane, the opening of the world. It is only a second or two but the lightning is all across the sky and from where I stand, the panther is revealed in that split of light, bony, lying on the ground with gray-looking fur and a wide, bony rib cage.

At first, I can't tell, she can't either, if it is alive or not. Ama sits down to wait, to watch it. The golden cat in the night is pale gray and large and wild-looking, ragged. From what I can see, it has the softness, too, of something that wanted to live and couldn't. It is beautiful, its skin loose on it, the muscular hunger of its body that does not seem to breathe. I hope all three of us are lucky, that the cat is dead and no longer suffering.

I look around at dark trees. I don't know where we are. I look around and it all looks the same to me, but Ama isn't lost like me; she knows our place. I would be lost without her. I have lived here all my life and I am lost. But she is found. It seems to me that looking for the panther and finding it, she is found, like people with a calling. As if the panther is a place and it holds her, as if they've always known and lived inside one another.

When she steps toward the cat, I say, "No, Ama, I'm afraid. What are you doing?" I start to cry again. I say, "Don't go near it. You don't know if it's alive," but my voice sounds small and pitiful and I realize I'm only whispering below my breath and I can't say it loud enough for her to hear. After a while I just sit down and I think of how she once said to me, "What do you know and what do you just believe?" I thought about that for the longest time. I know nothing, I only believe in things. And what I believe in now is the force of the storm, the mighty force of it, and the cat lying dead or half dead in the bushes and trees and that what we are doing is wrong but I know that we are compelled to it.

I can't see what Ama is doing, but I know. There are no sounds of struggle or death, but I feel it in my stomach like destiny moving itself around in a whirlwind, a dark wind that comes quickly, churning, then turns to leave and is gone. But the wind leaves you changed without knowing how, just knowing something unsayable has changed and it has changed forever and you cannot go back and you can never be the person you were only a day before.

I get up and go to Ama and the dead cat and I look square at her and say, "You have killed yourself, Ama." I'm surprised at how quiet my voice sounds, how strong I feel.

And she says, "I know it. Don't I just know it."

It is only a day or two since my sister went to town and bought herself a new blue dress and I am here with the woman who killed the cat and I think again, without saying it out loud, "Oh Ama what have you gone and done? You have gone and killed yourself."

There is no moon now and no more lightning, which means the temperature's changed.

After all this, after hunting and killing, I am tired and sleepy so I sit back against a tree and wonder what will happen to us with this beautiful cat dead before us, and even so, I can't help it, but I fall asleep. And once I dream I see Janie Soto, the head of the Panther Clan, so real-looking as she looks at us from behind some trees.

Sometime in the early hours before daybreak, I hear a plane flying over, breaking through my sleep. I open my eyes once and I see Ama sitting close by, and the light has changed and it is almost morning, I can tell. Fog ghosts up from water. It looks as though the ground is torn in pieces and cast upon the world. The sunlight comes crawling sideways across the grasses, on its knees, opening itself across the land. It smells of wet trees.

"I know what you'll have to do," she tells me before I'm even awake. "I know what you'll have to say."

And I drift back off to sleep, thinking I have dreamed these words, as I think I dreamed Janie Soto, hearing the roar of a small plane somewhere above me. I am grateful for sleep.

Then it's full morning, wet and hot. My mouth is dry. I lie still, empty and aching. I feel the sun on my left shoulder, then my chest. Fire is its power, but the center of it, I think, must be cold as death. Lord, please, I am thinking, don't let this thing be true, but I feel the pain of my bruises and see my scraped arms. My body, if nothing else, is a witness to what we have done.

All around me grasses shine wet as jewels with dew. Deep gray mosses hang over branches of trees. The first early shadows of everything are on the ground. Light shows its face to me, but it isn't all I see. I stand up and see the cat. Oh, it is such a poor thing lying there all curled lifeless on its side in the grass with the dew and mud and rain on its unshining coat. It looks so weak and small.

Ama kneels down and holds it like a child in her arms, lifts it up as if it weighs nothing, so the sky can see it, like an offering, then she brings it down to ground.

It has broken teeth, and fleas and ticks are still escaping the lifeless body. I can see its ribs. "It was hungry," I say, and around the neck, the fur is all flattened, and it looks nearly gone, worn away.

Ama cries just to look at it. I know why she cries. Because once they were beautiful and large and powerful. Now it is just like her, like the woman who wears boy's old shoes because she's poor and they are cheaper, and it is also like me trying so hard to stay out of Herman's way, trying to think what kind of life I'll ever have, and it is like the cut-up land, too, and I see that this is what has become of us, of all three of us here. We are diminished and endangered.

Its long cat face is scarred. Moss and leaves are on its back. It is a large cat, but thin. Very thin. We'd never have been able to see from far off just how sickly it is, though Ama must have known it. You have to look up close to see that it is a real pitiful thing. This hurts Ama more than the fact that it is dead, because maybe it is better off dead, and dead by her hand, too, the woman who loved and worshiped it, that's what I now believe. Now she just looks at it. It has a large dark spot on its side, a little near half-circle that must be a flaw or maybe an old wound—it looks like fire has touched it—but the fur there is darker, almost black. It is so sad a thing to see and yet there is still the beautiful curve of its back and the large, lifeless paws, their claws dangerous a day ago but now they are reduced, vulnerable-looking.

And I see the deer. This is not the broken-legged deer and this bothers me though I can't say why, whether it's because that injured one is still out there hurting or because the cat, in spite of its seeming weakness, caught a four-legged deer that was healthy enough to have a fighting chance at life and maybe it means the cat could have fended for itself, that it is not so sick or old as it looks.

I see around the cat's neck how the fur is mussed, crushed down, that Ama must have strangled the last bit of breath from it with her own hands, this is what I conclude, that she wasn't even afraid of its broken, dirty claws, and this last fact is what drives a final wedge between me and Ama; it is what makes me doubt her. I think, how could she be so cold-blooded? But I see, too, that she made it a bed of leaves in a circle of twine, that she offered it tobacco and food, that she did the correct thing while I was asleep. The cat was very poor and she made it a bed of leaves. She followed the old traditions of caring for the hunted cat, the prey, of giving it the proper respect. She even offered it pollen and corn, so its soul could eat before it left. But still I stare at her like she is something I don't know. I've never known her, truly. I feel this in my stomach, and that I do not like her and I'd run away but I'm here and in this thing with her and what good would it do to run now from this place where the ground is still wet from the storm with grasses lying flat and beaded with rain, and Sisa, with pollen on her whiskers and feet, dead before us.

I go over to what looks like a good spot and begin to scratch a hole in the limestone, to reach the water beneath us where waters spread and move on their way to sea. I cut through with a stick and when water rises into the hole and turns clear, I put the jar down into the fresh water and gather some, relieved to be away from Ama and the cat, and in the air around me I can feel a cold front coming in.

When I return, she has blood on her hands and her blouse. While I was gone, she has skinned back its head, but its eyes are still in it and it has big teeth. It scares me and I think maybe she is crazy; I look at her and try to judge whether or not she is sane. Then she starts to talk and she calls the cat "her." It is stiffening up by now. She says, all practical now, "I don't want to skin her before we get her back to the house but I might have to." And I don't know why.

The trees are dark and silent about us, but it feels like the ground is talking. I hear a kind of humming like it is telling us something. Maybe it's the power lines, so wrong in this place. Maybe it's all earth weeping for the cat.

After time has passed, after we look at it, I feel for Ama, she looks so dejected. I say, "Here, you better drink some water." I hand her the jar.

She takes a sip, only a sip, then sprinkles the rest on the big cat. It's a sacrifice on her part. I know how dry she must be. And the small plane comes over us again and circles in the sky and the loudness of it rankles me, considering all this trouble here on earth.

I look around to see where we are. Some pines are nearby. I don't know how they got here. There's a big shiny-back water turtle, the kind my stepfather Herman says is good eating but kind of tough. I look at all this while she places the cat inside the bag and she carries it slung over her shoulder, her hands holding tight to it, clenched, and she begins walking back. And somehow, tired as I am, I start out behind her once again, this time to follow her back to the house, and I see that we must have circled partway back last night without my knowing it. We are not that far from her place, not as far as I would have guessed anyway, but still she will have to carry the cat across the grazing clearings and up the road.

A hundred things are on my mind now, what if we get caught, what if someone sees us, because I know what Ama is doing, what we have done, cannot be right, not just that it's against the law, but that it can't be *right*.

"How can you carry it?" I ask, meaning not its weight, because now it weighs what a child would weigh, and this is what she says: "It is a sacrifice. It all is. This whole thing."

What whole thing is that, I want to know. Once Ama said

that we humans are nothing more than a vision the gods had. We are only one song, one of the births of this singular world, one of the deaths, too, all of it blown together by the winds of a storm. I don't know why I remember this now, but I do and I also think there is nothing whole about this, not any of this.

And then, as if she knows I have judged her, she stops a moment with her burden and stands looking at me and says, "Look at history and say this is bloody or this is death. Look at time, then tell me, because it is true as the stories say that this is everything the world turns on," and I know she means in this taking. I have never heard her be so eloquent. In some way I don't yet know, what she says is true. But I also know everything has been betrayed. And that it's all different now. Everything in the world is different and betrayed. In just one day, one act, nothing will ever be the same again.

I look up at the sky. There isn't even a sign of rain left over from the storm, not a cloud. Now the road, the white road with shells of fossils and what's old in it, is dry, the pale road flat in the sunlight. It burns my feet right through her boots as I walk and again a small plane passes over us, very noisy, very close; it must be examining the damage of the storm.

"You'll have to tell about this," she says as we walk. "They'll ask you about this and you'll have to tell them."

I barely hear her for the sound of the plane. Then it lands somewhere behind us. But with these words I know whatever it was that cast a spell on us is over, it is done. It is tied up tight as the rope around the bag and it is knotted. Sealed tight. That's what they say about fate, isn't it, that it's a sealed, closed thing. And now neither of us can ever go back to before and I know I will have to tell about Ama and the woodtick-bit old cat, so poor and endangered. The police will ask what I know about it. Not because they care but because it's a law, because you can't kill one of them.

It is over and there is no way to step back in time, to go back a day earlier, a day in which something could have been undone, could have unfolded itself in a different way. I try to think, but inside me there's only emptiness. The storm was not just wind and rain, not just a house with a shutter thrown open, a door torn off its hinges. It was not just a dying house with a broken window and branches and leaves blown inside it. It was a beginning and an end of something. I feel what it is but I don't have words for it yet. If I did they'd look like history and flowered lands and people with the beautiful ways we Taiga were said to have before it was all cut apart in history. History is the place where the Spaniards cut off the hands of my ancestors. The Spanish who laughed at our desperation and dying, and I wish it didn't but that history still terrifies and haunts me so that I dream it in dreams with skies the color of green bottle-glass. And somehow, against their will, I stole through.

I look at Ama and she looks different now. I mean she is older, she is darker, in this different world. I feel it, too, like she said, about us being the visions of gods and that maybe it isn't the ordinary world but someplace else we have entered and tracked. The insects and frogs behind us have fallen silent. Not just because it is morning but because they feel it, too, I know they do, the whole earth feels it. Whatever has ended, whatever has begun, is this strong in the air.

"Sisa," that's what we call the cat in Taiga. It is our name for them. It means godlike, all-powerful. The cat is the animal that came here before us and it taught us the word, Oni, which is the word for life itself, for wind and breath, and I think all this as Ama carries it like it weighs nothing, no breath in it. But now its breath is in us. Ama was strong enough before—she could have lifted herself up to the roof by her arms and hands if she had to fix a leak or she could carry buckets of water—but this is stronger than I've ever seen her and she is not even exhausted from the long work of this hunt, as if it was a natural thing.

She carries the cat all the way back, part of the time over her back, part of the time with the cat across her arms, large as it is, in the old gunnysack like a baby, and she walks like she isn't tired. She walks straight-backed even though she has a slight limp; she's cut her ankle or foot along the way and is leaving a trail of blood. Her blood, not Sisa's, because the cat doesn't seem to be bleeding that much, which surprises me. All this, after the hammering of shutters, the storm, the cleaning of debris. How long has it been since she slept, I wonder. Maybe she's crazy with sleeplessness. That's what I heard, that not to sleep makes you crazy.

On our way back, we pass again by Willard's brown trailer and the broken citrus groves. Red dragonflies eat mosquitoes from the air all around us. Willard's skinny white horse stands out there by the broken fence. It isn't Ama's horse and it's not like her at all, but she takes it. She takes the horse because she has been limping and she needs to carry the cat on it and she believes Willard will understand this. She apologizes to the horse as she hefts the cat, thin as a sick dog, but longer, to the horse's back. The horse shies beneath its burden. She talks to the horse. It breathes quickly, hard, afraid, but it does what the human wants; it is trained to do whatever people want. Red dragonflies float by, and the horse comes with us, even smelling the dangerous animal on its back, and we all walk in the place where there used to be black leaves, purple flowers, and a dark corner of swamp but now there's only grass in a clearing.

I am quiet. I don't help her. I don't touch the cat, not once. I am afraid to. It's not that I think it will spring back to life. It's that, even dead, it has power over us, some kind of sway. There will be punishment and retribution, I know, words they use at my mother's church. I don't like these words, but I can't think of any other. And I know, too, that Ama believes, without a doubt in her heart, that this is redemption. I can see it in her face, so calm, so quiet.

When we reach Ama's house, surrounded by ruined trees and those small surviving ones left standing as if nothing passed through them, I see that everything in the house is just like it was when we left, the white turtle shell sitting on the shelf, the rushes on the north side noisy once again with frogs. The chickens are out of their fence, pecking the ground between broken branches, one of them sitting on an old chair that sits on the porch.

Inside, Ama looks at me and tells me again, "When they come, you've got to tell the truth." She asks me to tell people she had to do it. I don't question her. A car passes by. Her bed is made and covered with a worn-out quilt. "The truth," she says, "all except for one thing." And again she makes me promise not to say what the cat looked like, that it was sick and starving. "Promise me now," she says. "Promise you won't tell that part. Not to anyone."

My mama's husband, Herman, says promises are made to be broken, but that's not how I think, so I consider this carefully. I look at her and weigh this promise before I make it. I have to think what it might cost somebody and I can't see any reason why it would matter to anyone but her, in fact I'd think it would help her to tell it, but finally I say, "Okay," and I look in her river-brown eyes so she'll know I mean to keep my word. But I can't help wondering if she's crazy like some people think. I don't look at her too long in case she can read this in my eyes. Instead I turn and look at the horse, the white horse with a red patch of blood on its side where some has seeped through the bag, its body tense as if it is ready to bolt. I go over to it. I touch it. I tell it, "Shhh. Everything's all right. It's all right," and it seems the whole world begins breathing around us.

And then I go inside and I can't help it, I fall asleep, even hearing the sound of the plane above us.

It's evening. I am sitting on the porch looking at her house when the police come with their red lights circling. I remember that some of the roads are cleared. At first the dying house seemed unharmed by the storm, but now, as the police come, I see her house is devastated like something happened to it after we left it. It's covered over with leaves and branches and dark things that blew in from the storm. It makes me wonder if, in the confusion and shock, I hadn't seen it right before or if another storm arrived while we were out tracking in the swamps and woods.

Ama knew they would come. She is ready for them. It was part of the bargain all along—or should I call it destiny. She is washing her face in a basin of water when they come, two cars, one with the sheriff and the deputy, one with a man from the U.S. Division of Wildlife.

Tom Sheedy, the sheriff, calls out to her. "Mrs. Eaton," he says, walking toward her. I have never heard her called that. I don't ever think of it, that she used to be married, if only for a short time. For some reason, it changes things, how I see her. It adds a measure of conformity to her, as if there's something to her I don't really know and it's ordinary. I see her again like she's a stranger, those small hands, her face calm even now as she dries her hands on a towel and pretends not to hear the sheriff. I look at her again like at someone I've never seen before, a woman I don't know.

Tom Sheedy says they have to take her in, to ask a few questions. He, who I have seen joking with my stepdad, is very serious.

"I know it, Tom. It's okay," she says as if to reassure him, still drying her face.

And the other fellows are looking around outside the premises for the cat. The June bugs are flying in the car lights of the police cars where they are parked on the road, lights still on.

"Hello, ma'am," Sheedy says to me. It's condescending.

It is Jimmy Eights, the deputy, talking now. "Miss Ama?" is all he has to say and he says it like a question. He knows her. Around here everybody knows everybody. But I don't know how they could have heard about the killing. And so soon. Someone must have told them. Someone must have seen her, and seen me, too. Someone must have called them. It means someone watched us. Maybe it was Willard, mad that Ama took his horse, the white horse that stands alongside the road now, its flesh pink and blue where the flashing light of the police car is still going round, hitting all the trees, making the world look unnatural and terrifying, and I can see the frogs in the road leaping in the headlights of the car.

"The least you could do is turn off the lights," I say to Jimmy. He's a half-breed. I've known him for years. And he goes and does it.

Ama has her few things ready, her clothes and her comb already wrapped up in the piece of red cloth like she knew ahead of time she would go away.

Tom Sheedy says, after they have searched high and low for the cat, "What have you done with it, Mrs. Eaton?"

She says nothing.

He looks around. "Where is the panther?" he asks her. "Where's your gun?" Sure of her crime. I wonder how they can be so certain.

When the wildlife official talks to her, her face is just a blank. She is silent, tired, almost moody.

They search around the house once again, come back with only the bloody burlap bag and the rifle Ama took from the three boys and place both in the car, and I think, they don't even have the right gun. But there's something small inside the bag, like maybe it's the cat's head or entrails or maybe just a towel or small blanket. It's not the cat, though. I can tell this.

"What did you do with the carcass and hide?" Tom Sheedy asks her.

She says nothing. She brushes her hands over her dirty dress, smoothing it down as if they are not there waiting for her.

He turns to me. "You're Herman's girl, aren't you? Where did she put the cat?"

"I don't know. I was asleep."

And then to my surprise, he doesn't ask me another question. He's not one bit interested in me.

Ama tosses the pan of water out into the moist soil. She stands, ready to go, and then, simple as that, she picks up the red cloth wrapped around her things and she walks to the car as if she knew all along what would happen. She doesn't fuss. I watch her closely. I can't read a thing on her face, not a look of surprise, not a look of remorse or guilt either. She is at peace, even with Jimmy Eights helping her into the car, more at peace than anyone I've seen before, even more than any of the women at Mama's church.

I see her too-large, scuffed shoes and her heavy scratched arms as she gets into the police car.

I feel the men watch me, too, as they take her to the car. I don't get up or return their look. I sit and look at the ground. They will come for me later, I am sure of this, but for now they think I am just a girl, that maybe I've just arrived here, or just woke up like I said. But as she goes with them in their car, I am already thinking of the story I will have to tell them. She doesn't look back at me, not once. It's as if she doesn't know me.

When they turn on the lights, the frogs are still jumping across the road. They don't try to miss them. They drive on through them and the cars run over them and I turn away and cry.

———

After she is gone I remain sitting in the darkness and listen to the bullfrogs and the sounds of water and insects, the sound of her little dying house that was built back before there were fences. It settles in the night. And I sit and wonder how she knew the police were coming, because she must have known. She'd put all her things together before we even went after the cat. Maybe it was the far-off thunder that told her. I sit and wonder how it is they did not find the cat or her rifle. I am afraid, myself, to go look for it in case I find it and they are still there watching from the thickets and I will lead them to it.

So I just sit for the longest time.

The porch, if you could call it that, is about to cave in. Once Ama painted the metal roof of her house red, the color of oxblood, but most of it is peeled off by now. It reminds me of her in that way, no paint or fixing up, worn down to within an inch or a minute of falling.

The house is sinking back into the earth and Ama would let it. It is the natural thing and anyway she isn't going to be there that much longer, she once said, as if she believed that she'd be leaving. "Where you going?" I asked her but she just shrugged and I thought it was a joke because I couldn't imagine her anywhere but here. Now I think she knew all along about the hunt, the arrest, as if she'd designed it.

From the porch I see the vines beginning once again to grow on the side wall, not the morning glory, but the persistent kudzu, an exotic species that does not belong here but takes over everything. It grows so fast, you can watch it grow. It grows a few inches a day, sometimes more.

After what must be an hour, at least, maybe two, I go out back to see where she hid her gun. With a flashlight I go search the blackness for the cat, the rifle, to see where she's hidden them.

There's a little spot of disturbed ground and I think she's buried it there and it looks dug into a second time, slightly opened, but I try to dig. Above me I see my dress still hanging in the tree like a woman, like something suspended. As I dig and smell the odor of clay, I will myself not to see the cat the way it was, the eyes with life in them, leaving as if life was water being poured out of a glass. I find nothing here, in this still-wet earth. And then, just before the flashlight dims, I look to see if there are any kinds of signs. I see what I think is a fresh footprint, a woman's, it looks like, a bigger foot than Ama's, but still small and kind of awkward-looking, and I know it's either the print of a deputy or someone else has been here. Watching. Or maybe it was the boys coming back to get their gun. In any case, a chill goes up my spine. There's no sign of the gun or hide, just the footprint.

The next morning I walk down the road to the pay phone down at the gas station to call my sister to come and get me now that the roads are all cleared.

The clerk, a woman from Mama's church, a woman in a red sweater and glasses, loans me a quarter and then watches me as I call and I realize how I must look, the dress too big, the cuts on my arms and legs, the boots unwashed, my face swollen. She thinks I was injured by the storm. "You okay?" she asks. "Lots of damage everywhere."

"Yeah, I just need a ride."

"Well, the phone lines are on again. You're in luck. And we didn't get much damage here at all."

My voice is calm and Donna, my sister, says, "Who is this? Sis? Is it you?" She doesn't recognize me, as I no longer recognized Ama. Then she turns from the phone, covers it with her hand, and calls out to Mama that I'm all right.

"Could you come and get me?"

"It'll take a while. I'm waiting for Dave to return with the car." Dave's her boyfriend. He's big and used to play ball for the Blues, a semiprofessional team.

In the store, amid the smell of engine grease, I look at the candy and soda and chips and their bright wrappers and they don't seem real to me.

"I'll pay you back," I tell the clerk.

On my way back up to Ama's, I see Willard's white horse has followed me. It gives me a start, standing in the road that way. It follows me back, its hooves noisy on the pavement, me and the horse walking up the road.

Then I go up to Ama's and start to dig a hole to bury the dead and fallen Spanish horse, still covered with mud. I decide I have to dig a little out from under it and next to it so the horse will roll in easily. I plan the hole so the dead horse will collapse into it, and as I work I begin to cry. I use the shovel to dig, trying to find a place where ground is easy to break. It is muddy and wet in places, and even though I ache, I dig and Willard's white horse, standing there, watches as I open earth, listens to the sound of the shovel. Then I hit stone and try to work my way around it. I worry it will fall into water beneath limestone and travel an underground river out to the sea and wash up somewhere as bones.

4
DESCENT

My mother used to say, "You trying to dig a hole to China?" And I guess I was. Every place that I could find a crack of pure earth I'd dig. It was in my mind to escape this world. I'd pretend I was tunneling out of prison or that I'd break into one of the rivers underground and float it away from here. I thought a way would break open, and I'd find an entrance to another world and I would enter it free and alone.

Sometimes I see things as they were before this world, in the time of first people. Not just before the building of houses, the filling in of land, the drying up of water, but long ago, before we had canoes and torches and moved through the wet night like earthbound stars, slow and enchanted in our human orbit, knowing our route because, as Ama said, it had always been our route. I see this place from in the beginning when it was an ocean of a world. Even sky was a kind of water. Land not yet created. And then a breeze of air, an alive wind, swept through, searching for something to breathe its life into and all it could do was move the water in waves and tides, and water didn't stand up, although it spoke.

It was before there were ants that survived the floods by gluing sticks together to make rafts that will float. At first, there was not even a stone. It must have been that a dreaming god, a begetter of some kind, dreamed up something solid and rooted. Then, that first island floated up like limestone from the ocean floor, the way it is now, in this time, and it began to breathe. Soon, green ferns pushed up their first coils from the ground and opened. The frogs emerged from mud and the island in the sea was breathing. The wind breathed through all of this. And all this was before anyone thought of heaven. The time might have been the age of the first trees, tall cypress or the mangrove trees that form land now.

In this watery, foggy world of one color and only the breeze of life, the great anhinga bird with its open, drooping wings, broke through the watery sky world with its beak, broke it like the shell of an egg. It, the sun bird, they call it, sat in light and draped its wings, and these wings, Ama said, called down the sun. And that first view of the sun from this world must have been as beautiful as it was blinding. And as the great bird rested, the panther entered through the broken shell, the hole of creation, all golden eyes and secret pride and lithe stillness, walking as if every cell of its muscular body was breathed awake and healthy. She, Sisa, God of Gods, entered this world with grace and sunlight and beauty. It was a world filled with the wind, with life-creating air. And everything in it began to breathe and move.

People used to believe that what rises up from the ground, or falls from the sky, opens its eyes and is alive, like first walkers and trees and birds. Now it seems it is the whole world that has fallen. Not the way light falls on the trunks of trees, not just shade and shadow cast by the light of sun, either, not even the first beginnings of life down in the tangle of roots and seeds. It has all fallen, this poisoned, cut world. It has fallen in a way that means this place is taken down a notch. Unloved and disgraced and torn apart. Fallen, that's what this world is. And betrayed.

Some say we, too, are fallen. We are Taiga Indians and no one has heard of us. We are a small tribe and we are swamp people. Once the Tocobagas were to the north of us. Calusas to the west. Tequestas with their pottery marked like kernels of corn to the east. Most of the other tribes, Seminoles, Mikosukkes, do not remember us now, but the old people say that, like them, we are related to the panther, Sisa, one of the first people here. And I am related to the panther, also. I'm from the people of the Panther Clan, which makes me a grandchild or niece to Sisa. Like Janie Soto and Annie Hide, my mother's cousin, I come from the Panther Clan on my mother's side. This is my ancestry. We are its descendants, all of us. We, my family, clan, and me, are one-third of the number of Taiga Indians still in this world. I don't like to think about this very much because it is too large for me, but sometimes this knowledge falls on me like misery.

I'm still digging when Donna drives up in her boyfriend's blue car and it's a sight, the roof dented in from a tree branch, the hood pitted with hail. I lean the shovel against the steps.

Donna gets out of the car like a queen and walks toward me. Her hair is curled and it lays softly about her face. She's pretty under her makeup. For a while she is quiet and I am, too, before she moves toward the car and opens the door for me. "Come on," she says. "But take off those muddy boots."

I am still wearing Ama's muddy boots and they look filthy

with earth, and I realize I must have slept with them on. I take them off and leave them by the door. I run back to the house for my shoes.

She's quiet for a while after I get in the car, but then the first thing she says is, "On our way back, we saw Janie Soto. The day after the hurricane. Just before they got the roads cleared." The first words out of her mouth. "We came looking for you. She was limping down the road. From making a phone call is what I think she told Mom, but she didn't say it in English."

Soto lives up above Kili Swamp where the other people, mostly old people, live. Soto, the woman who never goes to town or comes close to the world outside that invisible boundary line of Indian land. A woman who wanted Ama to live up at Kili with them. The woman who'd do anything, Mama says, anything at all to get us all back.

I want to ask Donna more, because it makes me nervous that Soto, the woman who is in charge of everything that happens with the panther, was this close to Ama and me. I wonder, does she know?

"She'd been making a phone call. I guess." Donna laughs a little, with tension. "It surprised us because she must have walked all that ways on her wooden leg and she could hardly walk, she was so tired, what with carrying a bag so big with one hand and with her cane in the other hand. We gave her a ride partway home."

"What were you doing there?" I ask.

"We were looking for you." She reaches over and touches me on the hand, but in a hesitant way, and I try to place where we were when they got to Ama's house, and I think I must have been in bed, dead tired, but where was Ama? I didn't even hear a knock on the unhinged door.

"She sat in the back and never said another word to us."

It isn't like Janie Soto to come this close to town. She wants to avoid the town people. All of the swamp people do.

Janie Soto is the old woman who is head of our clan and she has a wooden leg that is made of a tree that used to bloom. I heard that after she first started wearing the leg, it leafed out and blossomed. Green leaves grew from it. She walked with it that way, the tree still believing it was alive. And whenever I think of her, that's what I see in my mind's eye, the wooden leg sprouting leaves, budding with leaves and flowers even as she walks. Mama said that in the Bible, in Numbers, Aaron had a staff that bloomed and because of it he was made the first priest of Israel. Janie Soto herself is something like a tree, the clothing she wears is always dark green and brown. And she always wears the red beads, coral I think, that came from another place. She got them in a trade that was made between our tribe and another from before the time the Spanish arrived.

"We looked all over for you. Mama was in a panic," Donna says, both to let me know she loves me and to take sides with Mama against my thoughtlessness. "Mama thought you were killed in the storm. We drove over as close as we could get, four times, but at first the trees were on the roads. Then we got there but the house was empty. And later we thought someone had been there but we couldn't find you. Then Mama called the police."

I make her repeat this and I look at her while she talks. Not because there is a distant sound of chain saws but because I can tell by the tone of her voice, before she even tells me, that she and Mama both know about the panther and me and Ama. There's something in her voice, a suspicion or doubt. I imagine it was the police that told them where to find me, not that they'd have looked anywhere else. And I suppose Janie Soto knows and that's why she came along the road to Ama's. Janie Soto, I believe, might know what happened to the panther by her blood alone, they are that connected.

Then, she is silent. She doesn't have to talk. I know what she's thinking. It feels like the car is full of her thoughts. I can almost hear them. She wonders how I could do this thing. She wonders why. Now and then she looks at me with a weak little half-smile. She fidgets with her necklace, a gold heart on a chain. She knows what me and Ama have done even though she never comes right out and says it, but she looks at me different than ever before and she always will, the rest of our lives. I know this.

I feel the pulse in my neck. "What did they say? Did Janie Soto say what she was doing there?" My only words. Because I think if she was this close to the edge of town there must have been a good reason for it. But maybe someone was hurt by the storm.

"No. She was quiet but she was carrying a feather. A white feather."

"What kind of feather was it?" Although I know that Donna would not be able to identify any feather.

"It might've been a swan." She makes a turn. "And her bag. She was carrying a bag that seemed a little heavy. She didn't say anything except when we asked if she'd seen you and she just smiled at us. Something like a smile. Mama thought maybe she didn't understand us, so Mama tried to speak Taiga and asked her a lot of questions all the while we drove her up toward Kili Swamp, but Janie just sat there holding the bag on her lap and the feather in her hand. She had trouble getting her leg in and out of the car. We didn't make it all the way there to Kili because of the trees blown down across the road. Trees are still falling, you know. They get the roads open and then another tree falls. We had to let her out to walk the rest of the way. I offered to help her or carry the bag but she wouldn't have it."

I hardly hear a word Donna says or even the traffic of cars passing. I watch the world pass by as we drive, the broken, windblown world. I think of Ama and me tracking and moving in the almost-wilderness. Now what we did seems like a dream, like it could never happen here so close to the red-roofed houses and shopping centers set down here on the top of the ground, and not so far from Ama's either. I could almost forget there is a horse I need to finish burying and that Methuselah has fallen straight away from centuries of holding on to life.

And then Donna says, "What do you think she was doing this close?" She adjusts the mirror as if to see Janie Soto on the road behind us.

"Maybe someone was hurt."

But I weigh all this in my own mind and know it's not the case. When did the people up at Kili ever ask for help? I imagine old Janie trying to walk across the tree limbs and bodies of birds and fish swept out of the waters.

Donna turns on the car lights as if it is night. It isn't, although there is a feel of something like night. She is trying to see through some kind of darkness. All along the few miles to Mama's, I see what has happened to the world. Things have been ripped up. Street signs are bent, trees thrown down. From a water pipe, all that's left of a home, water is pouring. Fences are down, balconies torn away, cars are twisted wreckage. There is a cloud of smoke or fog hanging over the cane field and the workers' houses are a shambles from the storm, nothing about them was built to hold in the first place. The sun reveals the despair of the broken world, the stark unconcealed limestone glaring, the water and the ruined fruit trees. Men work like ants, trying to repair the damage, stopping to wipe their foreheads with rags, to smoke a cigarette. In jeans, white T-shirts, sweating, they work just when you'd have thought all work would have come to an end.

A heron flies over in the hot, musty air, its wings bent back, neck at an angle. I watch its flight, the suspension of it, the way it hangs in air, legs out behind it.

We go past where the land has been cleared and drained. It's only a few miles from Ama's house, I can run it in a short time, but there's a world of difference. The Indian land is still wet and fertile. But all the other land is poison now, like the pestilence of Mama's Bible that entered the houses as if to claim the firstborn sons.

At my mother's, in the streets of houses, there is only a thin green line of ancient trees remaining just behind the buildings. As we drive up, I see Mama and Herm are airing out the tornado cellar and in spite of myself and the storm, I smile. It is Herm's idea, to have a cellar in the torrents of falling rain even though it's the kind of water-soaked, flooded land that makes such a cellar impossible and yet he dug it out himself, cemented the walls, and they go into it, all of them, at his urging, his memory of Oklahoma storms and twisters, because he is convinced it's safer. But sometimes he has to use a sump pump to get water out of it. And the roots of trees are always trying to break in. Still, it's the only thing I like about him, that as unrealistic as the cellar is, he worries about Mama's safety part of the time.

"Thank God," my mother says, hugging me, as soon as I walk in the door. "We looked all over for you."

A towel and newspaper sit on the floor by the door so we won't leave footprints all over the house. She has never grown accustomed to the dirt, mud, and clay of this place, even though she's lived nowhere else. "Take off those shoes. You'll track in mud." The next words my mama says even though she's been afraid for me. Cleanliness is next to godliness, Mama always says. She's godly enough and her house is neat as a pin; it seems sharpened to a point.

I am thrown back into the world too fast and I reel from it. Inside my mother's house, the washing machine is running. The lights are on even though it is light outside, as if there is something dark fallen all around us that can't be seen but that everyone knows is here. The same kind of darkness that made Donna turn on her car lights in broad daylight.

I sit down in my mother's kitchen by habit, looking at the gray linoleum tiles of the floor, not saying a word. But the air is thick with everything that's not said. Outside the kitchen window is the devastation, the despair, the stark, unconcealed breaking of things. The fruit trees are ruined, oranges on the ground, but the house itself is untouched, at least it seems that way, unlike the houses with their roofs blown "all to tarnation," as my mother says, their walls pushed inward, pulled outward.

"I was worried sick about you," she says. Now that I am safe, she's able to be angry.

I say nothing. I only nod a little, not so much at Mama, but looking around the house where I have always lived. Nothing seems familiar, not the television, the blond coffee table, the school photographs of me and Donna. I can hardly concentrate on her words because it all looks new to me, as if I've never seen it before.

I look around my mother's house and nothing is familiar. It's as if I have never lived here. I see the world this place has come from. I see the walls of the fallen forest, the floor of clay dissolving in time.

"The sheriff told me what hapened," Mama says, almost gentle. She is looking at me and I realize how I look. I am dirty and disheveled and wearing Ama's clothes because mine still hang in the tree. My arms are scratched, my nails broken and filled with black dirt. All this in her clean little kitchen. But I am thinking also about Janie Soto and how on her one good leg she got to the phone at the gas station over trees and branches and blown-in building parts. And I am thinking of the Spanish horse and what to do about burying it, and that I need to get back and take care of the goats and chickens that live at Ama's.

"Why?" my mother says.

She means why did I do it.

This house seems lonely and sad. And I look at Mama and

try to listen. She's telling me what I already know. "There's a law, the government has a law against it."

"I know."

"You're in deep water." She's getting shrill now. "Do you know that? For killing that panther."

I nod at her.

"It wasn't your idea, was it? It was hers. It must have been Ama's. No one would ever believe you could do such a thing. People are coming to town from all across the country to investigate this and write it up; they've already called here eleven times to ask about you. They know you were with her."

I don't ask how.

"It was endangered, you know."

I nod at her.

"You knew that. I know you did."

Some people have even called to tell how evil I am and it's in all the newspapers, bigger than life. My photograph they got from the high school, illegally, Ama's from right after she was arrested and went to the jail.

"I don't know how they could put your picture in the paper. You're too young. Isn't that wrong?" my mother asks. "They're not supposed to do that, are they? I thought it was against the law." She rattles on, nervously.

I sit in my mother's kitchen, looking down.

"I can't believe you'd do this," Mama says. "You've got such a tender heart. You get mad at the way Herm fishes."

It's true. I do, for him leaving them on a stringer, keeping them alive until they're in the sink. I think it's cruel.

She says, "For all I knew you were in your boat at the bottom of one of the canals or lakes. And the way the river's flowing, you could have gotten washed all the way to kingdom come."

And Herman, my stepfather, says, "This time you've really done it, they're putting you in the newspaper, and some reporter's been calling here to talk to you."

He doesn't say, as usual, "I ought to backhand you."

My mother: "They shouldn't have done that."

"It's a federal crime," he says.

Then to me Mama says, "You weren't to blame. But you should listen to your father."

"He's not my father," I say, sounding more angry than I feel.

Now he says it. He says, "I ought to backhand you. I went without good shoes for you. I glued my shoes together for you girls. Now you're dragging us in the mud."

"Ama's a bad influence," my mother says, like it explains everything away.

I can't tell her—she would never understand—that it was an old story we must have followed, that we were under something that felt like a spell, that what I followed wasn't Ama, and that Ama followed something that wasn't her either. It wasn't that Ama was claiming something, but that something was claiming her. Ama would never have done this otherwise and neither would I. It wasn't even so simple as a mercy killing, even though, judging by the look of the cat, that was cause enough. It's not like me at all to believe in any such nonsense as stories or forces that would take over a person but it's the closest I can come to truth and reason. She was acted on. But outside, the rain starts to fall again, and as it does, it runs over this small square house and begins the long, slow process of disintegrating it, rotting it away. For this I am glad.

Without saying another word, I get up and draw a bath for myself and this is when I feel how dead tired I am. My muscles ache. My eyes burn with fatigue and unfallen tears. I get my robe off the hook on my bedroom door and I lock the door and get into the water, and see the scratches on my arms and legs and close my eyes and lay back in the hot water wondering what it would have been like in the earlier days to have been scratched by panther claws. I stay in the water a long time until it is time to go to bed. For a change, no one knocks on the door or complains.

I dry off and put some talcum powder on my body, under my small breasts and beneath my thin arms, and I tie the robe and go into my small room without saying good night, and I go to bed smelling fresh as lilies, those little flowers that bloom for only a day before they wither and the petals fall down seedless. I can hear everyone in the living room watching TV. They are together, as if to show that now I am outside this family. I am the source of their problems. I have brought them closer together, joined them in their judgment of me. I lie down on my back. My bed is more narrow than I remember, the house more small, as if I've outgrown it. I look at the moving shadows of the trees cast on the wall by a streetlight that, miraculously after the storm, is one of the few still working. The shadows are dancing over me. I can still smell the cat, the sharp odor, the damp fur, the smell of cut flesh and blood, all still with me like it's become my skin, and I am steeped in it. All around me are the houses, with people watching television and eating their snacks, and I am in the trees.

Later, in the middle of the night, I wake up. My shadow is on the wall of the room in this, my mother's house. I get up at once and look out at the bushes and they are glowing in the dark with foxfire, after the storm. Like a burning bush in Mama's Bible. I am so deeply tired and I'm sweating but my skin feels cold and I cover myself and lie back down and fall asleep. Sleep is another sinking down and it is a deep sleep in which I dream of people who do not yet know they are human. Maybe they are only now being born. It includes me, this cast of people, and there are the four women singing and they are the future, not the past, like I first thought. In the dream I am a green branch beginning to bloom, to grow something strong and human and alive.

Once when I was younger I went out and sat under the sky and looked up and asked it to take me back. What I should have done was gone to the swamp and bog and ask them to bring me back because, if anything is, mud and marsh are the origins of life. Now I think of the storm that made chaos, that the storm opened a door. It tried to make over the world the way it wanted it to be. At school I learn that storms create life, that lightning, with its nitrogen, is a beginning; bacteria and enzymes grow new life from decay out of darkness and water. It's into this that I want to fall, into swamp and mud and sludge, and it seems like falling is the natural way of things; gravity needs no fuel, no wings. It needs only stillness and waiting and time.

In the early morning, before it's even light, I get out of bed before everyone else is up and dress quickly, soundlessly, pulling on my jeans, and I go out the door and close it quietly. I take a shortcut past the houses, behind them, through trees. Some have fallen and are hard to pass. I head back to Ama's house before anyone will miss me. I think I should finish burying the horse.

Outside, it's a chaotic, disordered world where I could break a bone with more ease than not. I watch for downed wires. The birds are not yet singing or fussing about. The sky is overcast and I think of the storm, of looking up and seeing the circle of clear night and stars in the silent eye of that storm only a few days ago, and how I entered something so calm as to be unearthly and it could have killed me if it wanted to.

I see Ama's little hutlike house from the black trees, more dilapidated than before. She has not returned, as I already knew, because she has no bail, no recognizance, although Mama said they would keep her there for her own safety. There are people who hate her for what she's done.

When I see the Spanish horse, I am surprised it has hardly started to decay. The vines have already started growing across it. That's how hungry they are, these foreign vines, that's how fast they grow. I take the shovel handle and wrap it with cloth because it has started to splinter and it's still wet. Then I begin once again to dig. Because it's early and it has been cool, only a few slow-moving flies are near the horse.

Willard's white horse, too, is still at Ama's. It comes out of the trees and watches me. It's a true witness, the only one. I feel guilty in its eyes. I stop digging a moment, put down the shovel and go over to it. It's so dirty, I fill the bucket Ama washed in with water from the little cistern and pour the water over it and wash clean its sides with my bare hands. It curves its neck around and breathes on me, its breath sweet with chewed grasses, its dark eyes looking at me. It doesn't want to go back to Willard's. Maybe he's beat it and it's not so stupid as everyone thinks horses are, but I decide to take it back because I know they'll blame Ama for it. From now on, everything that goes wrong, every single thing, is going to be blamed on Ama.

I lead the horse back to Willard's. It seems like such a short distance when only a night or two earlier this space between places seemed far away and forever. I prop up Willard's fallen gate to try to keep his white horse at home. And then I return and dig once again at the hole, digging down centuries toward what is lost and covered up.

I wonder who is missing this horse. Maybe they think it is still alive, that it ran away in terror and will go wild out in the swamps like the Spaniard Cabeza de Vaca, the explorer who wandered these places for years. But no one has yet stepped forward to claim it.

It's not quite deep enough, the hole, and I am already tired. I dig down into roots and limestone, packs of clay. The hole I dig fills with water and I have to get into the chalky brown water and stand in it to dig. It's not deep enough but I am tired and so wet I stay in it partway and see if I can dig underneath the horse enough to get it partway down, my jeans wet and muddy, and then mound it over with stones. Then I get out and push it, as if I've lost my reason and think I have strength, but I can't budge the mud-caked horse that is solid as wood. I dig around the horse, close to it, thinking I can dig the hole out larger, until I can get the horse to fall into it, and I'm sweating and the flies are starting to swarm as the sun rises and I hear the sound of shovel, rock, water.

Smelling the wet earth, I know that somehow the police will dig this hole up again later believing it is where Ama hid her gun, or hid the panther. Maybe they will know the hole is fresh and dug by me and believe I have taken whatever was buried there, that I have stolen evidence. And even knowing this, I dig until my back hurts.

And finally, I think I can get the horse in and then, just then, a ledge of earth breaks off and the horse falls in with me, on me. I scream out and rush to pull myself back away from the horse, rushing out of the water, leaving one shoe underneath the horse, solid as wood, and then I sit, catching my breath, looking around me at the world that has been torn out of its ground, and the sun rises across the land. I sit, simple, plain, alive. Like a lizard in the sun, eyes closed and alive. I am still these few moments before I pour water over my arms and clean the mud off. Then, just then, the birds all come awake at once and they make such a clatter, a noise of life, that I, who have had trouble hearing since the storm, I hear them clear and sharp, their songs descending to touch me. I go inside and leave my remaining shoe beside the door and put on Ama's boots. The house is dark and smelling of earth and root and decay.

Two worlds exist. Maybe it's always been this way, but I enter them both like I am two people. Above and below. Land and water. Now and then.

5
JUDGMENT

On the following Sunday, because she wants me to be forgiven, Mama takes me to her church. Because I am obedient, I go with her. For her sake, not mine, because she has been crying, and I feel bad for her. But I don't believe in forgiveness. I think it's generous to a fault, even when it concerns me.

Driving, my mother says, "None of this is because of you," as if to convince herself, but I know she doesn't believe her own words or why would I have to go to church and be forgiven? Forgiveness means that whatever the sin was, you will never do it again, and that others will stop judging you. It means you are pardoned by them and you know the error of your ways. It's a gift they offer you. But it's a selfish gift because it makes them feel better than it makes you feel.

From the Chevy I look out at the dozers still clearing trees that fell in the storm, and at the houses with their roofs blown off. What once seemed solid looks like nothing more than broken toothpicks. Human creations don't hold a candle to wind. That's how I know something is greater than human will. And even though it's a tragedy, I feel better seeing how small we are. It makes me think that all our crimes against the world will be undone in just one rage of wind or flood.

The church my mother goes to has been spared by the storm. Saved, like the people in it. A good sign, everyone thinks. It's a rattletrap affair, brown-painted, home to the preacher as well as to God. Mr. Kedson is opening the folding chairs when we arrive, setting them down in a few curved rows. In the corner is an old piano with worn keys. A bulletin board behind it. Donated, like everything else. Everything smells of coffee. There are orange burlap curtains at windows, plastic flowers in vases at the back with the fresh-picked real ones in the front, donated by one of the women whose cutting garden survived the storm. I look around. They are women, mostly, women my mother's age, and if the church was a person, I think, it would be like them. It would wear too much blush and mascara and a too-bright dress.

This is a place where the women receive love of another kind than what they wish for at home. They receive doughnuts after all their meetings, too, but most of them won't eat the oily, calorie-filled things in public. They'll save them for the drive home. They are good women, nice women, but even so, I don't want to be here in this somber place that tries too hard to look cheery, where everyone is waiting for the Rapture.

My mother's voice, when she sings, sounds treacherous and untrue. I don't believe it always sounded this way. It's something that's happened in recent years, and I wonder sometimes if she stopped believing in anything here in this church, and only pretends that she still does, as if I feel all the doubts for her. In any case, she lies to herself. About Herm. About us. Maybe it's one reason I no longer trust anything, not her, not God, not myself. And I don't pretend to sing or say "Halleluia" at first. I just listen to "What a Friend We Have in Jesus," and as I hear the combined voices I think what a disappointment I am to my mother and her friends, Indian and white. I'm both a

Taiga, a person from this downtrodden place, and I am the smart daughter, the one they think will show all the others how we can make it. I was the one who would prove that we are not at the bottom of the world. They thought their kids would follow me. Now they hope they won't.

The church is full. Mr. Kedson, the preacher, is a clean-faced, bangs-wearing man and he lives in the church. He looks boyish and scrubbed, not much older than me. He lives in a very disorderly way for a clean-looking man but the disorder is the only thing I like about him. They, he and Mrs. Kedson, have two cats always sitting by the door in the same position, one asleep, the other always staring at something in the bushes. There are dead plants in the yard right next to the house, a child's shoe next to the pots of plants, a stack of old magazines, water-soaked and stained, up against the porch. This place wasn't hit by the wind. It just looks like it was, it's the way his life and family have unfolded, all unkempt and nothing tidy except for the room where they hold church. He needs air plants, I think, the kind that live without need or care. Or resurrection ferns that wait for a rain like dead things and then open up new and green and beautiful like they are doing right now out on the hurricane-felled trees, like they didn't know it was catastrophe that gave them life. Maybe, I think, I am like those ferns. Ama's like the rain.

Today they wouldn't have to wait for resurrection because it is going to rain and I can see it coming through the windows, moving toward us, and more than that, I can smell it. Everybody stands and begins to sing again and then, as I knew would happen at the house of God, after singing and crying, after uplifting words, Mr. Kedson beckons me to the front of the church. Mrs. Kedson gets up from the piano bench and I sit down on it, and it's still warm from her large behind. And all the people walk out of the seats and come to lay hands on me. They come, one by one, to touch me with their hands and I look at each one of these decent women, some of them crying, maybe even crying for me, and the few men looking faithful, and I receive them, but inside my skin I feel myself draw back, even though these are generous women, kind women. But theirs is a spare God, short on love, thin on compassion, strong on judgment. Theirs is a fallen God, at least in my eyes, and it's not for me I sit here, but for Mama, and it doesn't feel good, this sacrifice, I feel it in my stomach—it doesn't feel right, being touched by all these people, but I put up with it for her sake.

"Don't you feel better?" my mother asks as we leave amidst all the smiling, newly shining faces and drive home.

"Yes," I say, even though the strong perfume of one of the women has given me the start of a headache.

"You do?" she asks, looking at me to be certain.

I nod, and I feel the lie turn over in my stomach so strong I think maybe it feels this way when you have a baby inside. Maybe lies are like babies. They grow by their own design and sooner or later they have a mind of their own. But I see my mother is happy with this lie so I leave it there where it starts to grow a heart and new eyes. But this one hasn't yet formed a spine and it has fallen from the grace of a father in the sky.

When I wake up Monday morning at my mother's house of emptiness, it's barely light. I dress and go through Herm's tools and take out hinges and screws, open the door quietly once again to slip away.

The frogs are loud this morning as I walk to Ama's in the first light of the day. I take the road instead of the shortcut because it's a beautiful day and I don't need to hide.

At Ama's, I see that the dead horse is gone and there are tire marks in the mud. The prints go to the road and then there is nothing. It's a mystery where it went. Maybe the owners found it and brought a truck to cart it away.

What I do this early morning is put the door back up, screw the hinges, lift the door, missing the nail head, making the little holes where I will drive the screws, marking the place once again. The door is heavy, but putting it up is easier than putting up the doors to my self, my body, my heart, to keep Herm from fighting with me.

When I return home, Mama is already up, her makeup is on a little uneven, and she is starching Herm's shirts in a tub on the counter. She dries her red hands on a dish towel. "Where have you been?" She doesn't look at me.

"I went out for a walk," I tell her. I look around. No Herm or Donna. "Where is everybody?"

"Your dad is at work," she says, reading my mind. "Donna is staying with a friend."

Then I see the phone is off the hook and I know they planned it this way, not to be disturbed, not to have to talk to me, not to get any of the phone calls we have been getting about my so-called crime, as if I didn't already feel guilty enough. And it is the day when I have to face everyone, and now I am afraid. I'm nervous about going to school. Mama prepares me by fixing a bowl of oatmeal. "This'll stick to your ribs," she says as if I'm still a child and nothing has happened.

Later, when she walks me to the door, she says, "Hold your head up, you hear?" As if oatmeal and directions will carry me through the day.

She stands framed in the door as I leave for school. "You didn't do anything wrong. It was Ama that did it, so keep your head up."

I look at her and I won't tell her that I was wrong, too, that I should have stopped this thing, but couldn't. She believes, anyway, that I am forgiven, that I am taken back into the fold. But I am leaving it, walking out the door without a thing in my hand, no book, lunch, or pencil. It's not that I forgot it all, either.

A few steps away, I look back again and Mama's still there, anxious, watching, her face concentrated into a frown. I feel dread. I can't shake off the feeling that this is a dream and that I'll wake up and see my mother starching shirts and ironing and cooking, and everything will be just like it was a week ago. But time, the worst thing about it is that it doesn't turn back. You don't get two chances in this life.

My best friend, Jewel, doesn't drive by to pick me up as she usually does. I didn't expect her to, but I had hoped. I still do. I listen to every passing car to see if it sounds like hers. I know already that I'll be late. I will walk into home room with every eye on me, all of them seeing my guilt. Words travel; I am Ama's accomplice.

Jewel and I have shared and traded confidences all our lives. Sooner or later we would have been shaken out into separate worlds anyway. History, if nothing else, already came between us from before we were even born. We have been destined for different lives all along, Jewel for college, me for God knows what. Still, I long for her not to judge me. I have wished for her, of all people, not to judge me but this, my "act," has been the final building of our wall of difference; Jewel with the blue eyes, me with the dark skin, Jewel with the "good family," me with only my own intelligence and my half-starved hunger to hear about her life of lessons, piano, ballet, and every other coveted thing her mother could organize for her. Even though it also makes me laugh to think of her wearing a pink leotard and shoes in the midst of this swampy, mosquito-ridden land, of a piano soaked with humidity at every turn. They do it, though, lots of people, including Jewel with her family. That is what I envy. I have always wished to be part of a family like hers. Jewel with her father to pass something on to her, a place in the world. Me with nothing but what I can come up with from my own insides. There is no one, nothing on this God's great planet to make a place in the world for me. Ama might have done it. I thought she would. For this, I am disappointed.

For a minute I consider going back home to get my books,

but decide against it. It's a good feeling to be empty-handed, to feel naked as if a whole life was blown off my back by a storm. I walk down the road, passing fire hydrants, fences. I walk past the newly painted house of the sheriff, and before long, I go up the concrete walk and enter the limestone-colored brick school with its odors of floor wax, mildew, erasers, the smells of young people, all superimposed on top of a swamp. I enter the world of football and school rings, books, a place where we learn to examine stories and numbers, and I hate the smell of school, but I've been good at it, this world where we study war and the numbers that combine to destroy life.

When I walk into this school I see that this once-large world, like my mother's house, has grown smaller. There is no longer room in it for me.

Then I stop in front of my locker, dead still, and stare. On my locker, the word "Killer" is painted in black, and something inside me falls down a long stairway, hitting the sides as it falls. I stand before it a moment. The hall is empty of students. And then I slam the locker shut as if I don't care, and go to home room knowing already that everyone inside this room has turned away from me, and when I go into the room, I see that this is true. I hear them talking about me. It is intended that I hear. We are of that age, that winnowing age, the judging age, the comparing age. "There she is. Cat killer." Panther, our high school mascot. The idea of the panther is loved while the animal itself is hated, unwanted. Loved while it's been hated. There is no keeping their voices down or even putting their hands before their faces when I hear them speak as I enter the room. They will talk about me for years, the quiet girl, the one who thought she was smart, going out on a hunt with crazy Ama Eaton, and killing an endangered species, one of the last of the sickened cats in the glades and swamps.

The teacher silences the room, but she is uncomfortable and her eyes don't once look at me, not directly.

I sit down and make myself still inside, as if dreaming. I sit until the teacher comes over and places a book before me, already opened, but I am thinking how at school I have learned there's no room in sky for my mother's heaven; there's no room at the center of the earth for hell, either. It is new worlds I will have to look for. I sit without looking at the book.

When I go to my next class, the teacher calls my name and I can't speak. I'm unable to say "Here" or even raise my hand. Nothing to state that I have entered this room. I'm silent. It's as if I'm not here. All the time, inside my own mind, I talk to myself. I am not a cloud that has to fall, I tell myself. I am not a tree, broken by wind. I am not a building fallen with the storm. I am not brick, collapsed. I glance around, knowing I am not one of these people, either, not these people who are like vines grown over this land, smothering it.

This is the place where we study the fetus of a pig, and I wonder what suffering brought it here. Where we number the stamen and pistil of plants on paper, cut them apart to look through a microscope and identify the miracles of small things. Here, now, I am the specimen and they are all looking at me, watching my every move.

Too soon I am sitting in the lunchroom with students look-ing at me like I dropped out from the sky, like I am a cloud, after all, or a blown-down tree. I see Donna, my sister, with her tangle of friends, the white girls, Donna looking torn between me and them. I am going to cost her. Plenty. But, thankfully, she comes away from the other students and half-smiles at me and I feel relieved by her loyalty. She walks to me and sits down next to me in all the empty space around this long table. I sit straight, as if no one is talking about me, as if it doesn't matter, as if there is not a feeling of fear in my stomach. Donna gives me a carton of milk and her cookie, which I can't eat. I smile, though, and try to pretend nothing is wrong. Here is my sister, so sure of herself, created all on her own out of

POWER

magazines she's bought at the drugstore and she is bent down, trying to look into my eyes, telling me, "Don't worry what they say, Sis. It'll pass." I bring myself to nod at her. She squeezes my arm, then gets up and leaves me alone.

It will pass. I'm sure of it. I believe in time. But I'm wrong. In this gray brick building, time has changed and school is forever. In biology class, I look at a leaf with acetone on it, the perfect natural structure of it, the fluids moving around the thin-veined webbing of green. Leaf, I think, what an easy thing to be. Humans are not like leaves. We are a shambles of an animal.

But why should they be the ones who judge me or Ama? I know their mothers. I see them at the grocery store with rollers in their hair. I know what their fathers do to buy larger televisions for football, swamp coolers or lawn mowers for the homes where they worship, fight, and eat.

I've been good at this world, the one that hits you when you are born and makes you cry right from the start, so that crying is your first language. I've learned what I was supposed to learn, but now it comes to me that in doing so I've unlearned other things. I've lost my sense; I cannot sense things. Yes, we are a shambles. And maybe Ama found the way; she found it when all the paths were washed away by rivers from the sky, when all the buildings were blown down by the breath of a God. For just one day, that one day, she found a way out of that shambles, a way around it. And it's this I want to find. But now she has no path back, no way to return even if she wanted to be here in this America. She will always live away from this world, in something of a twilight that is not one thing or the other, not one time or the next. She lives in a point, a small point, between two weighted things and it is always rocking, this scale, back and forth.

I look around me and for the first time, I see things clearly—at least I think I do—crystal clear, the rich white girls are in one group, the dark, the black, the Indian in others. The Cubans in their proud clothes always look nice, those eight students, the girls with their swinging walks that I like, but the white boys think the way they walk means that they are loose and easy. Maybe everything is that simple to misread. I see, too, that once my eyes are open, I will never be the same.

When the bell rings, I walk down the hall in such a way that they will know it doesn't bother me that even the teachers look at me differently, not directly as before, but sideways, with a question in their eyes. I have disappointed them. I, the Taiga girl who had potential, who would be a new and shining model for the Indian kids who have always seemed indifferent to their school. Omishto, the exception. I can almost hear them talking through the walls and doors of the teachers' lounge.

Jewel has managed to keep away from me all day, but after school, just as I am leaving, she comes to talk with me. Suddenly she seems so young, younger than me, hugging her books to her chest. And I say to myself, I am not a child. I am not a white person. I am not the one who was wrong.

Jewel comes close and says to me, "It's true what they say about you, isn't it? You killed that panther? You and Ama Eaton." She is telling me more than she is asking.

I look at her, unable to answer. Her face is full of judgment. And more. I have betrayed her, I can see this in her eyes. Her small blue eyes accuse me.

I say simply, "Yes."

There's nothing else I can say, but I keep looking at her, a steady gaze.

She turns and walks away.

And I turn and don't watch her leave me.

Outside, the breeze touches my skin. I pull myself up as tall as I can. I will let them talk. They believe in my guilt. In a way they are right. What they believe is true.

I leave school alone, in all my skinniness, walking as straight and proud as I can, but at home I stand in front of the bedroom mirror and look into my own eyes, and then, as if this act has meaning and will change things, will change me, I go get the scissors from the kitchen drawer and cut my hair. I think maybe when I go back to school the next day I will walk past people and they will not know me.

Before dinner, Donna comes in and looks at all the dark hair on the floor. "What did you do to your hair?"

"My God," says my mother and calls one of her friends who cuts hair to see if she can fit me in and fix me. "Maybe she can even it up at least."

For English, we are to write an autobiographical essay. Out of habit more than anything, I sit down and try to write. What I say is this:

I am a Taiga. We are swamp people. There are only thirty of us now. My name is Omishto and it means "Watching." My mother doesn't remember my birth so she can't tell me anything about it and sometimes, anyway, I feel as if I am not yet born, not really.

I live with my mother and her husband and my sister, Donna. I am a Panther Clan member. I am sixteen. My sister is seventeen. Last year my brother was killed in a fire. I still miss him, though Mama says we shouldn't grieve because he's in heaven, so I try not to think of him. Sometimes I think I hear his voice at night. Jerry. He used to say he could read the minds of animals and I always asked him what they were thinking but he said he wasn't allowed to tell, but he always said they liked me. I know that can't be true because what is there to like about humans?

My mother used to tell me about the old Taiga people, the ones who live in the place where the road grows narrow, above Kili Swamp. She used to say that one day I'd want to go back in there, but she doesn't say it anymore. I went there with her for a while after my father left. I can barely remember. And once when she went after plants for medicine, she took me with her to see the people, my relatives. Someday I might go there myself. Maybe I would even stay.

I guess everyone has heard, I have a friend who killed a panther. Maybe you read about it in the newspaper, that I was with the woman who killed the panther. Ama Eaton. I think she could read the minds of animals, too. There is a Taiga story about Panther Woman. And I think Ama got lost in this story, although you might not believe this. It's an old story about a panther and a woman, told to me by Ama, told to Ama by Janie Soto who is the oldest member of our tribe.

This is how I heard it. Years ago, Panther walked on two feet. A woman lived in the dark swamp of the early world in those days. She was raised by wild animals because her human family had rejected her, but the animals favored her. It was given this woman to keep the world in balance. So she was a person who sang the sun up in the morning, and if she could do this it would keep the world alive. Like memory, she was there to refresh our thoughts and renew our acts.

This was long before there were cars. Long before the foreign seeds would open and grow. It was some time after the beginning of the Taiga people, after the world had aged. And this world came into being, and the people had broken the harmony and balance of this world we now live in. One day a storm blew with so much strength that it left an opening between the worlds. Panther Woman saw that opening, and followed the panther into that other world. She went through that opening and entered it. And no one enters willingly. What she saw there was rivers on fire, animals dying of sickness, and foreign vines. The world, she saw, was dying.

The unfortunate thing was that the door blew closed behind her and she had to find a way to open it again.

"You have to kill one of us," the panther, who was dying, told her. "It should be me. I'm not the oldest or the weakest, but I'm the one you know best."

A sacrifice was called for and if it was done well, all the animals and the panther would come back again and they'd be whole. The people in those days believed that all the hunted, if hunted correctly, would return again. In Taiga, the word for sacrifice means "to send away," and the animal returns to the spirit world.

And after she killed it, the woman put the skull of the panther in a tree so that it could see itself when it returned, could see its own path, and know the way back. It would see that she had killed it for that reason and it would bring life back to this once-beautiful place.

When the panther returned, this woman went back to where she came from and transformed herself into one of the catlike creatures. She went away with it to live in that place no one has ever entered, the place where a person could be lost for years and never find a hint of direction. Because it's the opening between the worlds, opened by a storm. Under the sky.

But that's an old story in a world of new people and no one much believes in stories anymore. And now the panther is endangered and it is protected by state and federal law. There might be less of them than there are of us.

The old people say the panther is our older sister. I think about this story. I think about the old people.

Even though I am young I remember not long ago when the water was very sweet and you could eat the fish here.

The person who's been most important in my life is Ama and she is the one who killed the panther. My mother says it is unfortunate for me that I was with her because it was a terrible thing and since it was the day of the hurricane, I was probably in shock because of the storm, and that must be why I went along.

But it was different than that, because I think that cat called to Ama Eaton, the way it did in that old story. And I went with her and I saw all this, but when I try to say why it happened, no words come to me. None at all. But I think Ama Eaton went through that opening and I followed her, and I remember that no one goes there willingly.

I read these words and I tear the paper into little pieces and throw them away. I have always been a good, obedient girl, but tomorrow, for the first time, I will hand in no assignment.

Empty-handed again, the next day I leave for school early, pass the houses on each side of the road. It is the season of storms. I am carrying my notebook, but I turn the wrong way on the road and I go to Ama's instead of to school. The way to school is too long, the way back home even longer. I go the hard way, taking the footpath through the trees behind the subdivision, and as I walk, I hope she is there even though I know she won't be. She has no money for bail, and there wasn't another soul in this world who'd bail her out. But I can't see why anyone would leave her in jail except that she's a dark woman and they find her strange. If it were a man who shot a cat, a white man, he'd be free to come and go as he pleased. He'd be called a hunter.

It rains for days. Torrents of rain. It rained small fish. Twice now the fish are on land. I've seen it rain fish before. Ama says their eggs hatch in the clouds and grow. Then, because they are heavy, they fall. When they do, the ground is alive with them, silver and thrashing. They make good fertilizer, Herm says, but I can't bear the thought of water creatures falling from the sky, drowning in air.

I can't sleep. I can't breathe. I sit up, suffocating like one of the fish, and try to take deep breaths. But when I lay back down, my breath stops again and so I give up on sleep and sit at the window, awake and feeling dread. It is the night before court and I tell myself this is a dream, it's only a dream, as if dreaming is less than being awake. I listen to the rain and see silver leaves in the flashes of lightning. In the next room Herm snores. And, as if I were still sleeping, behind my eyes I see shipwrecked men coming ashore, swimming in from ocean to land. Toward me.

On the first day of court, as we prepare to leave, there is a rumbling sound in the sky, a roaring in the distance, and the west corner of the sky is dark. Mama takes the umbrella.

On the way to the city we pass the place where Willard's brown trailer sits hidden behind trees. Another side of it is about to fall off. I look for the skinny white horse that's been driven insane by mosquitoes, but see not a trace of it before I realize the horse has returned to Ama's. There are signs of life, though; a red-winged blackbird sits on a cattail beside the road; a turtle is almost across the street, vulnerable even with its shell.

It is the rainy season when earth brims over. A swelling world in which even the wood of houses swells and grows larger before it begins to decay. Then, the rumbling sound comes closer, approaching with the low clouds, and it strikes, the hailstorm strikes earth with a vengeance. I look out and see the large hailstones falling, beating down the world. They hit the roof of Mama's car so hard it is like a war has broken out. She parks under a tree to wait. They strike earth and bounce upward. The branches fall on us, over the window.

"Oh my God," says Mama. "It's wrecking the car. I hope the window doesn't break."

But I think it doesn't matter. There is wind and in a while the hail lightens, and I open the door to remove the branch, throw it on the road. It smells fresh. As we drive, the hail is on the sides of the road like snow, I suppose, but I have never seen snow except in pictures. I worry about the goat and kid and the chickens, but the white snow looks beautiful even though it has dented the car Mama takes such good care of, the windshield cracked. All over the roads are bits and broken branches of trees with leaves torn off, and then, out by the cane workers' shacks I see a dead dog and roofs again broken, this time by the hail.

We pass the little square houses of sugarcane workers and bean pickers, houses painted pink and soft blue as if to lie about the lives of hard-worked, underpaid people who live inside the painted walls, and outside the plants look torn to bits.

As the land passes, I look backward at the day I followed Ama and it all seems dark and crazy. I am afraid to tell about it. How the clouds were ashes in the sky, that the wind blew or chased a heavy Spanish horse into Ama's dirt yard, that a barn owl screamed like a woman. How I worked to dig a hole to bury the horse, and how someone opened it again and the body of the horse disappeared. I don't know if I can tell that Ama was blown against the house and that what followed seemed natural and right even though it was wrong by law, but that another law was at work that day and it was older than human history. Would they let me tell that sugarcane and cattle and white houses with red roofs had killed the land and the panther people even before the storm, they are the true violators. That the cattle and houses we are passing are the beginning of this crime and that their makers remain unjudged and untried.

We follow the road into town, Mama's blue-gray car drives me through the streets, still wet with the storm. The city is morning busy. People are going to work in their cars. All of it moves so quick and fast with the storm just passed through. A few trees stand, alien and foreign, in a ground that not long ago was all theirs. The ground belonged to them and the marsh birds and possum. I believe they are surprised to be alive at all, those lonely trees, and nothing in this world acknowledges them. I look out the car window, feeling closed in and invisible. Shops are not yet open but an awning is being let out. We pass laundromats, fast food.

"You hungry?" Mama asks, as if I could eat.

I shake my head no.

"Me, either."

A woman takes a child into a building dark with decay and with bars on the windows. It is already hot, though the forecast calls again for rain and even though I am in my mother's car, I am in water, that's how it feels. My feet are in water, at the bottom of mud, sinking, but I see Ama again, looking me deep in the eye, saying to me, "When they ask you, just tell them what happened," and I am sure I no longer have a voice.

And then we arrive at the building whose walls are cold stone.

The trial of Ama Eaton draws a large crowd and we circle the block but find no parking. There are people protesting. White people. Indians. And there are newspaper people. There has been so much talk. The endangered cat. Treaty rights. By treaty, Ama could kill the cat. And it enrages the people who want to save them, especially when the panther has so many illnesses they hardly stand much of a chance. And I agree with them and with treaty rights, too. How can there be two truths that contradict each other? And me. I am on both sides now; that is the worst. What Ama did was wrong, and it was right. The cameras are flashing as we drive past, but we are, as yet, unseen. I feel ashamed of myself. Even in the car I lower my eyes and keep them lowered.

"I should drop you off and go park," Mama says. "It might

be a long walk." But she doesn't. She just wanted something to say. She doesn't want me to walk through this angry group of people all alone.

We drive on until we find a parking lot. It means we have to walk a good long way. We lock the car and then, walking, we are silent. I feel tiny as a seed being blown across a huge, wide world.

A crowd of people watches us as we come near the big white pillars of the courthouse. They know who I am. They are looking at me, judging me. I am sweating from the heat, my hair damp at the back of my neck, my heart pounding with fear. Mama walks faster, her hand on the back of my arm to push me along. "It's okay," she says.

But everyone sees us and it seems like Judgment has already written its name across their faces with a capital J. Ama Eaton is the killer of beautiful and endangered animals. She is the destroyer of the future, of life and possibility. She has taken from the world. She is a thief, robbing the world of one of the last few Florida panthers alive. And I am the child who followed, the quiet thing who has no mind, who went from a storm into a swamp of killing. They can't tell what I am inside. Neither can I. In the slow motion of time it takes to reach the steps, inside myself I am trying to find out what I really know, what is wrong or right, and all I know is that the birds are above us now, too many grackles looking for a place to settle in just two trees on this street and they displace each other, bickering. And I know that Ama, living near the water in the little, once-blue house, or sliding down the muddy banks into the water, that when she saw the yellow god-eyes moving toward water, catching light, it meant something that no one else could understand. They would never understand. It's not in them to know these kinds of things. They'd never know why Big Heart Eaton, as my mama used to call her, the woman who hated to have to hit a fly or cut a snake's head off, why it was that something moved her to take this life from the precious world. And they don't know our stories.

"Don't worry that they look at you, Omishto," my mother says.

It's the first time she's called me by my name. Maybe the first time in my life. And in her voice is worry about me. I look at her, wondering why she chose this day to call me by my rightful name. She is wearing too much blush on her cheeks, but I see beneath it her skin, not quite smooth and very pale.

As we go up the steps, one man comes forward, out of the crowd, and tries to talk to me. He is well dressed, but my mama says to the crowd, "Excuse us," and she puts her arms up and they part and let us pass through. I walk past in frozen silence as if I can't see them. I don't look up, not down either for fear of falling into what's beneath pavement, all the decay and sewers between here and hell.

It's only a moment, really, but it seems like forever, the steps we take into the courthouse. We leave the intense heat and humidity, and we go into the building. Inside, a man stands with a briefcase, clinging to it. I glance at him, wondering if he is going to become part of my life, this unknown man, if he's an attorney. But I remind myself that I am not on trial. I am just a witness. Like my name, Omishto, I'm the watcher. They have already told me if I tell the truth about Ama, I will not be charged with anything. They are going easy on me because of my age. But I will tell the truth anyway because she told me to. Except for how sickly it looked, not that it makes a difference one way or another, not enough to mention. I heard, too, that they asked jurors how they felt about insanity as a defense. I think what they mean to do is prove Ama insane, and I don't feel right betraying her in any way.

The inner walls of the building are cold stone. The corners seem dark. The floor has been polished. Although it feels empty, it's full of people. Those who work here seem pale and walk fast. They clean the floor. They enter rooms. Court clerks. Secretaries. Early mornings and again, in the evenings, their shoes make noise on the floors, tapping, scuffing. I hear the hum of lights overhead. That's how keen my hearing is in this room of stone, inside the big white pillars of the courthouse.

In the hall, two men are talking about how the snook fish left the salt and brine waters and swam inland when the water level was high and where was a good place to catch them but they grow quiet when they see me.

At the entrance to courtroom number four they check us for weapons and then we enter the place that has doors that do not look like doors, but walls opening, walls through which, finally, the judge comes out and someone says, "All rise."

Like sun rises, like wind rises, we stand up.

"In the year of our Lord," they say.

I can't help but whisper to my mother, "Their lord doesn't have many years compared to us." I say it because the tension is too great for me, because I feel both afraid and angry.

"Stop it," she says, and lets me know by her look what serious business this is and how I'm expected to behave, and I do, I will.

They tell us to sit down. How formal it is, how impossible. The trial proper opening with the honorable Judge Gracian. This building is a world cut in two. This building and what it contains divide one part of life from another. It has separated by scars, legal theft, even the stone of earth split and carried here to a building of justice, and then it covers everything broken all back over in words the way the kudzu plants from the old world cover this beautiful ground with foreign, choking vines.

I sit here in the dress my mother made over out of an older dress. People are looking at me. I am not pretty, they are thinking, I am not like them. You can see it right off. It's clear on their faces, what they think of me. And the dress. It is clearly homemade and nothing like anyone else wears. I have tried to be like them. But now, sitting here, I give it up. I would bequeath them an ugliness, a place outside their world, a darkness they could never light on, a memory of something that's from a history of destruction. They could not dare to survive it. They would have anguish. If there were thirty of them in this world, they would fall down in despair and hit themselves. They'd wish for life and death, both at the same time.

I see on the table a collar and the boy's rifle, which I know isn't the gun in question, not the one Ama used. In television courtrooms they examine the chamber, the bullets, the prints, but they must not do that here; they have no bullet to match it with, they have nothing to show for a dead cat. But the collar, at first I can't discern what it is. It is hard-looking and large, gray. It's twisted a bit, and cut, and I realize then, for the first time, that this is their evidence. That it's one of the tracking collars used by biologists and only now do I realize what has happened, that they traced us right to Ama's house because of the collar, that Ama took the collar to her house so they would find her. I remember the plane passing over us and now I see that the plane was a field service plane, that the cat was one of the studied, watched. That it was followed and we were followed.

The biologists are disliked by some for protecting the cats. By some. But there are others who think they do not do enough to protect them. All I know is that they, too, have lost cats. One of the panthers died by drowning in water after a drug was released into its neck. Another outgrew its collar and choked. One reacted to the drug.

And then I see Ama and realize she's been here all along and is nearly invisible in this room. She's made herself small at the table and almost clear. Nor does she look at the people in the room. She sees no one. She simply doesn't see them. It's as if all the people are not here, as if no one is here, not even me or my mother, not even herself. But as small as she tries to make herself, everyone, even me, watches her.

Then four of the elders of our tribe come into the room and sit down together in the back. From here I can see how the old people sit, quiet and still, almost stiff. In this place where words can lie, their stillness and discomfort is honest, and silence is a kind of truth. My mother once told me that when I was young, the old people wanted me to go back to their place above the swamp and stay with them. I think of them, always, as living at the threshold to our world. The people in the courthouse turn to look at them and the room grows quiet because even the white people respect them, how could they not, to see them so strong, so different, even in the way they move and hold themselves.

But it is Ama I notice the most. She hasn't been eating. I recognize the signs when I look at her. Large-boned as she is, she'll waste away, disappear, she's grown so thin. Her face looks tired with deeper lines than before. Yet strangely, at moments, something flickers across her and she looks healthy and bright, like she's light and not matter. At other times she sits, not listening, and looks at the wall, at the darkness as if she doesn't see this room, as if she's forgotten herself, where she is, in this room of law. She folds her arms across her chest, her eyes looking through the walls to the outside. I know she is seeing. She sees the room next to this, where there's another trial, a hearing maybe, a traffic ticket, a case of divorce or child custody. She sees beyond the walls to where the rows of homes are constructed, to where the horses and cattle stand in the fields, heads down, eating, always eating, until they stand at slaughter, are stunned, killed and bled away from life. She sees the cypress trees, the marshes with heat lightning and gases. She sees straight into the wild yellow eyes of the cat that was her relative, and in its eyes—even I remember this—she sees into death and birth and the place where the world is born and it is this, she believes, this light that keeps our people alive.

It was her lawyer, Mama said, that convinced her to have a trial. She didn't want one. She said what more was there to do but confess that she was guilty? But I realize the trial is about more than one thing, more than if she's insane or not, if she killed the cat or not, because now they are asking a biologist whether or not it was a true Florida panther and not another species, because if it wasn't it wouldn't be endangered and all she'd have been doing was hunting. And that would open up the laws, make a hole in the law that was to protect. She'd only be hunting. Out of season, maybe. And in the wrong place if it wasn't on reservation land. And without a proper license. And he can't say whether or not this panther might not have come from the union of a cougar or a mountain lion with one of the true panthers. Who is to say? Anything could wander in.

Later, when I am called to the stand, I am asked my name and what I do. "I'm a student at Walker High."

"Are you a good student?" The man tries to make me comfortable.

I don't say how well I used to do, how proud my mother was of me. I only nod, but my face reddens.

"What is your relationship to Ama Eaton?"

The law confuses me so I hope I get it right. "I am her friend."

"You are her friend." He repeats the answer back to me as if he doesn't believe it. "Despite your age difference?" It is a leading question, meaning that it's supposed to lead others to suspect our friendship, to think I have no judgment, to think she influences minors. To think she is strange to encourage a girl and I can see that this is unusual to them. I can see this. It makes me a vicitim of this woman who believes herself to be beyond and above the law.

I look at him straight on and say, "Yes, her friend."

"How long have you known her?"

"As long as I can remember. Since I was a child."

"Do you recall the day that the panther was killed?"

"Yes." I look at the prosecuting attorney. He is a heavily built, stiff man. He is looking for a weak place he can get inside. I do not look at Ama, not directly, but out of the corner of my eye I take in every detail. She sits, listening, but seeming as if she doesn't.

Then I take in my mother and I see her, the always wistful, hurt look on her face. A woman I'm afraid of becoming. She worries about what they think of me at school, in this room, in her church.

He asks me about the place. "Do you know where you were the day the panther was killed?"

"Not precisely."

"Was it on reservation land?"

"Yes, I think it was on the reserve." But I am not certain and they can sense this. It gives them an edge.

"How do you know it was on the reserve if you didn't know precisely where you were?"

"Because we passed over the road and the canals."

"So you knew where you were?"

"No, not exactly, I just knew we were on Taiga land. In the general area."

I look at my mother's face. Like me, she has aged. "I'm old," she said this morning. I saw that it was true even though she wore her best clothes. She has aged these past weeks, and she looks sad and I am sorry to have worried and disappointed her. She looks back at me. There is a helpless air between us, a wind of betrayal. Hers and mine. It's not that I betrayed her or she betrayed me, I know; we have been betrayed by something we can't yet name, neither of us.

"Did Ama Eaton know the panther was an endangered species?"

"Yes, she knew that." I don't say that she knew what would happen to her, knew they would judge her. She was guilty and she said it herself.

"Did you?"

"Yes."

I think of them, the cats out there in the cypress and mangroves and swamps humans aren't meant to enter, not most humans anyway, though it seems to me like a natural place. And I think of the cats killed by cars. A dozen of them since the highway went in. The high school team is named after them. They are mascots, nothing more. No one wants them around, but they like to see them just the same. They just don't want them out there by their places. They don't want to have to look over their shoulder everywhere they go. They say the cats follow people. They've never been known to hurt one person yet, but they will follow you. And no one wants them to eat cattle or dogs. There's no place human wants will let them be.

"You say you helped Ama Eaton. What exactly did you do to assist her?"

"I carried the water and things."

"What kind of things?"

"Just water mostly. And for a while a knife."

"Did you carry the cat back to her house?"

"No."

"Did you see the cat?"

I saw it thin and dying. Hungry. Pale brown, gray on its face, the dark circle on its side. I can see it even now in front of my eyes. I nod at him. "Yes, but only for a moment. After it was killed."

"Did you see her with the hide or the body of the cat?"

I close my eyes a moment. I see the police sergeant who said he was sorry to have to take her in. He, like everyone, knew her from before. "I never saw it afterwards. Not after we came home. I don't know what happened to it." That's what I tell them and I see, in my mind's eye, Ama combing her hair when they came for her, washing in a pan of water, brushing her dress down smooth. I see her walk over to the car to go with them. And I wonder, too, what she did with the cat's body, with the gun. Both are missing.

"How is it that you don't know where it was?"

I see the blood on the sides of the horse and feel sick. Worse, I can still smell it. And I know she brought the collar home on purpose—because she knew what it was—to draw them to her. But I don't know why.

"I fell asleep after that. When I woke up, nothing was there."

"Nothing?"

Everything I say sounds wrong.

I see her through their eyes for a moment and I doubt her and I wonder if she did, like some newswriter implied, eat the flesh of the cat. I wonder, too, what she did with the body, and if the whiskers, like they used to say, are really for healing, if the panther claws scratching the legs of a person truly helps them in this life, or at least used to help them the way generations before us believed. My eyes move toward the old people in the back of the room. Scratching the body. I think you scratch the body with the claws to let the light out, the human light, or to let something better than that in. I wonder if Ama believed this and I think she did.

The next day Ama doesn't smooth down her dress the way I do, self-conscious in this room of people, the way she did that day before getting into the police car. Her shoes, usually polished, are worn. She hasn't cleaned them, not even wiped the dust from them. She stands aside, beside even herself. Nothing of her tenderness shows on her, or her goodness, her mercy. But her bearing is straight. Her hair is neatly groomed. She wears a state dress; the jail provides the same kind of clothing they give patients in the mental hospital, like when my mother was in there after my brother died and later, again, when Herm took her there and she never took off her dark glasses the whole month. I always wonder what it was she didn't want anyone to see in her eyes. But unlike my mother, Ama does not look beaten down in the dress. Her back is straight, her shoulders square, and she has a strength, an honest strength.

Today the sun shines. The light in the room is bright and clear. It comes in through a single high window and lays itself down both on the floor and on the shoulder of a man who sits taking notes.

And then it is time again for me to talk. A new man is asking me something. I swallow, nervous at my own thoughts. "What?"

"Are you a full-blooded Taiga?"

"Yes."

"Do you think Ama Eaton is a full-blooded Taiga?"

This would make a difference to them, I see, though not to us.

I look at her and see that she is the kind of person that would kill herself to set the world straight again. Even if it breaks her own personal world apart.

I want to tell them the world is dying like us, little by little, and sometimes big, and that Ama believes in the oldest of ways and that she believed, yes, truly believed, someone had to do this, someone had to find a way to renew the world, and no one else would do it. Yes, it was against the law, but I saw with my eyes the boys driving through the place in their swamp buggies killing the land and the men wouldn't hold up so much as a finger to stop them, so maybe Ama took it all on herself to do. Even though nobody believes it anymore. And the thing is, the worst and most sad thing is, that it didn't work, that it seems like things have gone on as before, that belief has failed her, failed all of us, and the boys are still out there chasing down the world.

"Did she know the panther was an endangered species?" he asks me again.

"She knew what it was." I tell them this. She said it herself.

"How do you know that she understood this? Did you ever talk about it?"

"No, not straight out."

I feel lost. It's not like loneliness, it's something more, like in the deep night when you know you are alone and feel abandoned by everyone, the sea or nature or God, and I wonder why did I take part in something so terrible that when dark night engulfs me and I wish for sleep there is none. But I know, too, that I am a part of something that is maybe like God or the sea or nature and that whatever it is I've been part of, now it is slipping away and taking me with it.

She knew what would happen to it. She knew what would happen to herself. She knew it was a female. She knew they would judge her. She was guilty. She said it herself.

How can I say, there was a storm, the deer were flying, there was more water in the sky than on the earth so it seemed the world was turned over, the snakes were trying to get into the house. Me, I would have killed them. That's how scared of them I was. But not Ama because she never kills anything unless she has to.

There were ashes floating around us, I could say, and it was an unnatural day, but I can't say that what she did on that one day seemed like a natural thing and I can't say why. It was like how the world does things on its own. It kills them, I mean. Every last thing. It creates destruction so that it can go on. How can I explain this to them, that night and day were the same thing in that storm, that the very earth had slipped onto its side, and that this is part of the reason why she did it and why I followed her so awkwardly, unable to turn back, while she seemed to fly over the mud and stones and downed trees and the corpses of animals. How could I say it in any way that might convince them it had been coming a long time, a long, long time, and that it was a part of an old prophecy, an old story. It was some kind of a fixed thing, and there was no turning back. Not from any of it, then or now, even though the consequences were known by her, foretold, and even though I said to her without even knowing why or knowing the meaning of my words, "Ama, you have killed yourself," as if someone else said it through my mouth.

I look at all those sheets of paper in front of the lawyers. Even with this ray of light coming into the room, misfortune is an old thing here. Our misfortune. It's old and long, from before Ama's time or mine, clear back to when the first white men wandered lost in the swamps and grasses and forests. Misfortune would shine like two eyes in their dark night.

It must have started long ago, back when we lived in swamps with the mosses hanging down from trees and hid ourselves from soldiers. When we learned to travel water without a sound, undetected, so that we could live. We ate food without fire, lived without a trace of having been there. Or maybe it began longer back than that.

But I can't say the real truth; I can only say the facts. I don't believe in this court, but I don't lie anyway, not out of respect for the courthouse or the men in robes or suits, but out of respect for the truth.

My voice is only a whisper. They ask me to repeat myself and I say, "She knew there wasn't many of them." I do not even know I am whispering. And I say that she carried it back inside the bag and that we stole Willard's horse.

They ask me again what she did with the skin.

"I don't know. I didn't see what she did because I was tired and I fell asleep."

"Did she say anything to you about what she was doing?"

"Yes."

"What was it she said?"

"She said everything the world turns on is in this."

"What did you take that to mean?"

"That our lives depended on it."

The attorney, the defense, wants to prove how Ama believes. He asks me, "Is that your religion?"

"No. Not mine. Hers."

"Do you believe that?"

"No, I don't." I swallow and feel too warm. "Not myself, I mean. But she does." I can't even look straight at Ama for feeling like I've made her look crazy and abandoned her, betrayed something of who we are and who we once were, and who we are not any longer. Every word I say sounds wrong. And then, with surprise, I realize that I have lied, because I do believe what Ama believes. I have been lying, even to myself. There are times I do believe this, times like that one when I saw the four women. I saw them and they were there with or without anyone's belief, even my own.

I am quiet, but he is waiting for me to say more.

"Did she believe that gods retreated and the world was out of balance?"

I think, yes, they left us, yes, but I only say, "Yes. I think so."

"And it was her job to call them back?"

"Something like that. I think so." I feel tired, as if I could go to sleep.

"Were you with her that whole day?" Again.

Again, "Yes. I was with her the whole time."

"Did you try to stop her?" he asks.

As Ama asked me to do, I tell them the truth, though it seems damning. "Yes. At first," I tell him, but I am sorry to say it and my eyes are beginning to cry. And because it seems I am against her, I glance at Ama. She smiles, weakly, but looks into my eyes and her gaze is strong. "But she did it because she had to. You need to understand." My comment is unheeded. I close my eyes. I see her at the feet of the cat, at the feet of heaven, at the feet of justice, at the feet of all these fallen worlds.

Then the defense asks, "Why do you say this was something she had to do? What do you mean by that?"

I look at the old Taiga people, dark in the back of the room as if sitting in shadows, listening. I had almost forgotten them, they are so still. They are a shadow in the room. They watch me without seeming to look at me. "I mean they had a relationship. They knew each other. She knew the cat for years." I see by the way everyone moves in their seats and looks at each other that what I say sounds crazy to the people who fill the room. But I look at the old people.

"She knew the cat," he says.

"Yes." I don't tell how there is a story that a panther is killed and sent to the creator who renews the world but I tell him, "She protected it before. From some boys. That's their gun. Over there." I point to it. "She took it from them."

"She didn't shoot the panther with this rifle, did she?"

"No."

Inside the stone and marble and wood of this room is a silence deeper than any I've ever known. My words seem lost inside this room. My words have fallen like dust in the corners. And the beauty Ama has, no one can see. Only her eyes squinting, narrow with seeing. She, Ama Eaton, doesn't seem to look up or listen, even though she sees people in the room, I know she does, and I am remembering again how we saw the women coming in from the highway. Out of the heat. In their dresses. I saw them, I swear it, but it's nothing I can tell in this room of black and white law.

There is something else I want to tell. It lives in brush, bramble, darkness. It lives in the middle of black water. It leaves tracks and is unseen but felt. The strange world of it is private as another language. Its gold light of eyes is a secret door. It follows people but they don't see it. It is nothing they can imagine.

But Ama, too, is nothing they can imagine. The jury, the judge, the lawyers have never been in the wild places that are the places of Ama. In this way, it, this event, is not their affair. They can't know it the way you can't see your eyes closed in a mirror. Or how you can't see stars in daylight because there is too much light. And likewise, this world of theirs is none of her affair. Their lives are too narrow and brief for her. It is nothing she can understand or know or imagine. She has rarely been in the bleached and tamed confines of their world. In it now, she looks dead and tired as autumn grass. And to them, she looks crazy, but I know she is solid.

And the light comes into the room now like it did yesterday, the afternoon light. It is full and it lays itself down on the floor on top of my words and where they have fallen.

Now, he says she was trying to get power.

"Power," I say back to him. "What's that?"

"In the spirit world."

"What for?" I say. Rude. "To get something she wanted? She didn't want anything. To have luck in gambling?" And I sit back against this hard wooden chair and I think of everything I have learned so far in my life. I've learned time, history, division and subtraction, sentences and documents that were lies. That I have learned the wrong things settles down beside me and I want to weep. I think of the direction of the past. The records and histories that dwell in roads made of fossils. The past is distinct here. It has left traces everywhere. It's beneath us, a shadow, and its direction leads down, beneath the marble stairs, down under the floor, not down with the bones of the dead but with the unwatched beginnings of life. Sitting here, I don't dare look down as if I'll see something of that past. Instead, I look at the jury and I wonder, who is this jury? Who are they that will be her judges? I study the face of the man on the right. His is a broken, weak face as if he has given up on life. He is going to be her judge, I think. And the white woman with a creased forehead, thinking perhaps of her child or her job which I can tell is poor-paying. Maybe she thinks of how she does not get paid enough while she sits here losing time. She, too, will be the judge of Ama. A lean-faced black man with darting eyes. What do these people call life and what can I tell them that they will hear, that we traveled through the storm, through downed trees, covered in mud, that in the swamps that surround them, their houses, their children, an older world exists, a hungry panther, a woman who doesn't think like them? We are all around them.

"Were you on Indian land?" I am asked this again.

"Yes, I believe so."

"How far did you walk?"

"It was maybe eight miles. Maybe twelve. But not more."

"How did you know it was Indian land?"

Again. "Because I recognized it."

"But you said you don't know exactly where it was killed."

"Yes, but we didn't pass back over the highway and we went by Willard's place only once on the way out and once on the way back."

But the truth is, I am no longer certain of anything.

And at the end of the day when we return to the car, there's a ticket for parking improperly.

"Just look at you," my mother says. "You're a sight."

The first thing the next day, the unexpected happens. The tribal chairman, a man who brought us cigarettes and Bingo, has written a letter, and now he comes in to speak in defense of Ama. I know him and I think this is good of him. He comes into the courtroom, his hair brushed back in what Donna jokingly calls the tribal chairman's cut—we have decided all of them look the same. He comes in to talk in Ama's behalf; he says that she was compelled to do what she did, compelled by her beliefs, her history, and he hopes the court will consider this. And I see that they do, that they look at her, at us, and see that we are different kinds of people, that we are not like them, and I think for the first time that this is true. "This is a treaty right," he says, and he cites that the law is on Ama's side, our side, as if there are sides, never kept.

He says it is her right, by treaty, all our rights. He is speaking for himself, on principle, out of what will happen if she is found guilty, what will be broken. So he has a stake in this, and this, too, is wrong even while it's right and just, according to written law.

"Do you think. No, let me reword this," says the attorney. "Do you believe, do Taiga people believe, that if you—they— eat the meat of a panther it gives you power?" I see his face. There's not really much of a question in it.

The chairman sits straight. "No," he says. "I don't believe this."

"Do others believe it?"

"Well, anyone can believe anything," he says in a charming, relaxed manner. He doesn't say that the claws were once used for scratching the bodies of people in ceremonies.

But by the question, I see what they think. That she wanted something for herself, that this was all done for herself, which angers me. I sit and listen, and the truth is, I do not know what she did with the meat and bones and the gun. I look at her face. She looks small in the room. Again, I doubt her and I begin to wonder if she did eat the cat.

But it occurs to me that they have scant evidence. There's blood to be tested, only that. The gunnysack. No gun because the one they have found was registered to the father of one of the boys, who said it was stolen from his car and tests showed it hadn't been fired that recently. There's no cat. So maybe they think she stole the gun, but I know they will ask her, and they do, how she got this rifle and she will tell them, like I did, that she took it from the boys to keep them from killing the treed panther. She was its protector.

Soon they question her. "What is your occupation?" Ama is asked by a man whose role I don't understand. His jacket is nice. It has a shine to it.

Ama, still small, wearing her hair neat, tells them she has no work. Already she tells a lie. She doesn't tell that sometimes she fishes, that she trades a day's work anywhere for flour or meat or "what-have-you," as she puts it, that she is occupied from morning to night. That she occupies. House. Woods. Water. Land. And does it in a beautiful manner. Still, nothing is in it that they would recognize as work.

The room is stagnant, airless. Ama sits, quiet, her small hands in her lap, more still than I've ever seen, useless-looking here in this room. She's never bothered much about her looks and now it makes her seem hopelessly out of place. "Yes, I know how I look to you," she seems to say with every part of herself and I think a bit of lipstick might have made all the difference in the world.

"You mean you don't do anything?" he asks her again, to discredit her as a person.

"Sometimes I fish."

From tracks she can tell anything. She can read the tracks of all the animals. She has a different intelligence than the rest of us. But it seems like everything she says makes the room, the air itself, grow more tense and I feel the place closing in. A small closet.

"Are you on public assistance then?"

"No sir." I can almost hear her naked breathing as she looks away from the man questioning her and looks instead at the wall and she seems caged, but so does everyone in here.

In court she doesn't rub the top of her thighs the way she does at home when she is enthusiastic. She doesn't purse her lips when thinking or touch her chin. It's as if she's not really in this room. Only her body.

The lawyer, the prosecutor, asks her, "Do you, do Taiga people, believe you are related to the panthers?"

"Yes. We are." She looks at him, steady and intelligent, to let him know it's not just a matter of belief, but one of truth.

"Would you kill your own kinfolk?"

"No sir."

"Well what would ever possess you to kill that panther, if it was your relative? Would you kill your aunt or cousin?"

"No."

"But you shot the cat you believe was like your aunt or cousin?" He tries to prove she doesn't hold to this belief, not deep down.

"Yes." She looks off, away from him.

"Would you say you hold to traditional ways?"

For one second, she looks to the back of the room where the old people sit, listening. It's a brief glance. Maybe no one else sees it.

Then she says, "Yes."

"Even though you had a Dutch grandpa?"

"Yes sir."

"Even though you don't live with the traditional people?"

"Yes."

But she lives close enough to go there now and then and no one knows what that means anymore, tradition. Some people think it means old-fashioned or superstitious.

They, the people, are watching Ama, studying her. She's a curiosity. She is a human being of a different kind. She makes them doubt, I see that. She is not deranged as they want to think. She is not wholly wrong, not right. It's what you make of it, my mother would say. The word I think of is "pure." It was pure, her killing, her reason. A pure, clear motive. I look at them, everyone in the room, at the wooden table. They are making her wrong and terrible, and so have my own words. Without trying to, I have condemned her as much as they have.

"I killed it," she says, as if to cut things short. "I slayed it."

All those sheets of paper and she's saying it straight out and I can see they are convinced she is not sane. Or that she lies, that maybe she is covering for me or someone else, so they don't end the day here, don't listen deep enough.

Then the lawyer representing Ama Eaton asks her if it wasn't a deer she saw and followed in the dark. He wants her to say it was an accident. I can tell by his look when he asks her if it could have been the deer, if she mistook it. If she didn't think it was a deer. Maybe they had agreed on how the story would be told. But surely he knew she wouldn't go along with a lie. Now he wants her to be silent, but she won't. He looks distressed when she says, "No, deer are different in the dark. The color of their eyes. I knew what it was and I killed it," she says. That honest. Then she doesn't say anything else in the court. She doesn't want to be defended.

He looks at her in a way that says she is ruining her chances. And she looks at him as if to say, "I know it."

The lawyer—her lawyer—says it's because she believes in balance in the universe. Those are his very words. She never told him that herself. He found this out on his own, by talking to the anthropologist who studies us. I know this. He was seen going there. He is right, though, in a way. Because in the old story a woman went into the cypress to kill the cat so that the world might return to balance. But spoken in court, it sounds stupid and childlike, not at all what it really is. Inside marble halls there's another kind of truth and it lies down over everything, I see this.

I turn my head and look at the elders, and then at Ama.

I recall that one day Ama said to me, "See this earth here, this ground here? See those flat yellow rocks? Those are teeth of a larger thing. We live in the mouth of something," she said. "I don't know what it is. All I know is we're small as weevils."

And I believe she was right only she didn't know that part of what covers us is law.

I don't like the way the lawyer says "Their world"—as he calls it—is different than "ours," meaning the one he and others like him have been shaped by, have inhabited. He tries to make us different and not ever to be understood. In this way, for this reason, they might not find her guilty. She will be crazy instead. It makes her want to be guilty, I see this on her face. She resists his words, and he is the one speaking for her, but in every cell of herself she resists being what he tries to make her out to be. He stands in his suit, white shirt, and gray tie and talks about us. And the audience, as I call it by now, I can see that if they convict her now they would feel the weight of their own sins through history, of their own prejudice, that they are racist toward someone who is nothing like them.

And the judge—I think she must be his secret self. His eyes reflect contempt, more than they should, not in keeping with the crime. Still, he himself said, and it was in the papers, the environmentalists protesting, protesting him, too, because he said, "What's the big deal about a cat? Why's this cat such a big thing?" On his face, I see it's not the crime he hates, but her. And the jurors study her, a woman so unlike them as to exist in another world, another time. She is their animal.

There's a cold power in this room and it feels like a chill breeze but it is really made up of those who believe in secrets and twists of truth, but call for honesty. They believe in silences and omissions but want us to speak of things they don't believe in, to tell them stories they can't understand. They believe what we say will give them something, a glimpse into another world, not of their concern, a world that is a crack in the container of their history. And it was in this very building of power that our land and lives were signed away not that long ago.

In this room I feel like I am sinking. There is brown water, hip deep, and Ama and I are sinking into it in this very room. I see her through their eyes and she is homely. She wasn't always this shaggy thing they see before them now. She wasn't always lost in a world not her own, or as they think, lost in a world of her own making. I remember her laughing. Smiling at me. A day we went to the water. She seemed young then, almost my age it seemed, with radiant eyes and sunburned skin. I see her tall and strong and capable, not as she is now, her hands lifeless in her lap. I see her in the black woods with the clouds above us torn to pieces, the road muddy. It presses in on me, this vision. I see the way she looked then, when I followed her as she tracked, how graceful she was in woods, while behind her I stumbled and fell. She wasn't always this thing they see before them, her face dry and lean. She is changed, as I have changed. This morning I looked at myself in the mirror and I saw that, like my mother, I was older around the eyes, the mouth. Before all this I was like the wind, I was a slip of a girl, sixteen years old, intent on being a good student, a good daughter. Maybe the change is in the eyes, from what I've seen, because eyes go straight into the nerves and the brain and the body and they change it all cell by cell with their seeing. In one night of hunting we were changed, bone and marrow. As if such a task held a powerful sway over us. And I look at Ama and I see what has happened and what is going to happen. It looks to me like ruin was falling down around her, that it was there right from the start of wind and toppling trees and flying deer, in a world where fireflies were once so thick you could hear them moving in the air and in the brush.

Friday outside the courthouse I hear one of the lawyers say he couldn't sleep. There is sweat at his hairline and he looks pale. It is a rainy day and I pass between the protesters. I turn sideways to get through. My mother has made herself invisible as glass or air or water. Even I have lost sight of her. The protesters on the left of us are those who have returned to a reverence for animals and they are Americans who want her to go to jail and I would like to say to them that they are right, that it is wrong to kill land, animals, that it was wrong to destroy any of it, even us, but they are the children of those who were alive from the deaths of others and so I do not look at them even though they are right; they are taking up our beliefs and judging us, and to them I am a monster because for them everything has been so easy, but they do not see themselves or know their own history.

And on the other side, as if divided by choice, are the native protesters who have come to speak for Ama, and I would like to say to them, too, that it wasn't her right to kill the cat; it's no one's right to take one of those god-damned poor animals, and who in this place will speak out for the panther. But they are my people, too, and the point they want to make is an argument for our rights. According to American law, that is. But the truth is, the cat never lived by that law and never kept to the boundary lines of mapmakers. Again, both sides are wrong, but both sides, also, are right.

Then I see my mother and I reach out and take her arm and we go into the courthouse.

And it is on this day that two old women, two of the old traditional people from Kili Swamp are called in to speak. I see them come into the room. A translator, a young man with black hair, comes in with them. The first elder called to the stand is the woman called Annie Hide. I know her from when my mother used to visit the old people and take me with her, from before my mother's belief in the Rapture and the coming of the Lord. And I remember that she used to come to our house on Saturdays for fried chicken and gravy.

Annie Hide is a member of the Panther Clan. She walks to

the chair straight and tall and looks at Ama and there is something between them. Their eyes speak and I can't enter the current of their gaze. It's an exchange the color of rich, muddy water. I know a world grows there, in that water, the river flowing between them. Maybe it is a river of life or the deep water of our tribe and in it are our riches.

She is asked, "You are a Taiga?"

The translator speaks to her, listens to her reply, and then tells the court, "Yes, she is of the Panther Clan." And Annie, who speaks English, sits tall, her neck straight and long.

Annie Hide is the one who, at my mother's table, told us how the Seminole Osceola's head was placed on the bedpost of white children by their father, the physician who was with him when he died, to make them behave. She cried when she said this. For a time after the wars with the army, the people in our tribe gave in, not to the government but to the birth throes of a hatred and destruction we had never known before. Yet, always, we the survivors still had the sweet perfumed air, the winds from the gulf, the leaping of fish when they were fish. There was still a world of cats with eyes of light, deer with lovely antlers, bears that sounded like storms, wading birds with their twins on the skin of water. We saw the stars with their faces of brilliant fire. We knew the round, high world of eagles and all of it the food of creation before God and guns, orderliness and clocks.

Annie Hide is the one that told me and my mother that we who are Taiga, this small band of people, once nearly invisible, once nearly gone, that our ancestors knew to move along the water silently because we learned this from the panther and this is how, in dark nights and foggy days, we survived the invaders.

They ask her many questions, including whether it is improper to kill a panther and if it were done, what would be the right way to kill the cat in the Taiga way.

She looks at Ama with love. She is a doctor in a way. At least I guess you could call her that because she used to doctor people, and Mama said there have been more going to her of late than before. The people are more sick than in the past and the other doctors can't help them. Mostly it is the chemicals, Ama says, the same ones that have poisoned all the fish.

Once Annie Hide helped me, my mother said, though I don't remember. I was just a girl and I had a bad sore throat and fever. My mother took me to her and she boiled herbs and gave them to me and she said she was surprised at how quickly it worked, but some of those plants aren't there anymore. They are extinct.

Annie Hide remembers the old dances where we were scratched by the claws of the panther, the way the panther claw would heal a sick person. In those dances they used a claw that was held by Annie Hide's grandmothers since 1851. It was what healed the older woman when she was struck down by the fever in the epidemic that killed the others. She is certain of that, the way she was scratched on legs and arms, the sharp wounds of survival.

J a n i e S o t o is also called to talk. She limps on her wooden leg and is old and lovely to look at. Janie Soto, the woman who always wears red beads. Today her neck is empty. My gaze rests on her. She wears a dress the color of leaves, her skin the color of bark as if, on that right leg that once grew leaves, she is a tree that came to tell a story of the forest.

There is a story about how she lost her leg. I heard it from Ama, who was to be the person who followed Janie Soto. When Soto was a young woman she saw one of the ancient sea turtles. As it laid its eggs on the sand, it wept tears from its century-old eyes. Near it, a number of men waited for the turtle to return to sea so they could take the eggs. It broke Janie Soto's heart to see this breach of life, this ripped and gaping hole between turtle and young, to see the turtle that had no choice but to offer its eggs, and afterwards, that vision still in her eyes, she ran crying away from the edge of that water, and as she ran toward home, she stopped and submerged herself in one of the earliest man-made canals. She was crying there in water, trying to wash the vision from her eyes when a stone from the bank fell down on her leg and the stone wouldn't move. Try as hard as she might, she couldn't shift it, and quickly, so quickly, she had no choice but to cut off her own leg with her sharp-bladed knife or drown altogether there inside the water. Holding her breath that had carried her from the beginning of life, she tied her shirt tight around her thigh and severed her own leg. The hardest thing about it, she told Ama, was cutting through bone although it was already broken, and that eased her job. She saw around her the water turn red and knew she would drown if she fainted or cried out with pain, so as she cut, she thought with her mind and heart, "I offer this leg for the lives of animals."

Her leg is still down there, beneath a rock, a bone now, nothing more, and sometimes, like the animals she hears inside herself, it seems to call to her from its prison of water and stone.

When it's time for her to talk, he asks her, "You are a Taiga?"

The translator says, "She is an elder. She's the head of the Panther Clan."

Our clan. She is some kind of relation to me. But she doesn't look at me at all and my heart skips beats while I wonder if I have said the wrong things.

Unless they are silent, the old people have to say what they do even though it is a white court of law and they don't trust in it or even believe in it. And Janie Soto does, she says, "If she had killed it in our way the others would have been there."

"What others?"

She mumbles something to the interpreter and I am sorry I can't understand.

"What others?" he repeats.

She doesn't speak English. The translator says for her, "Us. The old people. The panther people."

"And what would she do with it? What would Ama Eaton do with the panther?"

Janie Soto looks away. Away from even the interpreter. "She would give it to us."

"The hide, you mean?" he says. "That's what she would do with the hide?"

"Yes. She would give it to one of us." Then her eyes lower. She doesn't look at the other people in the room. She keeps her eyes down except to look at Ama, for a moment, a moment of broken time. There's love and I feel it more than see it, her love and disappointment in Ama. She's watched Ama all her life. And I think she is angry that Ama didn't call for her, or take the panther to her the way it should have been done.

Ama looks back at Soto in that moment and I see how she loves and fears her, but Ama takes directions not from people, but from earth itself. She believes in earth.

I think back to the day of the hunt and how I dreamed or thought I saw Janie Soto and for a moment I entertain the thought that she followed us. Like the cat. Without us knowing or seeing.

"When was the last time anyone killed a panther?" he asks her.

The last panther killed, she says, was back in the forties.

She is the one Ama lived with at Kili. She lives for our future. Her father was the most well-known medicine man. He was taken prisoner by the U.S. Janie Soto is history itself. A quiet anger possesses her but it is one I understand. For what she's come to, for what we are now.

I look over to where Annie Hide sits, listening. I know her

better than Janie Soto because she is a cousin of my mother. And because she is softer.

Together, the two old women don't say enough to condemn Ama, not enough to free her either. But even so, the crack in that container, that jar of history, opens and it breaks. It widens between two halves of a single world. And now I feel that the breaking is all that's left. I can't put it out of my mind, any of this, and I too am broken and divided.

Ama, exhausted by now, looks nothing like herself. Her eyes look dark, tired, her skin ordinary. Her torn heart does not show. She insists on her own guilt so strongly that the judge doubts her. I can see that he believes she is crazy, a poor, ugly woman who lives alone.

But finally it is over. All they can think is there's not enough evidence beyond a doubt, except the cut collar and my witness, my only one, and I could be lying; Ama could be covering for me, in fact. Willard couldn't tell what it was we placed over his horse exactly. And the place, the reserve, is not their jurisdiction. Too, the biologist, when questioned, said it might have been a hybrid cat, in which case it would not have been endangered. They didn't have all the evidence in hand, not the gun, not the hide or flesh. It is a mistrial with a judge who is not in favor of the panther, a jury who doesn't think there's enough evidence to convict. And some of the people are angry that she is getting off, even though this woman, everyone thinks, should go, at least, to the hospital.

But the truth is, no one wants to enter this place between laws. And Ama wanted to be convicted, which is why they do not convict her.

She was wrong, I believe. Why she did it, whatever the reason, it was wrong. But she too is creature, animal. She is connected that close. It showed itself to her. It seemed we went against our wills, and who am I to judge, me being such a part of this other world, both these other worlds.

143

And it's over. It's over the way a person can just walk out of a storm, the way wind whips up the world, then disappears. That's how it is, as simple as that.

I sit awhile before I get up. I look out at the two old women, but I can't tell what they think. They pull themselves up and, with the young man, they walk outside the door and I do not see them again.

I look at Ama. She is not triumphant. I get up and go over to her. Court is over and I put my hand on her hand. Only for a moment. No words. I just lay my hand on her arm.

She looks at me. "It's not over yet," she says.

And then, as people leave the court, she says, "Look at them."

I do. Some of them are disappointed that she is not guilty. They look back at her with hatred. She is everything they despise. And in their eyes I know I have been a part of the final killing of the dying world and they hate me for it and I feel their hate, and I want to cry out. It's so easy, what they see, so clear-cut and easy.

"They are all waiting for Jesus to come and save them."

Outside the courthouse, they are all so well dressed. I look at them. My mother, smelling freshly of cologne, bright lipstick, puts her arm around me. I look at her and I see her. And not far away behind her are the elders. In court Mama didn't talk to the old people. Now she doesn't even look at them. Maybe she feels guilty that she does not go to see them. They look at her only briefly because it's Ama they are caring about now, but they look at Mama with love. She is the lost. Not Ama, but my mother who has made her choices and they did not include the tribe, not even me. I know full well she'd take a man over anything. It's her weakness, not loving, not seeing what I see, where we stand in history, what we stand to lose, and yet she is jealous of Ama. For a moment I am ashamed of her. But my shame, too, has no loyalty for I am as suddenly ashamed of Ama and of myself.

As we walk to the car, I see that buses are leaving town. There are the windows of stores with dresses on display.

And I could never have told any of them about that day the dead horse was sitting in the yard, peaceful as if it slept, not yet dull with death even though it was covered with water and mud and torn dark leaves.

In the car, my mother says, "I don't believe any of that stuff, you know." And then she tells me I look tired and ought to sleep. I close my eyes and pretend to drop into the green world of sleep as into an underworld that matches the one above it, but I only pretend. I am remembering, thinking of Ama saying to me that once, "What do you know and what do you just believe?" I cannot sleep for thinking of what I don't know.

At home, at night, in bed, the windows are dark. Even though it is raining again, the heat is heavy. I feel weighed down by it. Lightning reaches down like a thought, branching out somewhere, trying to go further than it can, and then it is followed by a great swell of darkness that comes in around the window shades and touches the walls. In the next room my mother sleeps beside her husband.

When rain lets up, toward morning, I think there's a faint wind but when I look up not a leaf is stirring. The wetness holds everything still, but I am awake.

By Saturday morning, it is sunny outside. My mother does not allow the sun inside the windows. It's her enemy. It fades the furniture and the rust-colored carpet Herm has bought her. Worse, it shows her wrinkled, tired eyes. So all the curtains are closed. There is a knock at the door. My mother is laughing and gay when she comes inside, a young white man at her side.

"Honey, this is a reporter from the news. He wants to talk to you."

I look at her. Then I take him in. He's young, dressed in a light blue jacket, a slight young man with eyes blue as his coat. I look him in the eyes and I tell him, "I don't have anything to say to you."

But Mama interrupts. She asks him, "Don't you want some lemonade?"

My mother is wearing a shiny blue blouse. She's made up like she does for company, like she knew he was coming. "Don't you?" she asks again.

He ignores her. He looks soft and his voice is young, boyish. "This was an important case," he tells me, trying to convince me, coming over to offer me his narrow, cold hand. "And people want to know what really happened. You're the only one that can tell us that."

"No," I say. I don't move. I look at him, then my mother returns with a glass of lemonade and ice. I turn to her. "What in the world are you thinking of? Letting him in here," I say to her, and I stand here, shaking so that I don't even know if I can walk away from the two of them.

"Well, Sis, you ought to talk to him. There might be something in it for you."

"What? Money?" I am cruel. "You'd sell my body if there's a profit in it." But I know she didn't mean money. She meant clearing my muddied name, polishing my tarnished reputation.

She looks like I hit her, but she turns to him. "This whole thing has been a strain for us."

"For me, Mama. Not for you. For me." And I walk out the door, out of the house, past the barbecue Mama's already fired up for dinner.

Outside, the grasses are already drying out in the overhanging heat of sun and low, hot winds. It means the roots of the grasses will shrink in the too-warm receding lake and creatures will walk away from life into their simple, invisible deaths.

At Ama's I sit on the steps. Night is falling. The stars will soon appear.

Story, I think. It's all any of them want, the court, my friends, as if there's a part in it they need or have to have. Even Mama wants the story.

6
THE PLACE OF OLD LAW

I am waiting under the tree, standing at the side of the road by the mailbox, and I hear the car coming. A rabbit races across the road and disappears into the green brush at the other side. The two men in the light blue car are coming for me, to take me to the elders to tell about Ama and the cat. The two young men are right on time. I am ready, nervous, with cold hands, though it is a humid, clammy day. I stand on the ground and move aside slightly as if to let the car pull over closer. My mother watches from the top of her steps. When one man gets out of the car to greet my mother, she's nervous. She touches her hair. She looks everywhere but at him or at the driver still inside the car, yet it is for them, this young man and the one barely seen through the fogged window, it's for them that she smiles, because surely she is not happy today of all days, when they are taking me away to talk to the old people, as if I am the one now being put on trial. My mother comes down the steps, wiping her hands on her skirt, and stands beside me. The man stands at the bottom of the porch steps with his hands in his pockets. He is tall with a rounded back and the bent shoulders of some thin, too-tall men.

"I'd like to come along," she tells the young man, even though she has not readied herself.

He is polite, but he looks away for a moment, at the car. "They want to talk to her alone," he says, looking now at me.

She knew this already. She doesn't argue. She nods at him and moves away as he opens the door for me to get into the backseat of the car. Then the car door slams and she watches us drive away. As the car begins to rattle along the road, Mama waves a little halfhearted wave. She turns for a moment as if to see whether the clothes on the line are dry, as if she could measure wetness with a look of the eye. She is afraid for me, but even at my age, I see how it is; the old people want me there alone. They need the truth. They, too, want the story. They know my mother, though. They know her better than I do. They've known her ever since she was a delicate, awkward child who cried day and night out of some heartbreak no one, not even me, ever knew. She once told me that one of the women came to her and told her to stop crying or she'd cry herself to death. Other children had done it before. Loni Merton had a child who lost her soul by too much crying and now they say the land over at the Mertons' place still cries with that child's voice; a person can hear it and it isn't the wind; it's the weeping of the land.

I look back at the woman whose body I come from, whose body I left. She is both sad and smiling. Then I lift my hand and wave at her. Even afraid of what I face, I try to smile. She thinks that I am leaving her. She thinks I am leaving home. This morning she said she had a feeling I would not come back. I couldn't say for sure if she was wrong or not, because I'd leave if I could, but I said nothing to reassure her, because if I spoke she'd hear it if I was lying. She'd know it before I would because she's heard my voice before I had one. But now my mother tries to smile with something like hope and goodwill.

In a way she is right; sometimes a person leaves something and can never return. That's how I feel, too, as I look back at our house. I see the once-white fence, needing paint, the unhinged gate, the weathered ladder with its broken rung leaning up against the house like they need each other just to stand up. And there is nothing at this place that I need. I don't need a house to hold me up. I don't need a ladder because there's no place I want to climb. Near the house is a tree felled by the storm. Its roots are upturned, its branches broken. I take it all in because I do know this—I will not be the same person when I return. A door has closed, a door that will never open again, to a house and a life I will never fully enter or dwell in again. It's more than childhood I am leaving, more than my mother's place. What it is I can't touch with words, so all I can do is try to carry this sad picture in my mind, try to memorize my mother standing by the broken-hinged gate in her flowered dress, my mother who has tried all these years to pass as white. I see her muscular calves and her white socks, but I can barely see the yellow kitchen in my mind's eye. I can hardly picture my own room, even though I walked out of it just moments ago, the room where I've slept for sixteen years of my life in a bed with a blue chenille spread, my head on the same pillow with its clean, white case—my mother believes in fresh linens—and the vase of artificial flowers my mother loves so much she even plants them outdoors, beside the front door.

As we drive, it seems my life becomes a blur, even my mother standing there waving is smaller, then she vanishes altogether behind a place where the road bends. I am at the beginning or the end of a great distance. What the distance is, I can't say. But it is a distance that ends and begins me.

For a moment, across the way as we drive, I think I see, sitting stretched in the dusty air, a panther, and my heart speeds up, my sight sharpens. But it is only a felled tree and a tawny-colored rock.

"I know your cousin, LeeAnn," the tall man says. He looks back at me over his shoulder.

I nod at him. I swallow. We pass trees and the leaves are still in the humid heat of afternoon. I think of LeeAnn and her thick mascara and how she likes to dance.

"I'm sorry about your brother, Jerry," he says.

"Yeah, me too." And then we lapse into a heavy, unbroken silence. It's a heaviness that weighs us down, and as we drive without talking, I look out the window at the trees going past and the mailbox of someone named Harper, its red flag up to signal there's a letter or bill inside. I try not to think of Jerry, who used to walk with me on stilts he'd made for us, and how we'd talk on tin-can telephones attached by a piece of white twine. I try not to see his big lumbering ox of a body, as Donna called it, and I try not to remember or think of the fire, the can of gas with the line of heat going straight at him the way they said it did. Like someone had started it from the road, is how I always see it. Or why. And I've always thought nothing about it added up, even though Mama could only say who were we to question things. I think of him now and the fact that there is a hole in my life where he used to be. And then I start thinking of the cat and how I haven't seen or talked to Ama ever since that day we came back, even though I am on the lookout always. I search the forests for a trace of her. I follow what looks like fire and it is only sun. I follow what looks like smoke and it is only low clouds in the trees. But I want to find her.

Her last words to me since then were, "They are waiting for Jesus." And Ama's a little crazy, but that doesn't take into account everything that happened, I know, because whatever fell over us, I was caught in it, too, and I couldn't have turned back or stopped the thing to save my life, even thinking that we were wrong. And it was only one moment in the course of time that stood between us and the rest of our lives. One moment that changed it all. And a gunshot. Nothing more.

We turn left and at the end of a narrowing road, at a place where it looks like no people have been in a long time, the car comes to a stop and I find I am sweating, stuck to the seat of the car. We get out of the car, close the doors quietly, and walk. The tall man—more of a boy really—lets me walk in front of him over the footpath worn smooth through trees, me carrying my little white purse like it has something in it besides change, a pencil and notebook, a hairbrush, Vaseline, Kleenex. My purse is cheap and I'm smart enough to be aware of it. Inside it is everything I bring with me to the place of old law, coins with the faces of presidents and *In God We Trust*s, a few dollars. These are the little parts of my tired life, pieces of an untoward civilization that is being unraveled all around me by its own half-shaped, barely lived life.

We walk on a trail that's worn-out earth. These young men, they stay to help the old people part of the time. Ama would say they're good boys.

It's dry here in the midst of a land where it seems all the rest of earth is moist and saturated with waters, rainwater, underground water, bog water, and swamp. But this place is arid and strange above Kili Swamp. I look around me. The leaves are gray with dust as if even the air here is dry, and a different wind blows. I look around me and try to locate where we are and know only that we are somewhere up above Kili, but it's a place I didn't know before, this place of old law my Uncle Ray used to tell me about before he was sick and saw people who weren't there. This place that is part of the territory of the panther. The place, he called it, where decisions are made.

We're in a clearing in the trees where the old people live among tradition and memory that is nothing more, as Ama used to say, than the bones of something recalled real and whole. The old people at the place of their law are living still in a kind of paradise even though it is surrounded by devastation. Nearby is a junkyard full of discarded things and the smells of decay and rot. It's a place of the old and thrown-away; even the dogs attest to that. They are bony old dogs digging through it all for some castaway food. But even so, it's like the people have stepped outside an ugly world and now they remain far away from it all, under the pale blue sky called remembering. It's where they hear what the creator tells them to hear and they hear it well because this sky is not full of the sounds of airplanes, this land is not cluttered with the sounds of cars or television. It's the place where they do what the creator tells them to do in spite of the world of old rags and parts of things that have fallen out of the ruined world all around them. And because of this, they still hold themselves in a beautiful manner; that's what we used to call it, "a beautiful manner." It's the way of living that holds tight to memory, creation, and earth. You can see this goodness of life on their peaceful faces, on their skin, even though not far from here are the old, rusted cars.

Seeing this, I feel as if I am home here.

When the young men leave, I realize that without them, I might not know the way back. They leave me standing, blinking in the light. But the sun touches my hair with its heavy hand of heat and I get my bearings. Specks of dust are in the light all around me, in a flooding light where nothing is hidden, where every line on the face of Annie Hide is distinct. And Annie Hide is the one who greets me first. She is a straight-backed woman. She smiles at me, this woman I remember from my childhood. Back then she was a tall and imposing woman. Now her legs are old, but they are still strong. Annie Hide is stately and still gives the impression of being very tall although she is short, smaller than I am.

There's a fire, even on such a hot day, and a thin flag of smoke rises from it. Heat wavers above it like a mirage, like the heat waves on the day I saw the four women walking down the road and for a moment, in my mind's eye, for just a moment, I see them again and I hear them singing, hear their turtle-shell rattles.

And Ama is here, behind the thin smoke of the fire. When I see her, I want to go to her, but I don't, not here, not now. She's happy to see me but only her eyes show it. I can tell she hasn't been staying up here, but I can't say how I know this. The way she sits, not quite at home, no longer familiar with the place. Her brown arms are thin but strong. She is wearing her best clothes and they are too large for her now. Usually her clothes are the color of earth or water or trees, but today they are the color of flowers, white and red, as if she's rejoicing. She seems dry and much older in her red skirt and white blouse, and I think she must have gone home to get them, but she is not at all so strained and colorless as she looked in the courthouse, and I think how much better she looks here, not so out of place or forlorn but something like a flower just before the petals dry and fall. Still, I can't help but think that she is dressed wrong for this solemn occasion, and she looks too unafraid, as clear as one who never sinned or broke any law, or someone fooled by the power of their own convictions. She greets me with only a slight nod.

Annie Hide motions for me to sit on the ground in front of the fire, on a mat that is coming unraveled, and she sits on the earth across from me, the fire between us. She sits on a folded blanket. I sit down, aware of my tennis shoes, self-conscious about them because they are so out of place here even though I know Annie Hide has worn them, too. I've seen her. Today, though, she's barefoot and I see her feet as she sits. The lines of her feet are beautiful and narrow.

I tuck my feet beneath me, keep the white purse at my side as if someone might steal it.

Janie Soto stirs the fire. It snaps. I smell it, woodsmoke and pitch.

At first I don't look at the other people, as if I'm afraid of what they think of me. Instead I look around at the place, the outlying trees with thin trunks, the stones, the swept earth. It seems I've seen it before. Maybe I remember it from when I was a small girl and my mother brought me here. In my discomfort, out in the open, I study it now, and there is no arbor with shading branches, no pan of coffee boiling, just the stark, full light of sun that shows the flawed edges of things. It reveals not just the fraying threads of mats and clothing, the rotting wood on the ground, but the smooth handle of the old broom, its straw worn down flat and close and dirty from sweeping the earth until it is a floor cleaned of pebbles, leaves, and twigs.

Through the ground, through the heavy pull of gravity, I feel the deep underground waters, all of it beneath the hot, bright sun and the fresh odor of this sun-warmed world, and I am sinking.

We sit on the ground swept clean as skin, me on the unraveling mat, Annie Hide on the blanket, and finally I look around at the people, only glancing at first. Farthest away from me is a dark, white-haired woman I have never seen before though there is something familiar about her face. Of course, there is something familiar about all of us, having come from the same world, the same opening in the sky so long ago. And these are people my mother used to visit. Now hardly anyone comes here but I see the resemblances.

Another woman rests on her heels, plump and soft, her dark knees bent. I don't know all these people. From what I hear some live far back in woods or swamps. Others, like Annie Hide and Janie Soto live here at Kili full-time, and this, I suppose, is the meeting place of everyone, something of a courtyard, the old grounds. And I remember something about the plump woman, that she is the daughter of Annie Hide. Mara is her name.

The others are old and dusty and worn to the color of the ground we sit on. Still, the eyes of the old people have light, except for one old man who is thin as a pole. Joseph Post. He is carried into the circle of people who sit around the fire on a canvas stretcher, lying down, his hands together across his skinny chest as if he's practicing for death, his skin so thin it looks like it could disintegrate or tear. He is placed on a blanket on the hard, clean ground. His eyes look cracked and white around the edges as if he's seen too much sun, or other things he should never have looked at. He is one of the two men, I remember hearing, who were said to have created storms. My mother told me about them. The storms obeyed their voices, she said, and I didn't believe her. In the past, they say, Joseph Post was able to sing even as he drew air into his lungs, an inward singing. That singing pulled the world into him, and when he exhaled, he sent the world back out, changed.

He knows songs, Ama told me, that would send animals to their hunters, songs of love and songs that heal diseases which rot and swallow and harden the body, except for the disease of very old age, which does all three things to the body and cannot be so easily unraveled.

There are songs that change weather, cast and take away spells. That this is so, this strength of songs, is known by so many people and tribes the world over that to believe it is not true is to be purely ignorant and lacking in knowledge.

Looking at him now, I wonder if he was the cause of the hurricane.

These are people my mother used to visit before her days in the First Sanctified Church of the Holy Ghost where, in the deep heat of revivals, some of the people handle snakes to prove their faith in God. These old people are from my mother's life before she heard God speaking to her in dreams, before she heard his voice talking to her as if he had all the time in the world for just one woman.

Ama, sitting next to old Janie Soto, looks as if she knows something calm and secret and just. For a minute I think, what right does she have to look that way? But then I remember this is the Ama I have loved like a mother, even if she killed the cat. And me her accomplice, I have seen with a dark eye what I wish I never saw and I'm weary with the vision and so, I believe, are the old people hereabouts. They've seen all of it, the drained swamps, the rushing cars, the near destruction of their world, all of it mixed in right next to the old, dark-leafed world they cling to as if it will save them, and maybe it will. Maybe when it comes right down to it, we're all looking for the same thing and we could call it salvation.

I look at the three other people I do not know, a toothless, sharp-eyed man who sits with one shoulder lower than the other, and two women, one plump and not so old as the others. Janie Soto, head of the Panther Clan, sits with a reddish-gold fur on her knees that I keep trying to recognize because I've seen it before, or something like it, and I think I must remember it from childhood. I also recall, just now, for the first time, that I was once scratched lightly with a claw, not enough to break the skin, but I can feel it still, or did I dream it, that they do this with children born into the Panther Clan, and that it happened here, in this place.

I see how they sit up straight and proud in the midst of this life and suddenly I feel something go out of me and I want something else to enter, but it doesn't; there is only the relentless pain of my open-eyed seeing all of this like they are inhabitants of a world gone by. They want it back like it's a wheel of life that will turn and right itself and I don't know but wonder if it can ever be that way in these times.

Annie Hide, my mother's relative who has come to the house for meals and said nothing while she ate, just watched me until

I was old enough that her gaze made me squirm and grow hot-faced as if I'd done something wrong.

Next to Ama, on her left, is one-legged Janie Soto. She, too, was in the courthouse and I recognize her, but she looks different here as she fans herself with a white swan wing, her dark hair piled on her head in a beautiful way. She is serious and inside the drifting of her own mind. She leans forward and stirs the fire with a stick. Then she arranges her skirt all around her, so like a lady though her skirt is a little dirty, and I see that here she has a beautiful grace that she did not possess in the court-room. She is tall and beautifully dressed except for her one scuffed shoe, but she removes this shoe. She is not wearing her other leg. For a moment I wonder where it is, the wood, the tree, that has become her way of walking. Soto's eyes are not quite brown. They are more like Ama's, the color of dark amber water, and her hands are large and dry but elegant even though I can see that they are, they were always, working hands. I heard once that when she was very young, a teenager, she'd married my grandfather's brother and helped him sell moon-shine in the bayous to the north of here. You couldn't tell it to see her now, her manner so calm and graceful, so clearly the head of the clan.

Far away a dog barks. The place itself seems alive. Here, the land itself seems to have a sound, the soft brush of a breeze. And the sun—if sun could pile up like snow, it would pile against my body, against the trees, the old people.

Annie Hide bends over and places a round stone on the ground, then she lights a cigarette and hands it to the old man who is so thin he looks like a fallen tree lying down on the ground, his face turned up to the sky. He takes the cigarette. They smile at each other though he can barely see. She opens an umbrella and places it in his hand and he holds it over himself, and for now he is the only one shaded and I look at him in the shadow and then I look at Ama, her small hands with all their strength. My heart goes out to her. School kids used to call her Big Ama and laugh at her. She isn't big, though; she has grown spare and in only a short time. She, Ama, is beautiful, too, with her bony face, her sharp and soulful eyes. I used to wish she was my mother. I used to ask her, "Ama, can I live with you?" She'd laugh and say, "I'm your outside mother. The other one is your inside mother."

Ama sits back a little from the others, just a little outside the circle. I try to read her expression, but her gaze says she's made a kind of peace with whatever is coming. She has resigned herself to it. I don't think she cares at all about the outcome of this trial by tribal court, but to look at her you'd think she is sure they will find her innocent. They will hear her out and they will listen to me and then decide her innocence or guilt and what will become of her. Here it doesn't matter what was decided in the marble building in town. It doesn't matter what's written on paper. The old people are the ones who know the laws of this place, this world, laws stronger and older than America.

I will speak in this full light of sun where nothing is hidden and they will listen, sitting still as rocks. My words will be important to them.

It is the story the elders need, even though it seems untellable to me. It's why they have called me here, to tell this thing that can't be told, to send words into a place words have not yet been, a ground not yet broken by them. And then, if the story is right, if the story is deep, if the story offers food, and there is something saving in it, they will take this in, consider it, judge it.

I look at Annie Hide and she smiles at me. I swallow hard, afraid. I look at the fire and see things in it, the faces of snakes and birds, deer with antlers of flame.

Ama tries to tell me something with her eyes. I know she is willing me to tell the truth. I can't think why because it is not only damning, but there is a multitude of things, other truths, behind this truth; history, belief, even the story of the panther who is the true owner of this place. But I will tell the truth, all of it, except the part I promised to leave out, and I hope that it's not the same thing as lying.

I'm thinking of Ama, but the old people are looking at me. They care for me, I know. They consider me, who I am, who I come from. They have always loved my mother.

I am both at home and a foreigner here in their presence. I am at home here in a way I don't feel; I am at home like a little tree with roots connected to these taller, older ones, reaching deep for water and mineral, and these big trees all around me are not the ones that were felled by the storm. In their eyes, I am the future, and I am not strange or savage or beautiful in ways they are not, living in the empty regions of an unloved world. Neither is Ama. I know they'd like to wash civilization off them and wash it all onto her just the same as the lawyers and judge in the courthouse wanted to clean all the wildness off them, onto her.

I know our survival depends on who I am and who I will become. But this is all too large for me. It makes me want to run away and this, perhaps, is the reason my mother tries to pass.

But I am also foreign here because I understand almost nothing that is said in the old Taiga language. I am inept and hardly know our ways. I am awkward and embarrassed about my shoes and white bag and sorry about what I don't know when there are so few of us that no one can even imagine what we will become as a people. This grieves the old people, I know. And now, suddenly, it grieves me and my eyes fill with tears.

Annie Hide notices how misplaced I feel. She leans forward, says something, looks at me and smiles. She looks tender. I don't smile back. I try, but I can't smile. I try to feel what she means, her intentions. She says it again, using my real name. "Omishto, we are just going to listen to your words. Don't be afraid to speak."

The rest of them seem solemn. I try to read their faces. "Read" is the word that comes to my mind as I look from face to face. It's my useless occupation; it's what I do. I read people, schoolbooks, blackboards, whether or not Mama's husband is in a mood. With Ama I have learned to read sky and water, land. Now it all seems meaningless and useless, this work of mine, this reading, but I do it, as if to find something true that lies beneath all the rest, the way I have tried so often to read Ama, even now as she sits quiet and unafraid, so clear, as if she never broke the shape of things. Now she looks calm and secret as if she knows something more than all the rest of us could know, something that could lift her up right off the ground, right up from before the fire and into the wavering air above it sure as the four women I saw that day before the storm, the women who seemed to walk without their feet on any solid earth.

And so, again, I tell the story. Each time I tell it, I want to cry for her and for me, for the panther people, for the future and the past. I feel like I have fallen from the sky and landed at the feet of that storm, suspended and dying on muddy ground.

I tell the story in a different way than I did in the court-house. It's the same story, but I tell it more true. I tell how I felt something in the trees that morning. I add how Ama knew when I was coming even though she didn't hear me, that she told me she had dreamed of the cat the day before. I tell them that she knew the cat, and how she saved it from the boys. I tell how we saw the four women. I saw them myself. "They were walking toward us and they were singing. I heard them shaking their turtle-shell rattles."

I tell of the storm arriving, and then, "The deer were flying in the sky." I tell the old people this, and I see that this is not simple, how the world turned over that day when I looked up through a hole in the storm and saw the night sky, clear, black, and star-filled. I tell them how the wind was so strong it blew my clothes off me and my dress was in a tree and I was naked, another thing I did not tell in court. And I tell how my body felt so heavy and tired after I ran to pull the algae-green boat up to land that I was sure I couldn't walk, but I could, I did, and I followed Ama after the broken-legged deer when I didn't know that who we really hunted was the cat.

"The old tree, Methuselah, fell."

They consider this deeply, the oldest tree and how it fell as all the centuries have fallen before us like it was the end of all that time. This is important to them. I don't want to tell how I looked back at the house between the gusts and gales and saw that Ama had been blown against the wall, but I do tell this, that I saw her still holding the hammer she'd been using to cover windows when time ran out. I tell that the snakes, so determined to survive, climbed the trees and the steps, and some were close to her as she stood there. And this is a sign, I can tell, in Ama's favor.

They nod and listen. The old man who lies on the ground seems asleep but I can feel his listening. When I talk, it seems that even the trees listen. I can hardly bear to say it, to tell the story over again about the strong wind that threw me to the ground with its body so solid, so strong, the breaking trees, how one of the Spanish horses, from the Sanchez place, died in front of Ama's once-blue house and how I wanted so much to bury it and I fell into the hole with it, but finally I succeeded in covering it only to find its grave partly open and the body of the horse gone the next day.

"And then even while I was looking, the deer dropped out of the sky," I tell the old people. "And one of them had a broken leg." At this I stop.

"Go on," says Annie Hide, not moving, not even to nod at me. "Just tell what you saw."

"It was cold after the storm. Ama wrapped me in a blanket." So kind, so caretaking.

And then I tell of our tracking, that I wondered or believed it all must have started there in her feet, when I saw her place her foot over the track of the cat, and that in the ground where birds had walked were stars, and the fallen trees made it impossible to know where we were and even who we were. And the place was changed in the same way time was changed. Nothing, not even outselves, was familiar.

Annie Hide and Janie Soto exchange glances. In their eyes they say something. I hear the silence and it is loud and frightening. "It didn't seem wrong while we were doing it; it seemed like we had no other choice, like it fell into the story of Panther Woman, a spell. She, Ama, called out to the cat all along, 'Grandmother, I am coming.' I half wondered if she wasn't crazy except I was going along with it and I couldn't have turned back from this thing to save my life and I don't believe that she could either, not to save our lives. And it seemed that this had happened once before. There was a familiarity to it. And when she killed it, I told her, 'Ama, you have killed yourself.' And Mama said that, too, later. She said, 'Ama Eaton has burned her own house.' "

Then I tell about how the sheriff and wildlife manager came. I heard their cars before I saw them in what I took to be evening although now I realize it could have been morning or even noon. And I watched them take her away.

As I speak, I see her again, sitting there in the car, straight and tall. I see the frogs in the headlights. And I tell them the police wanted the hide but couldn't find it, the gun either. I slept and I didn't know what took place between the time we came back with the cat and when the police arrived. All I know is they found nothing. They searched high and low and all they found was the boy's gun and the collar.

———

POWER

I can't bear the heat of day. Maybe it's the angle of light, the heat of sun, an odor, but suddenly the flies are bad even though I hadn't noticed them before. There are so many in the air, they pester a yellow dog sitting on its haunches nearby. The dog gets up and moves slowly away to a place that's in the darker, cooler shade. Above us the birds are busy. It's the kind of day a person would call easy, but here in this circle it is hard.

They ask me questions, each one speaking in turn. Janie Soto wants to know how we found the panther.

"She tracked it. Even after the rain. She can track anything, you know. She hears the animals, smells them."

Ama sits still and waits. She has accepted everything I've said, and even now she doesn't want to add or subtract anything from my words, and suddenly I realize that once again Ama will not speak or act in her own defense. She will not take any of their thoughts from them, their judgments either. She will let them come to their own conclusions. This frustrates me; I know she could speak and they would hear. She could make this act understood. It angers me that she cares so little about what will happen to her.

It seems to bother the old man on a stretcher, too. He looks at her and says, "You didn't bring the body of the cat to us." It's an accusation, not a question. But this is what she should have done. Even I know this and I'm still a girl. Because the panther is a sacred animal and they are the old people of the Panther Clan and all business having to do with the animal, even skinning it, must go through their hands, especially those of Janie Soto.

I look at Ama as if she might answer and tell them of her intent. But she says nothing.

Then he asks, "Did you know you were to bring it to us if one was killed?"

"Yes," she says, and it's all she says.

Janie Soto and Annie Hide exchange a glance. The oldest, Janie, shifts her weight. She is the woman who told Ama about the cat, the stories. This is the woman who has watched Ama all her life.

But Ama is strong. She doesn't mind the hands of death or even banishment. I'd like to think she doesn't believe in it the way she doesn't believe in law, but I know otherwise. Ama says nothing else, nor does she lower her eyes, and I see that the old man takes this for defiance and rebellion and it frustrates and angers him even more.

I think I should tell them that the one we followed was sick, its ribs showed, that it was dying. But I promised her I would tell none of this and a promise is a sacred thing. I feel like my dress hanging helpless in the tree, suspended by all the things I cannot tell in this life, and the worst of those things is that I believe I could save Ama and help her if I tell. But suddenly I know why she didn't take them the panther, at least I think I do, and why she made me promise not to tell. I'm sure of it. And I know why it is that I do as she says and leave this out of the story. The panther is this important to the old people. For thousands of years. They are connected to it, intricately, intimately. And I see that she could not have done what was right, could not have taken them the cat, could not have permitted them to see the poor thing. I want to tell them about it, but I can't tell how the cat was hungry even though the deer were dying and slow-moving, that there was something wrong with the cat. I will spare them this. It would cut their world in half. It would break their hearts and lives. It would take away everything that they have left in this world, it was so poor. If she gave it to them it would have been like giving them sickness and death. If they had seen it, it would have broken their poor old hearts that have already seen so much misery. It would have been the wrong side of mercy, that's why she kept quiet about it, I know, because it broke my own heart in two just to see that thing with the ragged, flea-bitten coat and broken teeth. This justifies Ama. And even sick, the cat was still sacred.

It is their belief that has brought them this far in their lives, all the way to old age. If they saw the face of it, that skinny cat dead on the black grasses, they would no longer believe or have hope. They would lie down on the ground and never get up again in this world where the cars pass through on the cut roads and the roar of machines breaks through the swamps among the dying fish. If I told, would the trees here bear fruit? Would the fish return? I think not.

Ama, who knows me, sees that I have just now understood, that a moment ago I wanted to tell, but now I will keep silent. She is relieved. A gentle look touches me through her eyes, a look of solace, of kinship.

I am hoping my face reveals nothing of what I feel and I look at the old women and when the man asks me once again why she didn't bring it to them, I lie and say I do not know why.

"Why did you go with her?"

"I don't know that either. I couldn't help it. It showed itself," I say. "It knew we were there. It knew we were coming." I say that I saw its eyes and they were shining in the dark underbrush before she killed it. Annie Hide, at least, understands what I mean, that I had no choice but to shadow Ama.

"How did she kill it?"

I tell him that she shot it once and that I'm not sure, but I thought at first she strangled the last life out of it, as if to keep the coat intact, but now think its neck looked the way it did because there was a radio collar on it, the collar the biologists had placed about its neck. That is all I tell.

The man doesn't believe my words. He asks again, "You don't know what she did with it?"

I tell the truth, that I saw nothing. "I fell asleep. I was tired. Whatever she did, she must have done while I was asleep."

Perhaps Ama is a scapegoat. That's what she is. Perhaps she will become the reason the fish are not there. She will become the sin and carry it on her back, the whole weight of all that's happened. I look at Ama and she is so peaceful that even though my words could save her from judgment, I don't say them because I see that this is how it's supposed to be. This is a design not of human making, but of something I don't know, no one knows. It came from the invisible.

In the old days Ama would be banished or killed. Like Abraham Swallow, the man who beat his wife, was judged and killed without a weapon of any kind, just with something invisible the old people knew, something that had wings no one could see, a whirlwind they sang into existence. I saw it with my very eyes and even then I tried not to believe in it. It was words and singing and air that killed old man Swallow, and it left no trace of evidence. I remember, though, that after this happened, people were once again afraid of the old law, even the young people who'd given up the old ways as superstitious. They used to laugh about what the old people said. But afterwards, whenever an old person looked them in the eye or walked toward them, they'd look away and be afraid because maybe they still believed it, the old laws, maybe they still had power. And after the death of Abraham, many of the young people returned to living by the old laws. Even the young men in the car. This is why they returned.

It is silent now. No one speaks. And while Abraham died because thoughts and words were powerful things, I think Ama could die through the silences, including my own, and all the silence frightens me.

We drink water from a ladle, pass it around. I take some into my mouth. It is cool and fresh.

Then Annie Hide surprises me. "Omishto," she says, calling me by my name.

I look at her. But something about her looks weak and thin. She says nothing, then looks away. She knows I am holding something back. And I believe she, too, holds something back. There's a decision she doesn't want to make and she thinks I am the key. She is kin to Ama. She is too soft a woman to pass judgment on others. Maybe that's why she's been chosen, because of the bigness of her heart. I look at her but I cannot speak. And she wants me to. She wants to let Ama return, remain a part of us, if she ever was. But I cannot tell the final part, the why of it that I have just now understood.

I feel dizzy, as if nothing is solid. But even in the heat, the air is on my face, and there's a faint breeze of something breathing, something alive that tells me we are in the presence of something large that is all around us.

Ama already knows her judgment, the condemnation that is sure to come, but she still looks the people in the eye, full and unashamed. She is sorry for her act, but she is not ashamed.

They are more serious than ever, sitting beside one another in the heat, speaking to each other in my language, the language I can't understand. My heart wants to break and every so often Annie Hide looks at me and says something—she knows I am holding back—and I am thinking Ama was wrong in what she did even if she doesn't know or believe it. She has committed a terrible act; she has sinned against the earth, the animals who are our allies, the one who was our ancestor. She has broken natural law.

I wonder, inside myself, how I can look at her, how I can still feel the goodness in her, but I can. I can and I do, even if I wish it were not so. I want to see her with a hard eye, to judge her and be done with it. But there's an eye in the heart and I see with the heart's eye and I know that something, even now, is fashioning her life, as it has fashioned mine, and has shaped even the lives of the elders who sit in the circle. She dreamed this and I don't know if a dream is wrong. For a moment, I wonder what if it was true, really true, that we would die, that the world needed this sacrifice to keep turning, and what if she was right? Not one of us would know this now that the world continues in its course, even in its broken way.

And then Janie Soto begins to speak, quietly, with dignity, in words I don't know. How failed I feel that I do not speak Taiga, even though Mama—in one of her better moments—said it was history, not us, that failed, as if history is a person, one that takes hold of us and decides who will survive, who will die, who will be whole and who will not. But in reality I know that history is nothing more than the aftershock of men's fears and rages and the wars those two feelings create. It's a tidal wave that swallows worlds whole and leaves nothing behind.

As Janie Soto speaks, in her speaking it seems that she feels the anger of betrayal and also its pain. She loves and is angered by Ama, the woman who was to be her follower, the woman who left, and when she did, a world cracked open. Maybe Ama is no different from any woman or man in any people's history, I think. She, like others, is capable of acts of beauty and horror and doom. And if she is capable of such things, then I am too, in this lengthening light, the last slivers of day, this passing time where the no-name birds fly over, the birds Ama said are just birds, just themselves, not names, but birds whole and delicate and alive. And maybe, too, Ama is just what she is without a name or judgment or destiny.

Finally, Annie Hide asks me, "Omishto, is there nothing else to tell?"

Without wanting to, I glance at Ama and our eyes hold for only a second or two, though it seems like a long while.

I look at the old woman.

"No," I say to Annie Hide, who has seen this exchange of eyes.

Bending over the fire with a stick, looking into the red-hot coals, Janie Soto is quiet. She no longer looks stern. She doesn't look at Ama. She doesn't look at me. It is the fire she watches, as if it will unfold something. Maybe she searches through the coals and ashes to see what is in the future. Maybe we are like woodsmoke or like water, only a wave along the surface, a tiny movement, a glint of light that is already gone when a person looks for it. Then she looks up at me for a long time. Waiting. I meet her eyes but only for a moment and I feel fear, in my stomach and heart.

And then, in the silence, Annie Hide pulls her sweater about her, as if she's cold in the still-hot sun. She wears no shoes and her feet are so old I've never seen anything like them, the dark skin cracked and lined but lovely, graceful, toenails almost oval and thick.

They don't look at each other now, none of them. Then Annie Hide begins to speak quietly and I want to understand the words.

"Ama," I whisper. "What are they saying?"

Ama silences me. She holds a finger up, to say, Listen.

The old people whisper to each other and I think they are whispers of condemnation, whispers of death, but I can't understand. I am beneath sound, beneath language. The old man seems to sleep but he is listening, I know. He listens so hard the flames from the fire move toward him. I feel suddenly cold. And then he says something. He sounds angry. Ama understands what they are saying, but tells me nothing. It sounds like they argue.

I am shivering. Maybe it's from fear. I look at Ama but her face is without expression. The way wind pressed against me, that's what this chill is like, a living thing. And in the heat of late day I feel it touch me as if it has hands. If it does have hands, they are thin and deadly as the hands of ghosts.

From the sky, the birds watch us, looking down.

The old people are weighing something, I can see this in their faces. What they weigh is hard, cold, and weighted more on one side than the other. They don't like what they have to measure. Ama has tested something. She has been the test.

There is one more statement from Annie Hide, who seems unhappy with what is being said. Then everything is silent, even the birds and the insects.

Ama's face is still so open I can't tell what is happening. I only feel it, dark and shedding. The air suddenly dead and cool like in a well, and I hear that word, "kill," and I think they are going to kill her. I panic a moment, afraid they are going to kill her before I remember that in our language the word for "banish" and the word for "kill" is the same word; it's the same because in the traditional belief, banishment is equal to death. It is death to be split from your own people, your self, to go away from the place you so love. And they say this word.

Then Ama looks at each of them in the circle, each one, and then at me. She is quiet, level of eye, and soft. Only Annie Hide lowers her eyes. Only she is uncertain. She looks terrible and tired, as if she has lost in her fight to keep Ama from being sent away.

As the sun goes down, Ama stands and straightens herself. Slowly she walks away from the circle, then from the swept earth and from the people. She takes a few steps away, but slowly.

I stand up to go after her. "Ama. Wait," I call out.

She turns slightly once, looks back, and then, as if she were going only to a store, to a neighbor's house, she walks away, not hurrying.

I stand to follow, looking back for a moment at Annie Hide.

"Omishto, you must sit down now," says Annie Hide in a voice that makes me do it. I sit down and put my hands over my face so that it's all dark, all still, and I try to erase from my mind the vision of Ama leaving, my own guilt.

I can tell that they are sorry, the old people. It's in the air, thick, like their shadows on the ground as afternoon sun slants in, like grief.

I look back to where Ama stands at the edge of trees. I'm shaken with sobs. I am being cried, as they used to say. It seems the trees speak one tree to another. I remain sitting. As Ama looks back, Annie Hide says something to her which must be "Go." She gestures, a quick movement of hand, as if to send away pain, and then Annie Hide, she's crying too, looks down as if her heart will give out, and says it again, soft enough that Ama cannot hear it.

Annie Hide's eyes fill with water. She doesn't like this decision that has been made. She doesn't like it that theirs, hers, is the power of death or disappearance.

Ama stands, her back to us. She stands still in a moment that stretches itself out and seems like forever. I am afraid to move in this moment that lasts so long as I look from Annie Hide to Ama and am motionless in spite of the feeling in my chest that tells me, also, to go. I sit as if the strength of the old ones is a magnet that holds me here, inside the circle created by generations and living and dying, that has boundary lines too thick to be drawn or made physical in this world, and I am only a speck inside it and all the God-teaching in my mother or in the world can't change this.

I am more, at this moment, than myself. I am them. I am the old. I am the land. I am Ama and the panther. It is all that I am. And I am not afraid anymore of the future or the past. But still I'm torn through. I sit and can't move.

The man who has been lying on the ground points a trembling finger. He lifts himself up, there beneath the umbrella, raises his head and points at Ama.

I look at the people sitting on the swept ground. Then I look at Ama, still standing that final moment in stopped time. Then, in her best clothes, without her knife, with nothing at all in her hands, not even a sweater, she walks into the evening shadows and the trees. She follows no path but goes straight in between trees on old paths no longer visible. There are no cries of birds now. It is silent. I hear my own heart beating again. That is the last I see of her. My heart feels like it's breaking. And when the sun lays itself down on the horizon, it is over.

———

Behind me, evening now, there is talking within the circle. Even though this is the place no words have ever been. And the people are stirring themselves off the ground.

I think they believe she wanted power. I look at them; they have hope, they have belief, they have what it has taken to endure through all this time. In part because Ama has not shattered this world with truth.

Soon, it's dark and the young men have returned and the people who don't live here are packing a kettle into a box, putting things in the young men's blue car. They make coffee. No one really talks. The man on the stretcher, Joseph Post, is taken into one of the little houses.

Now, in the dark, I break away and run toward her, but she's gone. I run into the first stand of trees, looking for a trace of her, for a sign that she has been here, but I see nothing and after a while I go back. I say goodbye to Annie Hide but not the others and even though it's miles from home, I do not want to ride in the car, and no one forces me or tells me what to do. I find the road away from Kili by myself. There are no cries of birds now, only silence. And as soon as I leave their view, even though it's miles from home, I run as fast as I can away, as if I'm escaping, and I keep running until I am winded, then I stop and rest, hiding in bushes until I regain my breath. Then, when it is fully dark, I go home to my mother's house through the straight young trees that survived the storm.

There is heat lightning in the sky.

My mother meets me at the door. "What did they say?" she wants to know.

I don't answer. I am catching my breath.

My mother is insistent. "What happened?" she wants to know. Growing shrill now.

"I don't know."

"What do you mean you don't know?"

"She left. I didn't understand them."

"Where did she go?"

"I don't know. I'm telling you." I am in my bedroom, pulling things out of drawers, putting them in a white pillowcase.

"What do you think you are doing?"

I say nothing.

Desperate for an answer, she hits me. Her fist against my shoulder. She tries to turn me around, toward her.

I put my arm up to protect myself. "I don't know, I don't know," I cry over and over, and then I am running away without my things, my hands over my ears, but still I hear her say, "What happened?" Then I hear her yell, "Where are you going? What do you think you are doing?"

I do not answer. I begin to run.

She screams after me, "You're not my daughter! You hear that? You're no kid of mine."

I run. I run to the bushes and sit, hiding, wondering would she hold me and rock me if I stopped, turned back, went inside the house. But I know she wouldn't. I am lonely and hungry, and I can still hear her calling me. She says, "Sissy. Sissy, come back. I don't mean it. Come home."

I sit, trying to breathe, hidden in the bushes until everything is silent and no more words chase me. Then I run toward Ama's and go down to the boat and take it out into the water. I go into its solitude and safety and take it to the center of the swampy water where no one will see me.

A light wind blows. I am exhausted and I fall asleep in the boat. I wake later, and smell the acid sweetness of a cane fire in the distance. I look at the world for a moment, in which I see that the surface of water is dark satin with a full moon up above it. I doze again and then it is first morning.

I decide to take the boat in to land and go look for Ama. I paddle gently.

Slow at first, I try to sense where she has been. I think there should be tracks and wasn't it Ama who taught me what little I know about reading the ground? But I see nothing and after only a short distance I stand and am still, watching, listening for sounds until it feels my ears are full even with my own heartbeat and the soft sound of my skin being shed, renewed, undone. I feel the silence of the air and I give up.

I turn and go back to the boat and sit in it and then lay down and try to cry and talk to myself out here where no one can hear my senseless words, words that are not really my own tongue, but are the only meaning I have.

And so, in the old boat I drop anchor and stay in the center of the lake and swamp we once lived around.

A bird screams like a larger animal has crept into its nest and grabbed it. The night is full of such things.

"I hate you, God," I say. But I can't look up. "From now on, you're on your own." But I say this last part to myself, only myself, and I think, why am I a human? Why do I have this thumb, these words? Why is it I am not on all fours in the forest or swamp?

I want to go backwards, to forget how to read. I want to know the land, feel it, to enter water. I want nothing more.

There is such a thing as walking death. It's when a person walks and there is no place to go. They walk until they are bare bones then walk some more. No one ever comes back from there. Four years of walking. This is what they have sentenced Ama to, and when I close my eyes, I see the old man point a shaking finger at her.

Something is climbing in the trees. The monkey, perhaps. A dog comes to the edge of the water but doesn't bark. I look at it, and as if stones are in the boat, sinking it, I fall asleep.

7
ONI: WHAT THEY BELIEVE

The wet air curls against me as I sit in the boat without seeing through the fog. I'm without my bearings, lost between the elements of air and water. It happens this way, that sometimes, when a person sits on a boat surrounded by water and fog so thick, so deep, there is a dizziness. It seems the boat has turned over and is rising, moving upward through sky like a vanishing cloud. Or it descends to new depths in the world beneath, as if to fall into underground rivers and be carried away.

Without her bearings this person loses her place in the world. She must sit still, without panic, and wait for a glimpse of something to emerge from the fog. Maybe there will be a clearing through which a tree branch is seen, or a shard of blue sky, a hole in fog that is an open place like in the first time when the panther emerged and came down to enter this world and all the other people followed. Or there will be the sound of frogs from below, or a crow above, or the scent of a flowering tree that smells for all this world like a paradise and draws you toward it from the center of water and fog. Or it might be a wading bird that appears out of the thick whiteness, and since its feet touch bottom, you can tell which way is up, which is down. You can tell where gravity lives. Then, only then, can you believe there is something solid in the world.

And so I sit here in fog and air and wait for something to become visible.

B a c k i n t h e days of the first people, the beginning of wind was the first breathing of one of the turbulent Gods, they say. This God's name was Oni. It is said that this word was the owner of wind, and the panther was the one who first spoke it.

"Oni. This is the word," Ama would say when we sat together in a blowing wind.

Oni, first and foremost, is the word for wind and air. It is a power every bit as strong as gravity, as strong as a sun you can't look at but know is there. It tells a story. Through air, words and voices are carried.

Usually, it is invisible. Only today I can see it. It is moving shadows. Its hands are laid down on every living thing. The plants that create it are held inside it and moved by it. In the presence of air, every living thing is moved.

It is greatness, they say. Like other Gods, it is everywhere at once. It travels by wind down from the sun, moon, and planets to this small place that has been blown into existence by something unknown and mysterious.

It is a breathing, ceaseless God, a power known and watched over by the panther people. It passes through us, breathed and spoken and immortal. It is what brings us to life.

It is the breath of life translated from trees. Because of this, there is no such thing as emptiness in our world, only the fullness of the unseen. It is the sea of creation we live inside. We are tossed about in its currents alongside the panther, the dark sleek otter, and the wild turkey whose tracks I have seen on the ground.

Sometimes Oni has a woman's voice, they say, full of tender

whispers and urgings, and sometimes it is the deep and bellowing rage of a storm.

What is spoken travels by air and the old people say even thoughts travel and are carried with it, and this is why, as I find myself in this boat in fog where any direction could be down, I tell the wind I need help and let my plea go out to the four quarters of the world my ancestors spoke of and I remember it was a cold wind that told our ancestors the Europeans were coming before they emerged from a dense fog in ships and on horseback like four-legged people with beautiful bodies who believed false stories, that the manatee were mermaids, that they would find riches and eternal youth if they searched far enough and long enough.

All the spirits of the world congregate in air, and I feel this is true. They are all here, in this fog and wet air where I sit closed in by them and waiting to see a hint of land. I breathe them and I feel them. In my breath is the singing of ancestors who live at the edges of sky. Like distant waves they reach a shore of the living.

It must have been wind, also, that told us how to glide past the Europeans, invisible and silent through these waters of grasses and the dark pathways and mazes between trees.

At school I learned that Darwin was sailing toward the great turtles while we were being killed on land and in the shoals. If he'd known how to listen to the air that blew him there, if he'd heard our stories and prayers and cries, would he have turned from his science and come to us? Would it have been a different world if someone had believed our lives were as important as theory and gold?

Sometimes air, full of plant and animal breathings, shows itself only in the ripples it sets moving on water or the grasses it bends. But today there is thick, close fog, and the full white sky lays itself down on the world as water rises up to meet it, to be taken in by it.

And so I sit, somewhere in this body of water, moved lightly by Oni, filled by it, closed in by it, and a breeze begins to blow. It doesn't blow the fog away from the world, not yet, and in this white air I am so lost and hidden that not even the mind of the swamp, not even the heart of the glades, the ears of water, the eyes of trees, can discern where I am, can distinguish the shape of me and my moss-covered boat.

I do not know the shape of what's fallen through this wet heavy air that comes in from the edges of land where winds live, terrible and soft and constant. Perhaps, beyond the boundaries of water, there are distant thunderstorms approaching, roofs whirling away from houses in twisting winds. But here it is quiet.

"What do you want?" I ask the wind that closes me in, but I fear that what it wants is more than I have to give. I've fallen into this creature of air. It is stronger than I am and I will do its bidding whether I want to or not because it has created me and my heart and mind; my body is only what the breath lives in, at its mercy like an old dress that can be blown into a tree. It was wind, after all, that set all these things in motion.

Lying here in the boat, the world reeling around me, I look into the thick white fog and think of all the people at the place of old law, and of my mother and sister. I think of words and songs, the power of every breath to keep life, and their thoughts move toward me with the wind, in just the same way older people say spirits are summoned.

I think of the old people who sat in a circle at the ash-colored place, the place that is what remains of a fire, the concealed people in the place where the road thins and vanishes, the people who passed judgment on Ama and maybe on Abraham Swallow. It seems that wind blows their thoughts toward me as I float. As if a small voice is speaking at my ear, one that tells me what it is my people believe:

———

It comes to me that Annie Hide believes she has felt the power of healing. It was a person of light that stepped into her body and wore her skin. Even now it shines out from her eyes with its own life so the light you see when you look at her she doesn't claim as hers. She believes she has been embraced by something akin to love that rose from seawater and from land like a bolt of fire. It has been this way from all the way back to when she was sick with yellow fever, a virus carried by unwilling air, by Oni that gives us life, a disease that killed so many of the Taiga. And she survived, she believes, by hearing the voice of that person of light inside her own body saying, "Be well. Go into the swamps." And what she didn't know—but obeyed— must have saved her as she went away, sick, on the raft, poling herself through the labyrinth of mangroves.

She knows that words are part of this strength of hers. They, too, are a person; they come from the birth throes of dream and thought. When spoken, words stand up straight as a stick before her, standing like thin gods, and if she stays by tradition, as if it, too, is a person, then something newly born and alive will remain in air, in water, in this world. That something will be here in times of need. Its movements will brush against a person as surely as if it had wings and was flying past, or as if something invisible was breathing on human skin. It will walk toward us and put its arm about us in that old embrace of something Annie Hide felt to be, knew to be, love. It is something that will sustain. She holds to the thought that if she lives long enough and can tell what she knows to a younger person, there will always be this shining in the world, an unbroken thread of light from a past where we were beautiful. It will curve around and into the present. And in another embrace, it will encircle the future and bring it all whole and together as one. She knows she must be strong in these troubled times that are every bit as frightening as were the times of our ancestors.

Annie Hide believes most strongly in words. They will get us through, she thinks. Song and prayer and wind are all the same word, Oni. Oni was the word the panther spoke to help the creator breathe us to life back in the oldest time when everything was only air and water. It was the word given to humans by the panther, Sisa, who came to this world first. Panther, here before us, was one of the beings who helped this creation breathe humans to life. As beautiful as she was, our cat older sister took a shine to us in this great circle of air, and set about teaching us this word and all its uses. It is the word the panther still cries out in the terrifying and beautiful dead of night where all the small animals break twigs, scurry, and hide.

"What our people would be now if not for all the things that have happened since that creation," Annie Hide once said to my mother, "I do not know, but I know what we are in spite of it; we are beautiful and strong and we are part of wind, because the word for wind is still the word for life."

Across the green, swampy world lit by fireflies, I hear her whisper, across space, memory, and time. "When one of us is born, Omishto," Annie Hide whispers to me, her voice carried by air, "the wind enters us and breathes us through a lifetime, through our first laughter and words, through our walking and cooking and planting. Then at death it leaves; it returns to being part of the rest of air and wind."

Annie Hide believes Ama is a righteous, innocent woman who lived by the rules of Oni and stayed away from the world that has wounded us with its ways. Whenever she looks at Ama, who is herself like a cat, she has seen something beautiful and strong, a following of heart, a woman able to live by animal rules, to stay inside a circle of being that, if it would remain open, would itself break into night-seeing eyes, paw, fur, antler, claw, sinew, leaf, all of the alive things that grow from living air.

"I will bring you home," I believe I hear Annie Hide say to me across the wind, "if you will let me."

The air begins to rock the boat a little and I still feel I am upended, but from the distance I hear a bird call out. It has a harsh voice and puts me in mind of the voice of one-legged Janie Soto, and this is what the air tells me, that she believes tradition has been broken, that we will be punished because we have violated the world according to ancient traditions, that the soul of the dead animal will curse the people unless it is appeased, that it will speak with the creator and express our crimes, even though in the early days when one was sacrificed, or "sent away," it spoke to the creator, the maker, in our defense. But in this changed world, it will call down ruin and helplessness like a dark rain upon us, and we—all of us—will die if we go against the will of nature, as we have already done even before this crime committed by Ama, a crime created by history, not tradition. Janie Soto, Panther Clan, knows that the laws of nature were in place from the beginning of earth, before the first breathing and stirring of people in the first place of dawn. There were certain powers, customs, and ways that humans were meant to live by. There was an order to things, a mystery of how every single thing worked together with the rest, merged and fitted like it was all one great body.

She knows that cutting the ground for the new highway was part of a terrible breaking that began long ago, the breaking of rules fixed from the start. Rules obeyed even by stars and sun. Janie Soto believes and knows that sometimes what we do goes up into the sky, and that sometimes it seeps down into earth and hides until all things go back to their beginning. She believes that our every act, word, and thought is of great significance in the round shape of this world and there are consequences for each. Because of this, we do not have the right to live in any way we desire; our way was made for us out of clay by the adept fingers of creation, the leafbed of its mud, from air and what lives in it. She believes, too, that the spirit of water is always beside us and so is that of our first ancestor, the cat, baring its teeth. Now that the cat is gone, the space where it lived is here, all around us, and it is crying out with emptiness. She can feel this phantom pain, like she feels the pain of her missing leg, the leg she believes she sacrificed so that the animal world would have continued life.

She believes the whole of creation heard her words of loss, "I offer this leg for the lives of animals," just as she hears the voices of the animals. And it's the whole of creation she has the duty to stand by, to speak for, and to arrange. There is pain in the world to the east and south and west and north, she has said. Where all the lives are missing, and there are no exceptions, can never be exceptions, to the rules that were set out for us at the start of creation.

Janie Soto believes Ama has offended the spirits. She has removed a panther from the world and in the wrong way. Ama has subtracted something from the world, and Janie perhaps had seen this, and she believes it was against Ama that she must speak and she has done so as she brushed the flies away from the tick-bitten dogs at the judgment of Ama. She saw Ama as a hole through which the life of the cat, a beloved creature she heard crying that night after the storm, left this world and became nothing more than a spirit grieving for the flesh it once had been, and for the flesh of its kith and kin. And Ama, too, was the one who was to have been her hope, our hope.

What Joseph Post, Turtle Clan, the old man stiff on the stretcher, his face old as the land, believes is that we have mysterious powers and that's what human beings are. He is the singer of songs, as if sound was always his specialty. He still believes angry spirits spark fires and break cups that hold the precious black liquid some of the old people drink at the old-time ceremonies. He has seen it with the dark squint of his own eyes.

Once Joseph Post could sing himself to the world beneath us or to the one above. He could sing himself into other people and get them to do his bidding. His body, he used to say, was not matter; it was made of nothing but song. He believes it is still possible to sing away evil which is as unbound as smoke in the air. Human will and voice, he believes, can work on the forces of nature as it did the time he and three other old men sang four storms into existence, attempting to keep intruders from cutting down the trees, and for a while they succeeded.

I have heard that Joseph Post's voice is so strong it will make a person tremble or love or fall to the ground. I heard him once and it was a sound so beautiful that the whole earth seemed to stop and listen, and I can still hear it now, traveling toward me through air.

But they say when a person is ill something has harmed the strength of their breath. Now Joseph Post is the one losing his breath, his voice. Now something has worn down those songs and their surging life. It is something from outside the people, their place above Kili, because the power of humans depends on the powers of earth, and all this earth has given way to farms and the death of water. Joseph Post believes it is as if something destructive, a large, clear-winged termite or maybe a gold-winged moth, has laid eggs that kill whatever they grow on, the leaf of this world. But he also believes that the surge of a song could make things happen the way they once did, could make earth change without so much as a hammer, backhoe, or dredge, if only he could return to something he was before the stiffening of his body, before the pain he can no longer sing or talk away. He knows there must be something that could fulfill the desires and needs of the people he is part of, and this something, too, could keep strong the panther, whose ability it is to help us pitiable humans. If only he could sing it, Sisa would not withdraw its help from us, would not be leaving us, leaving us humans alone in the world.

Still, sometimes he doubts all this. Not because he is a doubter or faithless, but because he has been made to feel small and impotent under the weight of history and the way the other men have treated him. But in Ama he believed there was a way, a way to break through all of it, and that there still is. That woman, Ama, who took so heavy a weight on herself and violated tribal law.

But through Ama's sin, if you could call it by that Christian word, he thinks there may be atonement. She is the between thing, like a wall that was built and stands between what is now and what could have been. If he could take down that wall, dismantle it the way he was once strong enough to do, the world would grow together again and become all the things it might have been. Ama, he thinks, is the sacrifice to appease offended spirits. His pointed finger directed something at that woman who is herself something like a storm, not a whirlwind, not something that chases after the heart of a man like Abraham, not the full-forced point of disaster where a house would explode from within itself and splinter in air, but a storm that brings thunder and lightning and rain, renewal. Ama is like that rain, he has no choice but to believe it, like rain that is nourishing but has to fall. And when it does, the world rises up once again and grows.

He thinks of the wind that travels all around in a circle. It's a person, he'd say. Its voice is thunder. It came up from the earth before us and it never wanted to end, so it is like a river traveling, going around, returning.

Lying here in the boat, the world reeling around me, I look into thick white fog and think of all these people. I think of words and songs, the power of breath. All these thoughts seem to move toward me in the wind, the way old people say spirits are summoned. From another direction than Kili Swamp, from town, it feels like the thoughts of my mother also come toward me, and what my mother believes is that salvation comes through giving herself to a distant god. If she believes hard enough and strong enough, she will stand at the front of the church and a sacred tongue will speak through her profane mouth and she will fall on the floor from the power of it and speak the language of God so that at last he will hear. She believes she can touch a poisonous snake, the embodiment of all that's wrong and evil and earthbound in the world, and not be harmed by it. This is salvation in the First Sanctified Church. And in the laying on of hands, she will find ways to heal diabetes, sterility, tuberculosis, even her own swollen fingers, the wedding ring she can't remove because, as she believes, she's filled with the venomous fluid of this world and with all the negative thinking she must rid herself of. She believes in these words: "Our father who art in heaven," and in this way she still believes in the air. She is certain that the old gods could not be real. If they were, they failed us when they let us be killed and sickened. She doesn't love herself, I know this, because she believes like they tell her in church, that it was our fate to be destroyed by those who were stronger and righter. She believes evil and ignorance are the natural state of humans, swamps, and animals, and we must save ourselves from it.

She believes, too, that goodness and mercy will take hold of her life that is worth nothing without Jesus in it, and she will be saved, I will be changed, and something might be as good as it used to be. My mother believes there is an afterlife and when she gets there she will be compensated for her miseries on earth. She has felt the hand of God upon her and she thinks we live in the time of Revelation. She believes God will save her from sudden gusts and whirls of wind, from a man she can't please, from every daybreak, and that if prayer can bring the dead to life, surely it can put her own life back together again if only she is earnest enough, sincere enough. She believes that prayer, that the goodness in the world, will rise up if only she believes hard enough and kneels down on her knees long enough saying words to her friend in the sky, "Our father who art," and I suppose this means, after all of it, that she still believes in the power and owner of breath, Oni, but by another name.

She believes, too, that I love Ama more than her—not differently, but more—and that Ama is the thief of other people's children and animals, a woman who had nothing at all to call her own, but ended up with Willard's horse, with Abraham's goats, and with me.

She fears Ama to the quick, and it's because she thinks Ama shows her what dark-hearted savages we are, like in older times, and Ama without even a decent pair of shoes that might have stepped any Sunday of any month into church and claimed salvation. But as hard as she tries to believe otherwise, my mother, I know, is one of us. And I know this, too, that she loves Ama like a wayward sister, and when she prays, it is Oni that passes through her.

The fog begins to lift. In places now it begins to move; it is moving away, crawling like an animal slipping away from water. I see in the way it moves which way the world sits, and in the eastern sky there is the first warmth of sunlight. It's as if I am dreaming Ama's dreams and seeing out of her eyes, knowing what she knows. And I think of Ama, the amber-eyed woman, and how she believes that she has saved us, that animals are the pathway between humans and gods. They are one step closer to the true than we are. She says skin was never a boundary to be kept or held to; there are no limits between one thing and another, one time and another. The old stories live in the present. She believes in stars and their gifts, that the wind speaks in intelligent trees that look bright as bonfires to eyes that are open. For Ama the other world is visible. It lives beside us in trees and stone. She can see it, like a path of light across water, and hear it in the swamps at night. She has touched it. The strange visitors she sees from out of the past are proof that time is not a straight line, that the course of time is a lie, and earth is still growing as it did a million years ago. And she believes her faintest move or thought is governed not only by spirits but by the desires and dreams of animals who are people like ourselves, in different skins.

This is what Ama sees when she closes her eyes and sings within the silence, that the world is withering up. And she believes that she killed her guardian, the sacred cat that taught us the word for wind, and that has always slept stretched out and long on the earth, that she killed it for our people to go on, traded its life for our lives, and that it will return, new and healthy, and so will the world of our people.

I still hear her calling it her grandmother. "Grandmother, I am coming," she said. I don't know if she meant it was a grandmother in the hidden world or here on earth, but I do know Ama believes she has done what she was here to do; she was summoned for this thing, maybe even born for it, as much as she wished she wasn't. She has fulfilled her destiny. She believes that the cat took notice of her, that it loved her and gave itself to her and through this way the civilized world that has no soul will crumble away from us like mud falling away from a rock in raw sunlight. In that falling our lives will be revealed, and try as we might we cannot hide from the true and evident powers of life and death.

In these times, she knew there had to be some act, however desperate, however illegal, to restore this world to balance, to bring young people home from their empty days in school and their nights before the television, the white wooden beds and lawns that need water. Crude, square lives familiar with all the killing devices ever imagined by men. And even if she and Sisa were the sacrificed, she believes she has brought the humans and gods together once again, joined them fitted together into the same realm, this world and the invisible world all of a piece, and that when we are quiet, when we are still as a tree, we can see it, put it together, hear it like a song from the swamps on lonely, breezy nights, hear even the voices of the tiniest of ants.

In this way, she is the same creed as the cat.

A n d t h e h i s t o r y and world of the panther, too, seems carried toward me by Oni. Panther. From across the surface of water, I remember the eyes of the cat, how they were the color of last light touching grasses, the color of fire and of planets in the black sky of night. Through the eyes of the panther, it has always been a golden world. In soft evenings light clouds drift and the sky turns yellow. Sisa watches this from the still point of her breath. And what the panther believes and remembers is that in the wild air and rank water of its existence, in the once-sweet wind, she, the cat, Sisa, is doomed, that humans have broken their covenant with the animals, their original word, their own sacred law.

I see it from Sisa's eyes.

The panther misses its companions, the blue-green crocodile, the many silver-sided fish, bear, and the delicate wood stork, all nearly gone. It wants to believe they will return. Sisa sees now that in place of the red wolf, the damp fur of the bear, the world has given way to cleared and empty space where the poor awkward cattle have no sheltering shade to lie down in but their own; they are clasped to the ground and along with their human-bred shadows they are eight-legged creatures of doubleness. Sisa knows that to eat them, even when she is hungry, is to be killed, but nevertheless they are food, nothing more.

The world has grown small where Sisa lives. It has lost its power and given way to highways and streets of towns where once there were woods and fens and bodies of water. The world is made less by these losses. Because of this, humans have lost the chance to be whole and joyous, reverent and alive. They live in square lots, apart even from one another. What they've forgotten is large and immense, and what they remember is only a small, narrow hopelessness.

The cat believes God has eyes that shine in the night, God has scales and fur, claws and sharp teeth, a long tail. God's shadow lies down on the ground like dust. The once-sweet smell of air is a gone wind. Sisa knows how tall grasses bow down, that love is a wailing sound in the night, and that life dwells in a lithe body, in silence and in hunting. Sisa thinks that if it, the cat, stays in the shadows of trees it will be as invisible to its enemies as a tiny speck of dust, something small and hidden there in the darkness all around our lit-up lives.

According to Ama and now according to me and what I feel traveling through Oni, the air, I know the panther remembers when humans were so beautiful and whole that her own people envied them and wanted to be like them. They admired the humans and the way the two-legged people stood beneath trees with leaves leaning down over them as they picked ripe fruits, how their eyes were fully open. How straight they walked! How beautiful the beads about their necks, the dresses women made in fabric that was the dark green of trees and the light colors of flowers. How intelligent the little shell and wooden bowls they ate from, how good they were at devising ways to catch fish with simple bone and metal, at making trails through thickets. They stood so gracefully and full of themselves, they sang so beautifully; it remembers all this, how they sang. The whole world rejoiced with their voices. They had breath and voices like the wind. Oni, that's the word Sisa's ancestors taught to these people. Breath. The panther believes that through blood it remembers when its own people surrounded the humans and gave them life and power, medicine to heal, to hunt, even to direct lightning and stormclouds away from their beautiful, dark-eyed children. They were its little brothers and sisters; she never preyed on them, nor does she now. Her work was to help them, to keep her eye on them, to keep them safe. But now they have turned against her. Now that they have no need for her, Sisa and her people, the panther, are leaving. They leave in sadness and grief.

Now so few of the humans have songs or presence, so many have such a heaviness that they can barely walk or move, raise themselves from their beds in the mornings. And Sisa believes, sees, that the world could end with their human misery, that she must somehow endure to the end, that humans are pitiable and small and broken, and along with them, the panther people, too, are hungry and sick.

In her visions and dreams, Sisa has seen the woman with small hands and the girl who went with her to this death. That was the woman who still sang and spoke to her the way humans were meant to do, the woman who remembered that she, Sisa, was the grandmother, the eldest sister of those two and all the rest. They met with one another, there in a world no longer their own, and they were all, all three of them, the sacrifice in this place that has grown small with rusty nails and oil drums in the shadows of buildings. But she, the cat, hopes that the world still has golden evening light, will have it again, and that the Taiga and the panther will recover and breathe again, that we all will sing once more in the swamps at night.

I t h i n k   a l l this as I lay in the boat, the aftermath of our lives bundled inside the wood of gone forests. And somewhere beyond the heavy white fog there are people half asleep, watching TV, eating, washing dinner dishes like my mother does after the evening meal, hands in soapy water, children already asleep in beds, in light pajamas. Do I believe the old stories, the things I've heard? Do I believe in things I can't see but know are there like fish inside the depths of dark water? Do I believe I am composed of muscle, nerve, skin, or that a heart I've never seen is beating beneath my chest? These are all questions of trust and faith.

I believe in prophets, old men, old women, a world with morning rain such as I see now when a light rain begins to wash the fog away.

A chill comes up through water and ground. As it clears I haul myself in to land in this boat that somehow remained untouched by the storm while all the fish skeletons were scattered on land. I go to Ama's, the little, dying house where everything is as she left it.

The rooster crowing is the only thing that hasn't lost track of this time and world.

And when I come to the house, I hear someone inside, rummaging, but when I open the door, it is silent. No one is there. I go to open the window, look out, see nothing. I try to make out a shape, but nothing moves. I feel a breeze of cool air through the window. It is wind.

In the house nothing is disturbed or taken, but all night I sit in darkness and listen, at times afraid it is an intruder, at times hopeful it is Ama.

8
THEY COME TO ME

At Ama's the porch is bare and worn. I decide to stay and take care of Ama's house, my house. I sweep the leaves away. I get on my knees and scrub the floor. Finally, the windows close. The perfumes of night and flowers and wetness come in the door. The sun by day. I find peace here. The rains come and the world blooms and the wings of birds are wet as if the rain comes from them. Rain with a breeze, a sigh of relief, a breathing out of the world that's held its breath.

Never have I had time for so much silence before, for what is born of solitude and listening. I sit in one chair, feet up on the other. Here in this place where storms sweep the land and lightning adds life, nitrogen impregnates the soil. Where the vines creep across the world, covering the place, walls, trees, old cars sitting outside houses.

Here where the fossils, the limestone, rose from beneath the sea up like a drowned body coming to the surface, I look for Ama even though I will not see her again because she is certain that if she returns to us it will bring ruin on us as sure as the storm that carried the deer up from their natural place on the ground into air and mixed fresh water with water from the ocean. I look for her in trees. I look for smoke but what I find is gray fog, cloud, the gray wall of rain, color stolen from the world. I look for fire and I find the angle of light at dusk. But Ama is out there somewhere.

One day a man comes, tall and pale. He doesn't think anyone could live here. He wants to buy the place. I take my feet off the chair, look at him, and laugh. He looks surprised, his hat in his hand. I look at the overgrown vines starting to cover the house. You would think it is only an abandoned building, the plants already reaching up after the storm, in a slow crawl.

He sees subdivisions. I see life. He knows the cost of things, but not their value. "It's my house. It's not for sale."

"Your house? Aren't you kind of young?"

And I realize how I look to him, young and unconvincing, and I feel my strength dwindle.

After he leaves I go inside and wait for the vines to cover me and this place, until no one will know I am here.

Time moves slowly. A few days seem like a week. Curled into the bed at night, I listen to the insects, to an animal stirring about in things beneath the window, its hooves or paws breaking twigs. In the run-down, falling, sinking house I sleep in Ama's bed and it seems I dream her dreams. I dream of men with long fingernails scraping flesh from the bones of the dead and when I wake I believe I have slept for centuries and I am stripped to bone. But I look at myself uncovered in the moonlight and I am like a new moon ready to grow. In the light I am young, pale green and shining. Through the window, the moon on my skin seems made of unborn light as it lays itself down on my arms and legs. I am surprised with my youth and suppleness because I feel old.

I get up and step outside to watch for the first light coming through the trees. I feel like this land. Something is gone, risen away from me, and I'm left behind, cool and clear. And when dawn comes, I sit out on the step and look toward the trees. I hear insects, a noisy bird in dark leaves.

It's the time when day animals stir themselves out of sleep and the animals of night settle into shadows and coves and branches as the world turns in a sea wave of darkness and sun.

When sun rises, the black wet trunks of trees are shining with morning.

N o t   e v e n   a   breeze moves along the ground. Above me the clouds. I wash my clothes in a tub and the soap smells good, the stiff clean smell of Ivory, then I go out and hang them on the line, even though it is so humid I know they will hang like lifeless bodies while water drips like sweet rain from the hems, as it does from my dress still in the tree. Because it's the rainy season, rain will fall on them. Suspended by their wooden clothespins, they won't dry for days.

Then I sit and look into the distance and listen to the air which is full of the sound of locusts and crickets.

T h e y   a l l   c o m e   to me, not only dreams but people, too. They come to me as if I'm in the center of all that has happened, the hub of a wheel, the calm eye of a great storm where all things around me whirl and break and are battered, but I can still look up and see the beautiful peace of a night sky.

They come to me and it's as if I don't know them. Yesterday the turtle came, sun on its shell. I wanted to understand what it wanted. I sat and watched but there was nothing, no bridge between us.

I do not know my own mother when she comes, or the sheriff. They want to know what I know, but all I can tell for sure is that there is a fracture in the world, a gap between Ama and those for which the world is silent and dead. I reach for words or thoughts that will fill this gap, stitch it together like thread sewing two unmatched pieces of cloth into one. It isn't that she was innocent, I want to tell them, it's just that she was not guilty.

I sit in the chair and try to conjure up my father, to understand him, to ask him for help.

"Come here, Papa," I say out loud. "Come to me. Show yourself to me." I wait for his ghost to appear. Now is when I need him.

I barely remember this man who named me Omishto. When I think of him I see the beautiful dark man of my memory with large eyes and Taiga skin, like mine, with its hint of gold. I feel the touch of his big warm hands on my small back, his soft smile. I am a little girl in this memory and he holds me up and dances with me, turning me around until I am laughing and dizzy and I fall back on the grasses among blossoms and smells of dampness. There my memory ends. He was a beautiful man, people say, and I remember him that way, beautiful and gone, first to another family, then to a death I didn't witness. Sometimes his image floats up in my mind, surfacing the way a fish becomes suddenly visible in still water. But mostly there is the occasional vision of his face rising up in my own face in a mirror. He's in my blood. Maybe, in this way, he does come to me, after all.

When he left, Mama said to me, "What do you have to cry about?" I think she meant because there was a white woman she thought better than herself waiting for him, his other baby already born. He had two lives all along. A double man, my sister still calls him, as if she remembers him a year better than I do. Later, he left that woman and their two kids and ran off with another. I know he wasn't a bad man. It was just that he believed all his own lies about love. But still he was a ghost to us. Mama used to tell people he died of heart failure. That's what she said. And I realize now that her words were true; he had a failed heart; out of all possible worlds, he always chose misery while believing he chased happiness.

Years later, my grandma told me that he had gone down to search for the caves of the lower Keys, the fabled snake-filled caves white people used to say Indians hid in, where our ancestors were believed to protect themselves, to hide from the invaders. I like to dream of this place, its dark, cool recesses away from them all.

I saw him once after he left us. I was only twelve, but I knew it was him. He was walking down the street, the beautiful man I barely remembered, a ponytail down his back, a nice shirt, a warm inviting smile. He turned and watched me with a sad, helpless look in his secretive eyes, a look both familiar and strange, and I knew right away that this was my father. I wondered if he watched me because he knew I was his daughter or if he thought I was just another girl to look at, one not as pretty as his others. He looked lifeless and empty, and in that one look, even at twelve, I knew that I was stronger than him and I was only a girl. Then he got into an old gray Ford and drove away, leaving, as he always did.

But I summon him now, now that I have been silent and alone, as if he's a better person in his death and he will come to me because I need him, because I'm alone and afraid. "Come to me, Papa," I say. But he does not break through the world of the dead.

———

The cars come though, monstrous down the road. Some days I hear them while I repair the roof, or I watch them from the chair on the porch, my hands in my lap. I look out at where the four singing women came walking that day from the direction of Kili toward town. The air smells abundant and fresh of plant life, clay, old rain. I could sleep, yes, even now, as I see the police coming toward me. But I sit and watch and wait. The old land seems to open toward the trees. The sky, too, is wide open. Not far from here is the pasture, though you could barely guess it. And the gas station, the place where my brother used to wash car windows and keep clean towels on the arms of the old worn couch where customers smoked and watched TV and waited for a tire to be repaired or a fan belt replaced.

I can see the gas station now and the windows are dark. I can see the sign with its black smudges of fingerprints. Because it's Sunday, if they remembered to turn the sign around, it says "Closed."

And then the police car arrives. The sheriff writes something down before he opens the car door and comes to talk to me. I know what he wants. Herman or my mother sent him to see if he could make me go back home. I know Mama prays for me at her church, saying, "Come home to me, girl," the way I have been summoning my pa. She loves me and so she says, down on her knees, "Jesus, send her home." And she tries to see Jesus the same way I try to see a vision of my father. I know she does. I've heard her kneeling by the bed, crying and calling out for anything that could save her.

The car door slams behind him. But the sheriff, as he walks toward me, has other things on his mind than just getting me home. I can see this. The sheriff stands before me, his foot in its polished boot on the lower step, the one made of cinder blocks. "How are you doing?" he says, being friendly. He's a big man, sweating in the heat. He manages a smile. It looks so forced I want to laugh, but I don't. I have manners, though I do not stand up. Instead, I shield my eyes from the sky as I look at him and ask, "How's your family?"

He doesn't answer. Instead, he says, "I've been looking for Ama Eaton. Do you know where she is?"

I look at him for only a second. I close my mouth and I shake my head no.

"Someone said the last time anyone saw her she was up at the Kili place. With the old people. Do you know anything about that? They said you were there." He sits down in the chair facing me, Ama's chair, as if he's a friend, his legs long, knees bent at a sharp angle. "Someone saw you there."

I want to ask him who it was that saw me, but I look him square in the eye. "No," I say, truthfully. "I haven't seen her." I wonder why doesn't he go ask the old people what they did with her, but I already know the answer; he'd have to find an interpreter and anyone who could interpret he wouldn't trust to tell him the truth. Even those who know English pretend that they don't.

I feel small sitting beside him. He takes up the whole chair. His physical presence is large and he wears glasses that don't look quite right with his uniform.

He becomes silent while he waits for me to say more. Even the insects have stopped as if to listen. As if nature itself wants an answer. "I saw her walk into the trees up at their place and that's all I saw."

I see it again, Ama walking toward the trees and water. Inside my memory, I watch her walk toward an old path no longer used, the last of daylight on her hair, her shoulders bright against the growing darkness of trees, the way she looked back at us, as if we'd call to her.

"That's all I saw. I haven't seen her since."

He doesn't believe me.

There are rumors and speculations. Some people say she was sent away, she was told by the old people she had to leave us for four years, banished into the wilderness, though I believe for her it would be like throwing brother rabbit into the thorn-bushes; it's her natural place. Others say she, like Abraham, was killed by tribal law or magic, by the spell of a thin, pointed finger, a song no one outside Kili remembers. I suppose that's what the officer wants to know. This is why he has come to talk to me. He wants to know if she was killed or injured. But even if it were true, who would they arrest? There was just the old pole-thin man, stiff as wood, who pulled himself up to judge her, who pointed his finger. They have no body, no evidence. In any case, there's no one they could go after, no one who would talk except me, and once again, it all rests on my words. Every-thing does.

Again, as if it's indelible in my mind's eye, I see Abraham Swallow run past me and Donna on the road. I remember ask-ing Ama how he died, how she said, "He died of fear." But fear is not something Ama is given to.

All this seems so long ago now that I have larger fears.

And even if they did kill Ama by some magic design, the police would never arrest any of the old people.

The sheriff is waiting for me to talk.

Instead, I ask the question. "Who told you Ama was miss-ing?" But I already know the answer to this. It was Herm who went to the sheriff and said Ama was missing. No one else would have known or reported it. He heard it from Mama. I can even hear Herm's voice saying to the sheriff that the damned Indians took the law in their own hands again as if their hands were better than the law and that he thought, by God, they might have even killed her.

And now, the sheriff is going to try to talk some sense into my head. I can see this by the set of his lips. He calls me by my real name. "Omishto," he says, "you've got to tell me the truth."

I look away from him. Omishto. It means I watch every-thing. It's true I miss nothing even though I don't talk much.

That's what bothers people most about me, that I don't say much even when I need to, that I'm all eyes. But my eyes don't miss how Mama is sad, and I don't miss how the sheriff is nervous with me, either, and me just a girl. And I don't miss liking that I make him so anxious to leave that he begins jangling his keys in his hand.

Then he puts the keys in his pocket. "Is there anything missing from here?" he asks. "Has she been here after any of her things?"

I look around as if I haven't already noticed that everything is as she left it just after the hunt, the bucket of water sitting outside, now full with rain, dead insects and algae in it. "No. She hasn't come back."

I can see the sheriff still doesn't believe me. He thinks I know where Ama has gone. He thinks I stay here now because I wait for her or that she's been here, that I'm in contact with her, that she'd come here for her things, at least, but I don't care that this is the set of his mind. Let him spy on me, then, the way he will. Let him sit in his car concealed in leaves and shadow and watch for her. He'll see me plant a garden, repair the house, pull up the kudzu vines so the other plants can grow again.

"It is the truth. I haven't seen her," I say again.

He tries to sound soft, to make his voice gentle. "Did she go to the old people?" he asks me.

And I look at him a long time. "You mean to stay?" I study his face.

He says nothing. He looks off into the trees as if he'll see something of her there. But I only shake my head no. Maybe it's a half-lie, depending on what he means. I don't tell him about the old law trial and I don't try very hard to convince him of anything even though a dozen thoughts go through my mind. I am glad he doesn't believe me. I'd like her found as much as anyone. I want them to go out and find her and bring her home. I am even happy he will look for her, that he and his men will go through the swamps to all the little huts and trailers where backwoods families live, asking them if they've seen a woman about so tall, and he will hold his hand up to her height, a woman with dark hair and old clothes.

"I want to help her," he says again. "I need to know where she is."

I tell the truth. "I don't know." And finally he knows this is all he'll get from me.

The air around us is heavy with unfallen rain and it is full of gnats.

The sheriff brushes his hair back with his hand and says he has to tell my mother where I am and how I'm doing. He says, "Your mother wants you to go home."

"She knows where I am." She does. I'm sure of this. "I'm not going back." I look at him and say, "Her husband is always after me. He hurts me. It's a bad scene over there." And then I look out beyond him, at the oaks and the darkness of swamp.

The sheriff, tight-lipped, does not ask me how, in what way. He does not say he will stop him. He doesn't seem surprised, though.

After a moment I ask, "What will you do about it?"

"Does your mother know?"

I think she does—I know she does—but I have not said so directly to her. There has never been room for such words, but she'd be blind to miss it. To say it outright would break her and she has always been so fragile, even her skin is thin as a doll's skin, her hands always shaking, her eyes never steady. Mama would deny it with the part of her mind that needs Herman. She would have to deny it. She lies to herself. I've never thought how weak she was before. It's as if now I'm not only seeing the sheriff, but Mama, too. Still, I nod at him, even knowing she'd feel torn between me and Herm. She'd be forced to call me the liar and rearrange the world as she always does, by her own needs.

The sheriff knows Herm. They are something like friends. Herm is the kind of man other men like. He is talkative with them. He stands beside them with his legs apart and gabs. They look out into the distance while they talk, not at each other.

I tell myself not to push it. Not now. I know their law will not protect me, and this knowledge falls like a stone inside me. Nothing of their world serves me. It's empty. It's a sinking stone cast out of a drowning boat. And suddenly, I'm enraged by this world that offers me nothing yet expects so much of me. I look at him direct as a beam of light and I study his face and I say, "Now that you know, what will you do?"

It seems like the first time I have ever looked at, really seen, anybody, and I look at him without my eyes wavering or lowering. I see in his eyes that, like Herm, like my father, he is a weak man. He has lost something along the way, strength or will or the ability to love. He does what he is told to do. He lives on the outskirts of town in a small house that I've walked past on my way to school. He's the kind of man who waves at everyone who passes. The house is a run-down thing that pretends to have a garden but the plants barely survive for lack of care. They struggle, choked in the midst of the large devil's claws and wild grasses that want to grow in this land. In the mornings he gets out of the bed that smells of his skin, and maybe his desire, and he puts on his uniform, and his wife sees him off to work.

I look at his polished shoes, the gun in its leather holster, the gun he feels for even when it isn't there because it gives him a sense that he is safe. I look at the way his face is wrinkled around his eyes, not at all unpleasant, the crease in his lip and cheek and beneath the brow where he sleeps. I see his stomach, his hips heavy from sitting, and I think, this is a man who keeps peace and maintains the law, and there is nothing he can do. He is sure to give my mother a report on how I'm doing and where I am—which she already knows even if she pretends she doesn't—because he has children and loves them and can put himself in her position. I've seen his girl and boy in the yard playing, becoming suddenly sullen when they see me pass by, watching me in all my skinny darkness like I am strange and foreign here in this land of all my ancestors.

"Well, what should I tell your mother then?" he asks as if he wants me to think he has not come as the law, but as a friend.

"You can tell her I'm here. I'm staying here." I say it so strong he can only nod and move away but just before he turns toward his car, in one fast second, he stops and looks at me. He stops a moment and turns. "Why would she do it, anyway?" he asks me. "Kill the cat, I mean. She knew it was against the law. The damn thing even had a collar on and the plane wasn't even a half mile off, and she brought the collar home. Why would anyone do that?"

I look at his gray eyes. And I think back to the day after the saw grass bloomed, the day when sky had its own struggles, and I see the deer all flying in the dark gray sky and how Ama was held against the little sinking house, her body blown and covered with branches, her eyes closed, and there were the powerful torrents of rain, the warm water of silver, wild rivers opening all across the land. I see the wind-trampled world, the power of wind. There was the ground of hunting, the cleared land, the poisoned fish cast out of water, helpless on the earth, and then I see the clouds of cane fire that some days cover the land from fifteen miles away. "You have to think of God," I tell him. "You have to think of history."

He looks at me as if I have spoken another language. And then he gets in the car and starts it up. After he leaves, I go inside and stand behind the closed door, listening to the sound of the car trail off and vanish in the distance.

I remain standing for a long time. Despite the hot, dank heaviness of air, I feel cold. I know he drives away, past the gas station with its smell of engine oil, its phone book with the torn-up, scribbled pages torn out by travelers.

Later, as the sky turns gray and darkens, I tell myself I am no longer what I look like, not a girl sixteen years old with straight dark hair, now short. Not a thin girl who doesn't stand up straight enough to please her mother. I am an old woman. The woman inside me is old and wears one of the old dresses with ribbons and crocodile teeth. My hair holds a swan feather, white and soft. My face is lined with all the events of a life. Maybe, like the land, there are rivers, mazes of canals, and swamps that run through my blood.

I l i g h t a lantern and watch the shadows move on the walls.

It's not that I am waiting for Ama. She won't be back. I know this. I am not waiting for anything. I am living.

In the morning when I wake, the sky is low. A light rain is falling. I go out in it and breathe it in.

This day I sit, looking again at the kudzu covering the world, dwarfing the native plants. I look up and watch the birds pull their necks inward when flying and as I watch them, I wonder if something is watching us that way, the way I felt the eyes on my back the day before Ama tracked the cat, the morning of the hurricane.

The clouds pile up when evening comes and the red sun is just beginning to descend behind the trees, liquid metal.

At evening, Herman, my stepfather, comes. I hear his car and look out at him. He has been working late. He is dressed in gray pants, blue shirt. He smells of hair creme.

I open the door and step outside, to keep him from entering the house which I have claimed as my own.

He is impatient and tense. He wastes no time, no words. He says, "Girl, you got to tell what happened and stop all this nonsense." The first words out of his mouth.

I shrug. "There's nothing else to tell. I told it all."

I look at the kudzu vines covering trees at the edge of Ama's yard and beginning to cover the house.

"You're lying," he says. "I know you. It'd kill you to tell the truth. She's been coming here, hasn't she? You know she has." He is entering one of his fits of rage. His face darkens, his eyes shine, his neck tightens. "Look at me when I talk to you."

Not to rile him up, I decide to say nothing. Instead, I pick up, take the lid off, the bucket of chicken feed and the scoop, take the key out of my jeans pocket, and walk out toward the chickens as if to feed them. He follows me. He is even more angry that I am walking away from him.

"Come back here," he says. He tries to grab my arm.

I pull away and unlock the padlock. I go inside the chicken-wire enclosure that keeps out predators and lock myself in so Herm can't get to me. The chickens cluck and bustle around my feet, the black hen, the red rooster, the yellow chickens. From inside the tall cage, nothing looks familiar, not even Herm.

He comes to the fence and puts his fingers in it and stares at me up close. "God damn you," he says. "Your mother has been crying for days. I ought to backhand you." He shakes the fence, but I know it's me he wants to shake. He would hit me if he could get at me.

But I stand up tall and look back at him.

"You won't ever lay a hand on me again," I say. I step closer to him, as if I'm not afraid. "Never. And I'm never going back."

He steps back and I see him grow smaller than I thought he

could, heavy in the stomach, his back weak. I am surprised by this. But he says, "Just you wait." He turns and walks away. He gets in the car and slams the door, hard, defeated, although he pretends not to be. I step back into the shadows and watch him drive away and I am taller.

As I watch the car disappear down the road, it occurs to me that he loves my mother, Herm does, in his own small way. He cares that she is crying, that I have hurt her. For a moment I feel guilty that I have stood up to him because, in that moment, I feel sorry for him, seeing him diminished. For a moment I think maybe he's not so bad. But then it comes back to me, the time he made me strip naked and lean against the wall while he beat me with his belt and I tried to cover myself with my hands, cover my breasts, my private body, even though the belt buckle was breaking my skin, leaving its designs like snakeskin patterns, and I believe I have been too kind to him.

I stay in with the chickens for a long time looking at the soft feathers shed on the dirty ground, the yellow eyes of chickens as they walk about in jerky motions pecking at the ground as if they could get inside it and disappear or crack the egg of earth open and let something beautiful escape.

Darkness lights down, an occasional car passes, and for this night I don't know why, but I remain with the chickens. It calls to mind the story from Mama's Bible where the young man lies with dogs and they clean his wounds and he heals.

I sleep like an animal, huddled in the corner of the cage, and sometimes a chicken cries out in the night and I hear it and wonder if they dream of being birds that fly, if their ancestors were beautiful and wild.

The first time my mother comes to see me, it's late afternoon and I'm cleaning the dishes. She comes in without knocking. She looks around the room, at the floor, the corners

I've cleaned on my hands and knees. She's looking for something the way she never dared look when Ama was here. "She's probably got roaches along with all the termites. I don't know what's held this house up for all these years."

It's true. The walls are crooked, the floor slants. It's far from clean. Even though I have been sweeping and scrubbing, it's not the kind of house you can clean. Mama opens a cupboard and looks inside. Her eyes are greedy when they move to the dishes, a taking-inventory kind of look, as if she might find something she could carry home with her. I dislike this about my mother.

"Why don't we go talk outside," I say. "It's cooler there." Which is a lie. With the new palms I've placed on the roof of the house, the inside feels like the deep cool shade of trees on a breezy day. The truth is, I don't like the way she intrudes on Ama's place; it's become a sanctuary to me and Mama's presence violates it.

She looks at me. "Why don't you be nice?" She goes out, clutching her bag, and I draw her a glass of water and follow.

I don't like the word "nice."

"Why can't you ever be nice?" she says again.

We sit outside, on the two chairs, both of us looking out into the trees. I am wondering what happened to the monkey in the hurricane. I haven't seen it since that day. With all the things that have come to pass, I had, in fact, forgotten all about it.

"I suppose she's out there somewhere," my mother says, sitting in this small, brief clearing, looking out into the world of cypress and oak hammocks and palmetto and swamp. "I suppose she's still alive, don't you?" She turns to me and looks at me closely.

I feel she knows what has happened to Ama.

I nod at her, but what I really want to do is to go live in the deep trees myself, out where the first hint of evening darkness is flying toward us.

She doesn't look at me when she asks, "When are you going back to school?"

"I don't know."

"You can't stay out of school."

It's not that she ever cared about me and school before. Suddenly it is important.

Then she asks, "When are you coming home?"

Now when I am first myself is when she wants to hold on to me, wants me to feel wanted. It must be hard for her to bear, that I am becoming so fully another person, that my skin, made of her skin, is a boundary that closes her out and now she wants in.

It wasn't that I decided to stop going to school. It was just something that happened. One day became another. One day it seemed easier not to go. Not because the others disliked me, either. I could bear that. It's that I thought about what I was learning there; isosceles triangles, pronouns, false history. With all that in mind, one day I decided not to go. Because it didn't mean anything to me anymore. Then the next day I decided the same, and the next.

"You can't let those other kids drive you away. People always talk. There's always talk and gossip. All your life. You might as well get used to it."

For Mama, the gossip is what would have hurt the most, but not for me. It wasn't the way I was looked at or what the kids called me, either, like Cat Killer or Swamp Nigger. It was something I didn't have words for, but I say to Mama and I look at her when I say it, "All along, Mama, it's been someone else's life I've been living. Other people's lives. Now it is my own. From now it's going to be mine." And I see that it's true when these words come out of my mouth, words I don't recall ever having thought. It's true. All along I've lived in their world with order and cleanliness and the many other instruments of despair. It has been my life. And now I want no share in it.

I have just been born, just now risen into the silence of evening.

We sit in the silence of early evening. She lights a Doral. Anger rises in her voice, "How are you going to eat, for God's sake? How will you ever get a job, for Christ's sake?"

"Leave me alone, Mama."

She doesn't believe her ears. "What?" Her mouth open.

"You heard me. I'm tired now. It's time for you to be getting home."

She's silent, her lips tight.

And suddenly what I say is true. I feel the pull of gravity and exhaustion. I want to go lie down and sleep. I don't want to do anything but that. The air is wet, thick as a body, and I want to lie down in it.

She is crying now. "I don't believe this." Then she tries to tell me what isn't true. "You were always a happy child," she says.

"You've got to go, Mama."

"What do I have to do, send your father back here again?"

"He's not my father."

She is shrill now, angry that I've hurt her. "You think she could do no wrong. Ama. You think the ground she walked on was holy. Look what she did. She killed it!"

"No," I say, bothered that my mother uses the past tense as if Ama is already dead. "What she did was wrong, I know that. But I understand it. That is all I'm saying, all I've ever said; I understand why she did it."

"Why then? Tell me why."

"I'll talk to you about it later. Not now, Mama. I'm too tired."

Not now when I have just been born.

I get up and go indoors. I know Mama wants to hit the door, to go from window to window yelling, but this time she doesn't.

I hear the car door slam, the car screech away.

And then I try, myself, to fathom why. The truth is, I can't tell. I don't have words for this yet, not yet.

Two days later, Donna comes to me, driving Dave's car. I smell summer the day she comes, as if she carries it with her, a hot wind walking to the door along with her. As always, she's in a hurry. She is wearing her blue dress and a gold locket, and she has come to let me know what a terrible daughter and sister I am. "Poor Mom can't stop crying. She cries and prays and then wipes her eyes with a hanky real quick so no one will see her mascara run."

I laugh when Donna says this. I can't help myself.

She looks at me a moment, and then she laughs, too, a genuine laugh, which lets me know that I am, at least in part, forgiven by her. Donna leans back when she laughs, she throws her head back and shows her square white teeth. I've always loved how she gives in to happiness that way, as if it sneaks up on her and catches her unawares.

I'd like it to be the way it once was between us, to sit with her and laugh as hard as we used to, to have her hit her thigh when she laughs. I want to believe that our laughing would change things, but suddenly I'm afraid I will break down and cry and not keep with the strength of what I am learning and becoming in this world, so I only smile and look at her. Her hair is clean and neat and fragrant.

She says, "The preacher stole church funds. He was arrested."

"No." In truth, it doesn't make any difference to me, but I know it will hurt Mama—she believes strongly in tithing—so after the laughter I am serious. "How did he do that? Who caught him?"

"It was in yesterday's paper."

Then the laughter fades. Donna changes the subject and looks serious. "You can't stay here, Sis."

Donna always has limits, her rules and standards of behavior. All I can say is, "Why not?"

She examines a broken fingernail. Then she looks at me quickly, puzzled. A cloud moves across the sky behind her. I see the sweat stains on her blue dress, beneath the arms, at the back, and there's a little food stain she has tried to scrub away with a Kleenex or hankie. She's not perfect, though God knows she tries and with desperation that she will be stuck, that she will be like Ama who is not pretty or lighthearted, or like our mother who doesn't even remember our births. "Sis, I have to tell you this. They think you're crazy. They're going to send a doctor out here."

The light on her hair is shining red.

It's so hot I feel sick. I'm not smiling now. "A doctor?" I ask this quietly. "They're going to send a doctor?" I think of the state hospital in Consodine, the white brick building that contained my swollen-faced mother and all of the other women sitting there smoking before a TV, one woman removing her clothing to walk down the hall, the shaved-head, mute stripper, the women who walk up and back, arms crossed before their chests, always crossed like they are protecting themselves.

I know what they do to take you to the hospital. I've seen it. It's what they did with Mama. The sheriff has the order. He comes to the door. He handcuffs you and takes you away. Then, at the hospital, because it's a regulation, they chain your legs together in case you might try to escape, in case you're a danger.

Donna puts her hand on my leg and looks at me. "You've got to go home. You can't stay here. They will have you committed. Herm's trying to get a court order."

I look at her like she's the one who is crazy. "Isn't that illegal now?" I consider this. It would be easy for them to lock me away. I would be the teenaged victim of Ama Eaton, the girl who helped kill the endangered panther, then had no choice but to testify against her own friend, the girl who was ostracized, photographed, and hounded. They'd expect it, for me to be crazy or guilt-ridden at least.

But I say, "I'm not coming back with you, Donna."

"What about school? You have to go to school." Her hand on her hip, even though she's sitting.

"No, I don't. I'm dropping out."

I see there will be no heart-to-heart with my sister, the girl I admired and followed around when we were little, when she'd try to pretend she didn't know me. I was an embarrassment to her even then.

"I can quit school. I'm sixteen. It's law."

After she sees her words will do no good, she is in a hurry to leave. She is always in a hurry. Ama calls it time sickness, a disease of this time and world. Everyone missing life in their hurrying. But maybe the world exists in layers and all time is here at once; I am my ancestors, and they foresaw me. They foresaw, too, that one day their descendants would become part of an enemy world.

As much as I wanted to laugh a moment ago, I want to cry now, out of loneliness and misery and the confusing possibility of my two possible fates, each distinct, each real. One fate exists in the white people's world, the other exists in the older world of my own people. Our lives, any of us, could break and fall outward in any direction, but for people like me there are only two ways to fall.

She plays with the locket around her neck on a chain, the way she does when she's nervous, or sometimes she twists her ring. I think how gold was the thing that created one of those worlds and destinies, that the Americans invaded us for gold.

Tears come to my eyes. I want to pour my heart out and tell her how lonely I am and how afraid I was last night when the barn owl screamed like a woman being killed.

And I want to tell her I might go to the end of the road up above Kili Swamp to where the old people wait for us, have always waited for us to go home, to be who we are, and that she could go with me and we'd live like we once did, like we were meant to live, and it would be peaceful and strong. But she would never go, I know this, and maybe I wouldn't either, out of fear that I will fail them like Ama must have done, fear that I am weak and not yet formed enough to sing or learn what they know, and fear that I won't be able to give up Coca-Cola and movies.

But even with all this inside me, I summon the strength to say, "Give Ma a hug for me, okay?"

Just before she goes, she turns and puts her arm around me and it feels good. It makes me want to weep, for that soft human skin, the warm touch of a hand. I can't remember the last time a person touched me so and now I think how lonely I am. I want to bury my face in Donna's shoulder, but I stand rooted to earth, and rooted this way I feel tall, even though she's taller and more womanly, filled out in breast and hip.

"You can't stay on the run." Her last words to me.

I tell her, "I'm not on the run. This is my place now. Ama always said it would be mine." I sound so strong, so solid, but still I want to hold Donna and laugh, to ask how the church got any money in their coffers anyway, and my heart pounds with fear for what I do say and fear that my own strength is wrong or false or will pass from me the minute Donna drives Dave's car out of here. Fear that I will have to do what I say and be true to my word.

And then she is gone. I watch Dave's car rumble down the road.

It is still light. I lie down on the bed listening to the house settle and wonder if I'm crazy like they think I am. It is true that I'm an unknown. Like in algebra, I am the x to be determined in the formula, and I almost wish I were crazy, that I'd only imagined all of the things that have happened; history, God, orders followed, lives lived to the precise line of what a person is supposed to do, obedient people who look on while others are killed, who look away when asked to help, the cup of misery they choose for themselves and then share with others.

All the hopes and fears I could pull out of the world enter me now. The woman inside me, can I betray her, the one I am becoming? I know only this, that I am Taiga, that the future depends in some way on me. We were the sacrificed, each one of us; now there are only thirty of us left in this world and we are hemmed in by sadness, living in a world that's become foreign.

I rest on the bed and even though it is afternoon I drift into sleep and it is like being inside a slow, warm current of water.

Suddenly I sit up, damp and sweating, my heart beating too fast. The crickets in the house are singing. I sit up straight. Janie Soto had the hide of the cat in her lap. I know this with certainty. I remember the swirl of fur, the dark spot, shaped like a circle. This knowledge has come to me through sleep. It has crashed through the ceiling of my sleep, fallen inside this room. I recognize the dark print on the side of the cat. It is what I saw on her lap that day. And how did she get it, I wonder. Did Ama give it to her or send her for it? But I think not. I remember dreaming I saw her that day after the storm in the brush, and now I think she must have heard the cry of the cat and followed us. According to Donna, Janie Soto was going from the phone that day. She carried a bag, a white feather. She must have taken it, carried it home in the bag on her own. These thoughts make my heart pound. I get up from the bed, thinking how Janie was the one who argued against Ama's freedom at the place of old law. Janie, the traditionalist, who spoke against Ama. Janie, the woman closest to the panther. She wouldn't have known it was sick, that Ama could not do what was right. She would have thought she was doing the right thing, taking the hide, she the oldest member of our tribe, the head of our Panther Clan.

Outside the little house, later, the world is alive and the sun is suspended in the western sky. I see shadows of trees moved by a breeze and the world is beautiful and I am still and quiet, the light of sun on my skin, and then a long wide dusk lies down on the land and sleeps. I scan the evening sky. I think of them talking to the doctors, the sheriff coming for me the way they did for Mama, like I am a criminal and my crime, my sin, is that I have fallen into an older world, into wilderness, that world where Ama has gone to cast her lot.

There is orange light from the descending sun. I watch the world darken until no sky is present.

When I go to bed, I dream the panther, its legs bent, its teeth poor. I feel dizzy with its scent, the smell of it and of blood. This, too, comes to me. In the dream it is standing in tall grasses, stalking with its night-shining eyes, lean now, healthy in its home inside my mind where it is closed in by whatever I am, who I belong to, the shrinking world, its growing smallness.

From the dark house I look out at the night sky with visible stars and stillness when I hear the car approach, its radio playing so loud it bumps up against the world. I hear their voices. Someone calls, "Hey, bitch!" I stand inside, just behind the window. It's the three boys. In the moonlight and with the car lights still shining on the house, I can see that one of the boys has a rock in his hand. They are looking for Ama, the scapegoat, a woman to be stoned. Not for her sin of killing the cat but for the sin of humiliating them. Two of them have their hands in the pockets of their school jackets and I think they might have guns.

"There she is," one says and I see he is pointing at a window of the house, seeing, like everyone does, what's not there inside any of the places of Ama.

I slip out the back window into darkness, and go into the trees, barefoot in the presence of snakes. Where earth touches sky, where I touch everything, I crouch and watch them from the leaves, unsafe. I see them as the panther must have seen us, foreign, alien, strange as a new element, like a meteor fallen from space.

I see that boy in a baseball cap, behind the light, eerie, half-lighted, the car lights turned on the house. He points to a window and throws a rock and glass shatters.

The boys have no way of knowing Ama's gone; they don't hear about our events. Our world is apart from theirs.

I recognize them from school. One is on the football team. His girlfriend cries when he doesn't make a score, when an opponent pulls him down by the legs. Winning is important to him. That's why he's come back. The younger one, with the rock in his hand, is new this year. The other is a friend of a boy I used to be sweet on. A million years ago, it seems. And I am afraid of all of them, each and every one. They have families, good grades, friends, and for some reason I can't fathom they are able to be good and honest, evil and dangerous, all in the same one person, at the same time, in the same skin.

"Bitch! We see you," he says again.

I can barely breathe.

They do not come out back to where it is dark, not yet. They stay near their car so they can get away. They stay near the road so they will be safer, in sight of each other. They don't split up.

And all night, even after I hear their car tear away, I cannot sleep. I look out the window, keeping watch, ready to leave, certain the boys will come back.

———

In the morning, with shaking hands, I go again to look for the rifle. The ground has been disturbed, I know this by the binding weed that grows over what has been broken. I pull at it and at the kudzu, clearing the vines from earth and trees with my hands, and with the splintering handle of the shovel, I dig, searching for the rifle. The dark soil of one place gives off a rich smell, but beneath it is only stone. The police have already searched for it and given up, but I hope they have overlooked it. Then, in one place I hit what sounds like wood. I work carefully. Digging, I find what I expected, the rifle box, empty, already beginning to rot. Someone found it before me. But beneath the vines, I find Janie Soto's red beads and I take them from the ground and hold them in my hand. It gives me a chill to find them. I puzzle through the many ways they could have gotten there and know she is the one who took the evidence. She, so strong against Ama, has tried also to protect her. I look at the beads, straightening the strands carefully. Red coral. Traded in some long-ago time with another tribe. Red as fire, red as blood. I sit down on the ground. She, Janie Soto, is the only one who has ever worn these. They were handed down to her from a long-ago past. I put them on myself.

Then I remain sitting outside by the place I dug, looking at the exposed root ends of plants, and I feel the cool air come up from the earth. Beneath me are many underground rivers, all flowing west to the sea. There is strength inside the earth, movement, and turning over. It smells of wet trees.

The second time Mama comes, a few days later, I think her car is the sheriff coming to take me to the hospital. I go outside into the trees to watch while the car parks, then I see it's her. As she gets out of the car, I don't even know her. That's what I tell myself, looking at her. She looks bent. I don't know my own mother and her feet in tight yellow shoes. I look at her,

her stiff walk. Then I go greet her and in spite of what I'd like to tell her, all I say is "Hey."

"Hey," she says. Mama and I sit down outside, she on the step lower from me so that I can see her hair, gray at the roots.

"You're a sight," she says.

I imagine I am. Sleepless. Dirty. Awake, thinking that Janie Soto had only part of the story and I have the rest.

"You look tired."

She leans forward. "Are you still waiting for Ama to come home? She won't come home, girl. She has been banished and she lives by old law and you won't see her for any of those four years."

"No, Mama, I'm not. I know she won't come back."

I know this because Ama believes the old people and accepts their verdict, their judgment.

Then, her face in her hands, "I know why you don't want to come back. I don't blame you."

Mama cannot look the world in the eye, but she looks at me, briefly, nervously. There is something in her look I can't read, don't know.

"I know that he hit you. I knew he had his eye on you. I just didn't want to see it." Then she's quiet a long while. We sit in silence. Then she says to me, "You've been eating of the tree of knowledge."

I'm quiet, uncertain of her meaning.

"Knowledge can be such a sad thing. You kick in with it and life is changed forever by what you know."

"Mama, I'm not coming home. I'm at home here. I'm awake, Mama," I say, no other words to tell her how I feel, the world stretching around me.

"Yeah, I know."

I study her face, surprised she knows anything about me, and I think how little of her that I know. She has never let me know her.

"I wish it was me," she says.

I am quiet, but I look at her. Both of us soften. After a while, she says, "I went to live at Kili once. You never knew that, did you?"

"I remember a little of it."

"You weren't no more than three or four."

Then the mama I know opens a mirror and puts on eyebrow pencil. The humidity has swallowed up her makeup. "Yeah, I was there," she says, searching her face for flaws, and there are many. "I went to live with the old people. You were a baby. It was Donna, you, and me. They saved our lives. When you were little and there was no food, and your father was coming after us, we went there. Your dad was on a bender. He was going to kill us. They saved us. Janie Soto said if I stayed she was going to teach me things. If only we'd stay. She practically begged us and it's not like her to do, not her style at all, but she would do anything to get us to go back. She wanted Ama. She practically raised her. It nearly broke her heart that Ama didn't stay. But I can see why. It's so much for them to want."

This is the first I've heard of this. I look at her with interest, a woman whose life I do not know, the woman who bore me and told me she has no memory of my birth, because in those days they put women to sleep to give birth and sometimes they remained asleep for years. We, my mother and I, have never so much as talked about anything. Such as who we are inside. As people, I mean.

"I would have stayed, too, but one day I just woke up and I thought, what good would any of this do us in this world? What good would it be for us? I could stay there, and then we'd be the ones all foreign in the world, and stared at, maybe even hated, and so I left. But they saved us."

And neither of us say it, but we both know that now I am the one who is foreign in this other place. I'm stared at, suspect, hated.

I touch my mother's arm. The heart is full of stolen dreams. Like memory it holds vanished worlds and streets and abandoned ways. My mother has her dreams and memories, and she stays and talks. I get up and fix her a glass of tea. The way she likes it. The daylight recedes before us. As night falls, she drowns in the darkness. I see only the outline of trees. In the darkness, the time of day when I come alive, I see only her scarf, her hand. I sit on the step above her and watch the heat lightning in the distance and I have wings and I know I will fly and I understand something Mama does not.

She takes her hands away from her face. "This is not the best place for you, Sister. I don't know if you are safe here."

Yes, I think, I am at the far edge of her world, teetering, ready to fall over.

"Donna told me about the hospital," I say. But I say nothing about the three boys.

She does not act surprised. "It's Herm's idea. Yeah, he's talked to them. They think, by his words, you are in trouble, in danger."

Psychologically, she means. "They won't find me here if they come, Mama," I say. I think maybe I will hide in the same place that hides Ama.

I take up her matches and light a citronella candle and watch it flame on the step. Willard's horse is standing beside the house where it comes to stand every single night, slightly lame, and I see it shake its head, newly freed once again.

"Serious trouble. Those were their words. I want you to know I don't agree with them or Herm."

"They won't get me, you know."

"I know. Nothing or no one ever could."

After a while, Mama is quiet and I'm thankful for it. She lights a cigarette. I hear the horse snuffle. In the candlelight, Mama looks worn out. With the always wistful, hurt look on her face. Then she gets up to leave and it's still dark. The air is thick and smells rich. I put an arm around her. I walk with her to the car.

She asks, "Do you need anything? Money or anything?"

"No, I'm fine." I open the car door for her.

"I'm leaving him, you know," she says, getting in the car. The light inside her car doesn't work. I close the door and stand while she turns the key. The car starts, the lights come on, and she's gone. I watch the taillights and know she will not leave Herman, and I stand and watch her go and I think of salvation. The church is saving Mama, the old ways are saving the people at Kili. Ama is saving a world. But I am saving myself being here, and in all these savings, the path of things is changed forever. And I can't help thinking that it's God Mama believes in, but it was the old people who saved us.

In the morning, the sun is too hot and bright in the sky but there is a whirlwind on the ground and the dead leaves and pieces of grass and trash from the road are picked up in it, carried in a circle.

I remember hearing a story about my grandfather. On a day this hot, in a heat wave where animals and people were dying, Grandpa went out with a United States–issue gun and tried to shoot out the sun to make it darker and cooler, to bring on the night.

It's a motionless heat. I sit out under the trees fanning myself with Ama's fan and I am looking at the sky, trying to call the clouds in toward me when I see her. It's Annie Hide, my mother's kin. From up the road I see her come walking toward me, the slow heavy-footed pace of an old woman, walking in from the distance, the same direction from which the four women came, the heat on the road making her look like she's walking on water, the way they did, her wide blue skirt like the ocean water of the gulf being touched by a soft wind. She doesn't seem real and I wonder if she isn't just a mirage. I stand up and feel dizzy with the heat and I wave at her and go out to the white road and wave and walk toward her. It is not such a long walk, but it seems long and far away as if I pass through time instead of just that little distance of space across the heat rising up. She has come a long way to me. I look at her and it seems there is a world of difference between us, but truly there is not. A generation of difference only, the generation my mother fell into like into a crack of the earth. I wonder who and what I would be now, in this day, if not for the crack in that world, the generation of my mother's that lies between us.

Annie Hide, or her apparition, is dressed in the old dress, the band across her chest with a circle of beads and threadwork, and she looks like mystery come out of the heat of day, but the spell is broken when I see the tennis shoes that would make anyone else look silly. I see, too, how she chews on sugarcane, one tooth decayed from where it is placed between her teeth, a little circle of enamel dissolved away.

I smile at her and it is the first time I've smiled in a long time.

She is the healer, the one who takes care of human wounds and broken things. Annie is the peacemaker, the mender of fights, the woman of a different mission than Janie Soto. I do not fear her the way I fear Janie Soto. Perhaps this is why she is the one who comes to me.

When I reach her, she says only, "It's hot." It's all she says. She breathes heavily and wipes her forehead with a red bandanna. She takes my hand in hers and grips it tight in her hard, old hand, as if I will get away if she lets go of me, and together, hand in hand this way, we turn and walk to Ama's.

I sneak a glance at her. I expect her to be dusty in her old skirts, but she has a fresh, clean smell, and I feel restful in her presence.

When we reach the house, she says, "Let's get out of the sun."

She knows, without my saying it, that the palmetto fronds

keep the house cool. Her voice is old, thin. I help her up the steps and she's heavier than she looks. Her hair wrapped, piled, and pinned on the top of her head is darker at the old ends, gray near the sweating scalp. The skin of her forehead is brown and softly wrinkled.

She sits at Ama's table and arranges her skirt. I pour her a glass of water. In both her hands, she takes the glass I offer. I sit down across from her in Ama's blue chair. I look at her old knuckles as she drinks the water in a hurry, thirstily, and wipes her mouth on the back of her hand. I take the glass from her and refill it. She needs to rest. She sits and breathes softly, her eyes closed. It gives me a chance to see her, to look straight at the face of the old woman I am said to resemble. There is sweat on her forehead and upper lip, her skin is worn. She breathes the air, Oni, she's carried through life to a near end.

Then she opens her eyes, places an old hand on mine. Her hand is warm. "You should know what I am thinking." A bird flies over and makes a long crying sound, a complaint about the heat. "I am thinking we threw her away." Her eyes are sad. "She was strong. She was important. We threw her away."

I sense in her a kind of helplessness. "I know it," I say back to her. Don't I just know it, though. I see Ama again, how she was sacrificed, how she went off silently, how I have not seen even the slightest trace of her, even a flash of the red skirt through trees or brush.

I take a sip of water.

And then she says, "I think I saw her." Her accent is soft but I drop the glass. It breaks. Is this the reason she has come to me? I try to pick up the pieces of glass. Annie Hide catches my eyes and smiles and I see she is a kind woman. "Yes, I think I saw her. It was two days ago. And she had new shoes and a hat."

With this my hopes fall. I know it isn't Ama she saw, not with new shoes and a hat. But everyone wants to see Ama. It's as if she's become a mystery or stands for something. So-and-so thought they saw her in town. The boys thought they saw her in the window of this house. I think of all the places she could be and how I have searched through the trees and swamps knowing in my bones and blood that I would not find her, but looking, still looking. For even a trace. Herm believes she's dead. Everyone has their theory. But these are only their stories and they need their stories, even if they aren't the truth. Stories are for people what water is for plants. And if anyone truly knows where Ama is, they are silent. Ama is a woman in the wilderness. Maybe she laid herself down on the ground and reached into clay, put a foot in it, then knelt down and laid her knees and palms in it, a hip, a shoulder, until she sank into the mud and earth and closed her eyes in the shining clay and stopped her own breath until there would be another time four years from now, when once again she could surface. I think she could do that, become earth in that way, and I would rather know this than believe she was in a city, walking down a street with a newspaper in her hand. Ama has always been what is hidden.

I don't tell her it wasn't Ama she saw, the way I didn't tell about the condition of the panther. She, too, needs hope and faith.

Then Annie Hide asks me, touching my hand again, "Are you all right here, Omishto?"

And I'm no longer strong. I start to cry. She puts her arm around me and I fall against her and cry. She smells familiar, like woodsmoke and human life. "There," she says. "There." As if to speak a place. "There," as if to show me something is here, inside me now, and that it's the way it's meant to be. And for one moment, in a glimpse, I remember something of what I am. And this, I'm sure, is why Annie came to me, to remind me of this.

We sit together as the shadows thrown by afternoon light fall across us. And before long there is a darkness outside with the sounds of frogs and insects.

Annie Hide stays the night. I fix myself a bed on the floor and I lie down, close to earth. I am something dim inside my own memory. I know that not even the mind of the world, the heart of the waters, can distinguish the shape of what's fallen over me, the shape I am being given, as if it's a gift.

While Annie Hide sleeps and breathes and snores gently on the bed, they come to me with their sounds, their wordless voices, their needs, the water, the trees, the animals, as if by her presence she draws them here. On this side of the uprooted world the animals walk, the turtle woman who swam with us in an earlier world, a universe of worlds, lays her eggs up along the edge of the canal, moves forward, lays more eggs just like the turtle I saw from the road. I dream and watch. I dream that I, like the turtle, am swimming and I wake up sweating and tired, my arms tight.

In the morning when the first sun comes through the trees, I get up and heat water. Annie Hide gets up stiffly from the bed and smiles at me sweetly, her hair in disarray. I give the old woman hot tea. And with nothing said, she ties her shoes and just before the heat of the day comes toward us, she goes back on the road and walks away, heading home just in front of the day's heat, and I watch her. Without looking, she knows I watch, and without turning, she waves.

9
WHAT I HAVE LEFT

I dream old people are looking in on me, brushing corn pollen on me, and I grow like the roots and stems of plants, as if I am coming up out of the ground to the light after a dark season and growing a new skin like a lizard or snake, shedding an old one.

In the old days it was said that the shining fish would come up from the water just to partake of our faces as we washed. The wind played a song in the reeds just to draw us near. The whole earth loved the human people. Now it all pulls away from us and hides.

In the old days when we were beautiful and agile, we asked the animals to lay down their lives for us and in turn we offered them our kinship, our respect, our words in the next world over from here, our kind treatment.

In the old days it was said that we were humans.

What people believe, falsely, is that all this can no longer be so.

All day, for days, I sit and feel the feeling in my stomach and heart. In daylight, I am awake and light without the shadow of a single god.

In the golden light of dusk I sit and watch. The leaves are blue beneath the moon. The flowers of earth grow like the reflection of white stars in the darkening, lowered sky. They seem alone on the trees. Light comes into my body, goes out. There is the smell of flowers, the black night behind it all with a breeze passing through. Inside the singing of frogs and insects, I sit beneath the arms of trees with something turning over inside myself, and then I go inside and light the lantern and listen to the trees.

Some nights I don't sleep and the bats fly to and fro above the black water. I'm awake as I watch the morning sun chase the moon from the sky. I hear whispers. I think she's out there, or maybe it's the cat, full and healthy and alive. I turn and the sound is gone, and when I look I can just make out the trees in the moonlight and above them the full moon that pulls at earth's water, that has more power finally than the dikes and canals that have changed this world.

In the mornings, I wake newly born, full of life, yet unable to tell what I hold as if my body is a sacred container of stories, of storms recalled, of the smooth teeth of animals and the words of ancestors. There is something sharp inside me, and unformed, that will smooth itself as I grow older.

I think, it is snowing somewhere north of here. In another place there's rain. A thief is running from a crime. There are countless houses being built. Planets are turning in the sky like eggs in a woman's body. Farther out is the world of stars, black holes, other universes, but there is no more cat, no more Ama, no more anything that would give us strength, even though I know it is coming back, all of it is coming back, because time is like waves of water, with darkness becoming light, light turning into darkness. The world is like an ocean wave carrying the cast-off debris of our lives before it turns and comes back.

One morning, the fog rolls in from out of the storm and I see five black otters crossing the road. They stand up, come up a slight rise, walking on two legs like humans on their way to the center of life.

At s c h o o l we heard about imploding stars, stars that fall inward the way I am falling, but there is no place ever to touch down, there is no bottom to inward falling, and though I cannot track the past, all of what was, I know this; this earth, the swamp, it's the same thing as grace, full of the intelligent souls of cat, deer, and wind. I am stronger in nature. There is something alive here and generous. And now, at night as I am walking toward Kili, this is what I enter.

The moon makes everything visible. Something is on the road. At first I think there is blood on the road, an animal has been injured, but I walk closer and see that it is one of Mom's red scarves dropped on the road, a shock of red on the white road, fallen from her car. I pick it up.

Something is around. As I walk, I feel it. A presence, peaceful and strong. Naked and revealing.

Walking to Kili, I think that at Kili, in their memories, are a thousand storms. The people there remember how to heal themselves and each other. They remember what they were born knowing. Nothing replaced or erased it like it has done with me. Me, I am a dissolved person, like salt in water.

I've lived a narrow life so far, I've lived by fear and the loss of what was beautiful and strong. But at the end of the road is a different story. On the little patch of land up behind the swamp, they are still human. The world they live in is still alive. They remember the stories that are the force of living, how Panther Woman went into the black trees and returned, finally, with magic words which she withheld until the time when the world teetered on the rib of death and then she spoke them.

This, perhaps, is the time. Now that the world is dying. Now that land disappears behind us, not like the mangrove trees, the creators and guardians of life who move away and leave behind them land, soil, fresh water, countless fish and insects and plants, but like a storm leaving chaos behind it.

Last night I dreamed the snakes and lizards. Their new skins, freshly exposed, shine beautiful and bright. I whisper to myself as I walk and the moonlight touches me, "I leave this world. I leave war and fear. I leave success and failure, owned things, rooms of the light that was once a river and is now reduced. I leave the radio, the manners of living." And this act, this leaving, takes all my courage, all my strength.

And leaving I become their enemy. It was always this way for those who tried to escape. I will be their other side, the shadow they cast, invisible, dark, dangerous. But I am not sorry. It will come to me, that world, and tug at me. It will impose itself on me. It will be here, all around me. But I will no longer be dissolved salt.

I walk to Kili in the full moonlight. Annie Hide and Janie Soto live in a red house. I stand in front of it. It is the color of blood. I stand and watch the clouds building above it, moving into the clear, black sky, and I want to talk to Annie Hide but my heart is pounding in my throat. I remain for a while, watching, looking at the clouds, at the silence of the houses set down there in the night, the moonlight on the walls. But I hesitate to go closer; the old people need their sleep, I tell myself. I will come back. I turn and go home. Home, that's what I call it, Ama's place. The sound of my shoes on the dirt road seems loud. Again, something is around. When I get close, I hear something in the brush, and I stand still and look so hard and long that the trees seem to disappear from my sight.

"Ama?" I say. I am hoping. I step toward the sound, not afraid, and the trees are real again and I see it. Standing still, looking back at me, the golden cat, large and with the tawny fur loose and healthy, lean-muscled. I don't move. It could kill me, swallow me. It thinks the same thing of me. We stand motionless and look at each other in the near morning and then I say, "No shi holo." I mean no harm, Aunt, Grandmother. I think this is the mate of the one Ama killed. Or maybe, as Ama maintained, it is the same one returned, fully grown and beautiful, or the one that was born alongside me at my beginning. As I watch it, as the trees open their ears and eyes and listen and watch, a breeze moves through and with it the spell is broken. The panther turns and walks away, slowly. It is not at all in a hurry and I want to say, "Run, we are dangerous people, every last one of us."

And then it's gone and I turn and walk home and as the sun rises, everything turns red, bathed in dawn.

Indoors I go to sleep and when I wake the sun is full in the sky. It's hot and sultry, the walls wet with moisture, the sound of gnats in the room. Outside, the chickens are noisy, hungry for their missed morning scraps, and when I get out of bed the skin on my back and the back of my legs and arms is burning and tight. I look at myself and see that I am scratched all over with clawed, red lines, dried blood, and I feel a moment of cold terror. This is what they used to do in ceremonies, scratching the back of the legs. This is how it used to be. I get up and close the shutters as if a storm or an intruder is coming in even though it isn't, and I cover myself with one of Ama's dresses. And I feel fear as, with my skin hurting, I walk down the road to the pay phone at the gas station. I put in my last coin, listen to it click, and dial my mother's number.

Donna answers, sounding tired, as if she is still groggy with sleep.

"Donna?"

"Yeah." She's still sleepy. "Who is this?"

"It's me. I need you to get Herm's truck and come and get Ama's chickens and goats for me, would you? I'm going home."

"Sure. That's good," she says, a little more awake now. "How are you?"

"I'll crate up the chickens for you."

"Okay. Good. It's for the best."

She thinks I mean something else. I don't correct her. "I know," I say.

Then I go back to the little worn-down house to pick up my things. I crate up the chickens for Donna, and then I sit for a while on the porch and look again at this world, and I'm still sitting on the porch when I see the four women walking up the road toward me, singing in the heat. Their rattles shaking so much louder than the insects. I see them so strong in their old dresses, singing their old songs, I know I could touch them with my hands and they'd be solid and I could smell them and they would smell like clean water and wet earth, and then I pick up my bag of things and go out to where they are and turn left on the road and I walk with them a ways, toward the old people, and then, because I know where I'm going, I pass them and I look back once to see if they are still coming with me and they are.

I don't grow tired, even in the heat. I walk past the young trees still standing after the storm. A car comes up the road and honks and I move aside and see the driver brake suddenly and turn to look back at the four women.

I walk on limestone that rose up from the bottom of sea not so very long ago. The Spanish had floors of silver, but nothing, I think, I know, is more valuable than the floor of the sea.

The four women and I go toward the place above Kili. The four women walking as if on water. They move as easily, as gracefully, as Ama did on the day of the hunt.

Even though we are no longer close to the big lake because it's been drained and stolen, I still feel the wind of it. The wind of it is troubled, looking for its water, its home, looking for the fish and animals it breathed into existence.

And I walk toward them. They are waiting for me as if they knew all along I was coming. Annie Hide and Janie Soto sit together, across from each other, on logs. When I arrive, I go sit on the ground beside Annie Hide and she smiles down at me. I can hardly breathe and soon there is a drum, the younger men drumming, and I stand up with the women and I am awkward and Janie Soto takes the panther skin off her lap and comes over and hands me a fan made with beautiful white feathers so pure, so clean I know it has just been made, and she says, "Dance with this," and I dance and as the wind stirs in the trees, someone sings the song that says the world will go on living.